# Vatican Wealth and a Pope's Pipe Dreams

## Monsignor Robert L. Getz

ISBN 978-1-48357-870-5

## Dedication

To all of the dreamers and visionaries who have blessed my years of church service. To those who inspired me in caring, serving, and love of God's dreams of brotherhood. Most importantly, I thank the Lord who has inspired my dreams of peacebuilding through prayers, reflection and writing.

## Acknowledgements

Twenty-two years of working on my novel, as my pastoral duties allowed, brought forward a number of people that I want to thank. Early reviewers of the story were Olivia Lerma McDonald and J. Ronald McDonald, and a dear friend whose suggestion developed into an additional character in the book.

More recently, I am thankful for Denise Chavez, Delano Lewis, and Dr. Nancy Archuleta for their encouragement.

My deep gratitude goes to the team who helped me bring the novel to the marketplace. Thank you, Donna and Dave Curtiss, Dr. J. David McNamara and Christy Anchondo for your valuable contributions.

# Contents

## Introduction by the Author

My novel was born the day I thought about what might happen if the Pope emptied the Vatican vault, and sold all of the Church's treasures in pursuit of world peace. The idea of purchasing world peace made me smile. How would such an enormous event take place? How would the Pope go about making it happen? Where would it begin and how would it end?

*Vatican Wealth and a Pope's Pipe Dreams,* is a result of that inspiration, and twenty-two years developing how a workable plan might unfold.

*Vatican Wealth and a Pope's Pipe Dreams* is a case of life imitating fiction. I created the character of Pope Francisco in the early 1990s when the possibility of a Pope named Francisco from South America was unbelievable.

The story is set in the Vatican and uses the Church subtly and respectfully. The reader need not be Catholic nor have an advanced degree to understand the novel. There is a glossary provided at the back of the book with a list of terms that might be unfamiliar to readers. When you find capitalization in the book that deviates from the norm, it is always used as a sign of respect.

The premise of my novel is to change the world's thinking and to provide a pathway to world peace. It is a work of fiction. The novel comes at a time in human history when the inspiration generated might make a difference. The strategic plan is methodical and believable.

The story unfolds as Archbishop Gutiérrez stands before the microphones of the international press corps in the hallowed halls of the Vatican. He is there to announce to the world what Vatican insiders have come to call the Pope's pipe dream.

Upon hearing the news, the world seems to stand still for a weary Russian peace negotiator living in Moscow. He has waited a lifetime to bring peace to the world.

The first project is a daunting one – historically attempted too many times to count. What makes it different this time is that there is an agnostic Argentinian billionaire in the mix.

A previous working title focused on three of the main characters: the atheist, the archbishop and the agnostic. Add to that group the first woman inside the Roman Curia, an African woman who becomes the president of a new pontifical university. The leader of the group is the pipe-dreaming Pope from Buenos Aires.

The novel develops with strong introspective appealing personalities with secondary characters that add interest and controversy.

As if building organizations dedicated to world peace is not enough, the protagonist establishes a first-ever vowed religious order consisting of both men and women consecrated to peace.

The novel concludes with an unpredictable twist.

The book's powerful message comes at a time in human history when I hope that the inspiration generated has a chance to make a real difference.

The novel, *Vatican Wealth and a Pope's Pipe Dreams,* raises questions for the reader rather than offering simplistic solutions.  The story pushes the reader to dream "what if?"

# Prologue

The young boy rushed into the crowded cellar room. He stopped at the old woman's bedside. He shouted to her repeatedly, "Grandma, Grandma."

Her searching eyes were distant as they darted around the empty space of the ceiling above her bed. She searched for his voice with her eyes, unable to move her head. He was losing her. He watched his grandmother's face pale as her chest stopped rising and falling. He sobbed as he clung tightly to her. She spoke in short gasping breaths, repeating "Viktor, live for peace," until her voice faded and stilled.

She stopped breathing. The room became silent. The only sound was Viktor softly weeping. The older people tugged at his shoulders. "Son, she's gone."

His legs were numb as he tried to stand. Clutching the edge of the makeshift bed as he moved to stand, he placed his cheek to hers one last time. Viktor wanted to hold on tight to his grandma even as she grew cool and still. His tears choked his words. He fought the hands that pulled and tried to drag him away. Viktor stood beside her bed as a silent sentry. He wanted to be close to her one last time.

Viktor had seen death before – from bombing, hunger, and cold. He lost an aunt and two young cousins last winter. This loss was the greatest pain of all.

After whatever time had passed, someone took him by his hand and led him, exhausted, outside of the dark basement into the sunlight. They asked him to go bring his mother.

Viktor's little feet were like lead as they slowly shuffled through the wet earth and rubble of the street in the warm light of spring. After only a block, he sat down heavily on a fallen wall and looked up into the blue sky. He wept again. War had brought such destruction, death, and sadness to Leningrad, and into everyone's life, his life was no exception. The scars from the war were long lasting. Viktor found no solace, other than the sunlight warming his face. He agonized. His grandmother's words echoed in an endless loop in his mind, he recalled for the first of many, many times in his life: "Live for peace, Viktor. Live for peace." Losing his grandmother's voice was like a dagger in his heart, to his spirit. She was gone, never to fully explain her desires for him. He never forgot that moment.

# Chapter 1

## The Archbishop

Pope Francisco, with a nod to his security, stepped quietly into the private chapel of his archbishop. He unobtrusively observed Archbishop Mario Gutiérrez deep in prayer. The Holy Father made the sign of the cross, prayed a blessing over Mario, and stepped out into the hallway – knowing he would not have long to wait.

As he waited, the Pontiff thought about the impression the archbishop was about to make on the world stage. "It doesn't hurt, Lord, that Mario is movie star handsome. The cameras will love him."

Archbishop Mario Gutiérrez moved slowly up and off his knees, his eyes lingered on the Blessed Sacrament. In recent days, he had been most at home here in his private chapel, which was his favorite room within his Vatican quarters. During this adoration visit Mario first knelt, then prostrated himself before the Holy Sacrament. Finally, he sat in the total silence that pierces your heart and your soul. The deep silence comforted and prepared him for the task ahead. A new resolve grew within him. A sigh escaped him that came from deep within his soul. Mario was about to embark on what he thought might be the greatest adventure of his life. He had no way of knowing that this was only the first step of the journey that lay ahead for him.

The archbishop crossed himself as he left the chapel, thinking that he wanted a few minutes to stop by the office of Pope Francisco prior to the scheduled press conference. He stepped outside his chapel, and saw the Pope had come to him, which brought home to Mario the significance of this day. The two men embraced vigorously and together prayed passionately the Lord's Prayer. "God love and be with you, Mario," were the parting words of Pope Francisco.

Mario's path to the Vatican began with a childhood of privilege. In Argentina, a country divided effectively into the "haves" and "have-nots," Mario was born into, and lived unmistakably, in the "haves" category. The Lord called Mario at the tender age of 16. He attended the Jesuit seminary in Buenos Aires. His parents and his sister María Elena were bursting with pride when he was ordained at the cathedral in the capital city. After ordination, he served as an associate in two large poor parish churches among the crush of the capital. Immediately after his priestly ordination, Mario made the decision to live among his parishioners. His new home was a one-room tin shack in one of the poorest ghettos of Buenos Aires. It was at that time Mario began to understand the day-to-day struggle for survival the poor and vulnerable faced in his parishes. It was then his love and devotion for the poor grew.

Sixty percent of Mario's parishioners lived below the poverty line. Others were workers with low salaries, such as teachers, retirees with below-subsistence level pensions. Many participated in state-subsidized employment plans, which paid only a few hundred dollars per month. Basic food costs were out of reach for most. The kids in Mario's parish neighborhood did not take wearing shoes or a daily bath for granted.

An International poll from years ago discovered citizens of the poorest countries were among the happiest people in the world. The same poll actually tried to determine the secret to Hispanic happiness. Mario smiled at the recollection. He had found this to be true among his parishioners. Obviously, their economic woes were not a deterrent to leading joy-filled lives.

Mario distinguished himself in his parish work, in his further studies in Argentina, and at *Di Propaganda Fide, Museo Missionario* in the Vatican, also recognized as the *Congregation for the Evangelization of Peoples*. His work among the many antiques, paintings, photographs and objects in the museum exposed Mario to all missionary activities in the world from 1622 when Pope Gregory XV set it up until the present time. While he was in Rome, he completed his doctoral studies in law at the Angelicum, and taught there for a short time. His career guidance in the Vatican came from the Office of the Secretariat of State, specifically from his mentor, Cardinal Casavantes.

Gutiérrez' spirit still lived in the ghettos of Buenos Aires. He clung to his connectedness with the poor. His commitment resided with all struggling people. He remembered them in each Mass celebration, especially the joyous celebrations of Mass among African, Southeast Asian and South American congregations.

His heart was restless for the equity the Gospel promised. Yet that sense of fairness was so hard to define between the "haves" and the "have-nots" living in our world. He was driven by the hungers his parish families lived through, as the families worked together to simply eke out the bare necessities through their labors. Many in his second parish assignment hauled concrete and bricks in the rich areas of Buenos Aires' commercial district to make a living. Peace with justice had eaten at him since the cry had arisen from Pope Paul VI in 1967.

Mario's long robes rustled as he moved forward with a confidence that complemented his 6'1" stature. His years of priesthood and negotiating the halls of Vatican diplomacy and bureaucracy lined his handsome, lean face. He prayed, as he thought about his journey thus far, "Thank you Lord for bringing us to this point in time, continue to walk with us, please."

Now as he rushed into the press conference, where he represented the Holy Father, he hoped to open the eyes of the world to peace with justice.

His spirits lifted higher by his time in the chapel and Pope Francisco's encouragement. He was as ready for this moment in history as possible. He shared the Pope's dream for peace in the world. A dream some Vatican insiders referred to as the Pope's pipe dreams.

As he stepped up to the microphones, one thread of thought from Matthew 6 echoed in his thoughts: "Blessed are the peacemakers for theirs is the kingdom of God." Mario, taking in all the people, the mixes of race and gender and clothing in the pressroom, thought, "The kingdom of God mixes God's children from the four winds. These are surely the raw material of the kingdom!"

Many reporters who routinely provided Vatican City media coverage were present. Nicknamed the *Vaticanisti*, the veteran reporters were gathering upfront at the press conference. More women than usual were in the room. Major international networks, some Chinese, Russian, Japanese and Middle Eastern journalists were present. The numbers surprised Archbishop Gutiérrez. The Vatican had already prepared and released his welcome statement along with a brief explanation of their plans to build a university dedicated to peace. He planned to spend about thirty minutes answering questions.

The press shouted questions from all areas of the room as the archbishop entered. He stepped up to the podium and smiled. A veteran *Vaticanisti*, "Your Excellency, is it true that the Vatican museum and all the artistic and unused treasures and Church property are going to be sold in order to establish this new Peace University? And, if so, how will the sale process be handled?" Archbishop Gutiérrez expected this specific question. He rehearsed this response a number of times, believing the question to be close to the opener. "Thank you, Heavenly Father."

Anna Malooff was a new face in the Vatican media assembly. A reporter for World Wide News for the last 12 of her 45 years, she was well recognized as a feature journalist. Anna's specialty was Asian and Middle Eastern events. This was her first time in the inner sanctums of Vatican City. Her Lebanese Catholic background, gave her some insight into the workings of the "Catholic Headquarters."

Anna raised her hand just as the archbishop finished his response to the first question. When the archbishop nodded to Anna, she stated her name, affiliation, "Archbishop, why this focus on a peace university, rather than, say, interdenominational ecumenism, or world poverty, or Catholic evangelization efforts?" "Ms. Maloof, peace is the major focus of Pope Francisco. He frequently prays for peace and speaks about global peacemaking often."

Anna followed up. "Your Grace, is it not true few women leaders or saints are recognized for efforts in peacemaking?"

"Historically, St. Catherine of Siena was a famous peacemaker with the Popes in the 13th century, and Golda Meier was a strong voice of Israeli peace in recent history." The archbishop thought the World Wide News woman perceptive with an understanding of the prospect of peace.

All the details of Pope Francisco's dramatic plan were in the hands of his trusted archbishop. Mario met with countless Papal consultants over the last few weeks as news of the planned peace institute leaked to the world press. His forehead and palms were perspiring as he faced the cameras and microphones; his mouth like sandpaper as the conference went on. "Please, Lord, help me finish this," his heart pounded in prayer.

Mario was able to handle five other languages besides his native Spanish. Many of the questions came in French, which he had studied in school. Thankfully, the archbishop spoke Russian, a language he picked up in travel and in reading everything from the "Motherland" available to him. In fact, Russian history was among his favorite hobbies. His English came from study, reading and travel. His knowledge of the Japanese language was a result of his five-year diplomatic assignment in Tokyo where he was part of the Nuncio's staff. His command of Italian came from living in Rome and ordering in the restaurants. He was still dabbling in German through self-study and reading newspapers.

The Russian reporters surprised Mario, not by their questions so much as the fact that they were present in the Vatican with their camera crews. He had not expected this response from the Russians. The Holy See had an unofficial apostolic representative in Moscow on the corner of Tikhvinskaya Street and Vadkovsky Lane. Russia had a permanent representative to the Holy See based in Rome. Russian skepticism of the Vatican and of world peace gestures was familiar to all. Unless they initiated the programs, the Kremlin generally did not involve itself in others' efforts. These reporters seemed very interested, however. Russia certainly had historical experience in dispossessing churches of their properties! "Let go of the past, Mario, this appears to be a genuine interest in new peace possibilities."

"When and where will the sale take place, who will handle the sales, and what are the expected revenues?" Another response he and his staff had worked out in advance, thank God. "The international firm of Lamentier, Ltd., headquartered in Zurich will handle the sales. Many of you are aware of Lamentier's diversity in multiple market areas. The family has received many Papal decorations over the last two centuries. The firm has a stellar reputation and their skills are unsurpassed in this arena." Mario left unsaid that the thought of handling a project of this magnitude had already caused the senior Lamentier to announce his retirement in favor of his second son, Alberto. His eldest son, Anthony, was a professor of theology at the *Institute Catholique* in Paris, a priest and a scholar of excellent repute.

"The Vatican will establish a schedule for inventory and for show-placing of items in the global marketplace. There are many items taken from the vault scheduled for return to countries of origin. Rightfully so, the return of these pieces will enrich the museums of the owner nations. Other objects identified as valuable to individual collectors or collectives will be part of the scheduled auction. It would take at least five years to complete the processes. A multitude of issues will need to be resolved, to include taxes, import tariffs, and statements of authenticity."

"Lamentier, Ltd. worked feverishly these last weeks to identify a team of supporting consultants. Oppenheim and Burke of London were brought onboard to identify the best markets. Oppenheim and Burke will also inventory not only the Vatican, but also the assets of the Church around the world. Plans are in place to engage a public relations firm of worldwide reputation."

"It is too soon to make a wild guess at projected revenues. We expect Lamentier's fame, reputation, and their marketing imagery, skill and public relations will be priceless."

As Gutiérrez concluded the press conference, reporters heard his deep sigh of relief!

The archbishop wondered what moved Pope Francisco to conceive such a plan, as world economists rushed to their drawing boards and computers to begin their own calculations of the impact such a sale would have on the global economy. There were no experiences yet in world marketing which compared to the Vatican sale. The sale of the crown jewels of Thailand in 1976 created a stir among collectors. Yet, even the crown jewels did not compare. This collection of art, manuscripts, jewelry, antiquities and other treasures was without equal in the world marketplace.

"Peace at any price" was a muddled thought of Archbishop Gutiérrez. His mind was unable to comprehend the magnitude of these sales. What will the cost of investing in peace be? The amount will equal the cost of establishing the new university dedicated to peace with all of the overhead and associated costs. "Worth every penny of it," he thought.

The archbishop's next step was to search for property. There was not enough acreage for a campus location in Vatican City. The price would be exorbitant even if they found a city site. Finding property was difficult, and the city distracting. Instead, they planned to create a campus with a setting that would lend an atmosphere of peace to the University. An academic campus was not an easy parcel to find in city life today.

Gutiérrez contacted Adolfo Morelli, a favored and formidable realtor recommended by the Holy Father. The archbishop also knew Morelli personally for many years. He was a distinguished Catholic, knighted with the Order of Malta and a member of Opus Dei. Señor Morelli was the designer of Club International's vacation and conference sites around the world. Morelli would sift through the perspective offers and locations. The main directive was for the property to be located outside the city, and close to the Vatican.

The Holy Father's instructions were "Good archbishop, be certain you locate this dream beyond the noise and smokestacks of Rome. Fair as the city is, we need a place that speaks peace to hearts and minds." The pope spoke lovingly of hills, valleys, and horizons, likening it to the Holy Land in the time of Jesus. Our Savior never seemed to do too well in the larger towns and cities; it was as if the lack of peace saddened him. He seemed to lead His followers to hillsides and roadways that were simpler, clearer and cleaner. We want this University to echo that peace and clearness of nature."

"Mario, do come back with some good possibilities. I trust your aesthetic and gospel sense. I will be praying for Him to lead you to the right location. I will be reminding Our Lord, and you that we do not want to pay top dollar for all that beauty." The Holy Father spoke with charm and a chuckle.

"Holy Father, after dealing with the economics, the art world, and the press, locating a site will be easy."

Thus far, the archbishop had not selected a university design architect. Beginning a university from scratch was a rare as well as an exceptional opportunity. They hoped to find a site with pre-existing buildings. Still, the remodeling would include major renovations, plus the addition of new facilities too. Where to begin!

The first phone call to Archbishop Gutiérrez came soon after the press conference concluded. The call came from Cardinal Steiger, Prefect of the Office of Seminaries and Universities.

"Good day, Archbishop Gutiérrez. I wanted to be the first to congratulate you and to offer to be of service."

"Thank you, Cardinal Steiger, that's very kind of you." Gutiérrez knew almost the exact words that would be coming next; he prayed, "God, give me patience!"

"Of course, you know, Mario, your faculty will be cleared through our office, and that the Holy Father will expect only the most orthodox teachers and experts for such a visible international institution. Let me know soon when you are free to meet so we can begin to set up the process for selecting the initial staff. This promises to be a most interesting project."

"To say the least," thought Gutiérrez.

"Who would leave it in the hands of such a drone?" he thought to himself, as they continued on the phone. Surely, the Holy Father had to be aware of Steiger's reputation as a church politician and spotlight-seeker. He was effective in a harsh sort of way, but more likely was looking for some kind of control, financial or curriculum, over the whole thing. Gutiérrez recognized Steiger as a manipulator. He planned to deal with him early on; otherwise, the situation would drain too much of his energy. "Sweet Jesus, help me keep my peace," was Gutiérrez ' closing thought as they set a meeting date. This would take all the wisdom and cunning of God's Holy Spirit! Gutiérrez would have to talk this situation over frankly with the Holy Father. God's grace could work through all the human schemes imaginable, as history had proved so well ever since the time of Jesus' crucifixion.

Mario fully appreciated the autonomy Pope Francisco had given him in the staffing area. Staffing the dream had troubled Gutiérrez until he remembered another excellent mentor of his. What a nightmare this would be without the good monsignor! Thanks to Divine Providence, Mario asked one of Rome's most renowned university administrators, Monsignor Raphael Rondeau, to head this area.

Rondeau's area of expertise was sociology and history. The monsignor was on the faculty of the Angelicum and lectured all over the world on the Church's development of social philosophy. He held professorships at three world-renowned universities and was fluent in seven international languages.

Rondeau worked well with a curriculum committee headed by Sister Marta Schloss of Nigeria to develop a list of perspective, world caliber academicians and scholars in the area of peace. The monsignor reviewed their credentials and availabilities, and suggested salaries for the specialized faculty. His team collected resumes and dossiers, and handled all legal clearances. He screened the unsolicited professors and specialists who applied. Gutiérrez considered what such an elite group brought to the university.

Although, Sister Marta had set up the first Catholic University in Nigeria, establishing this University of peace would be the accomplishment of her vocation, her lifetime. Sister Marta worked directly with Monsignor Rondeau.

Sister gathered five collaborators from Catholic universities around the world to lead the screening committee for staffing. They had six months to prepare a preliminary curriculum. The screening staff numbered twenty to start. Every critical step of elimination and inclusion was reviewed, many by Monsignor Rondeau. It would take time to build an experienced staff in such a non-typical area as peace. Only a few applicants' backgrounds fit perfectly into the "peace" portrait with the clarity and confidence they were seeking.

They planned a simple core curriculum in the first year with plans to expand the syllabus year by year with students working toward an undergraduate degree in a variety of peace specialties. Expansion would continue through graduate-level courses as time brought credibility to the university.

The inaugural faculty would be first-class. Staffing required a fine balance to minimize stealing professors from established chairs and universities, to picking deep curriculum topics, keeping a reasonable budget, and bringing together an internationally recognized faculty under one roof.

The ability to speak multiple languages was essential to the curriculum staff and faculty because students who enrolled came from all over the world. Sister Marta concluded they would begin with seven or eight major international languages in the early stages of development. They would hire consultants in the languages of indigenous peoples worldwide. To mesh the differences of student languages with the native tongues of the faculty and curriculum staff required wizardry. "Where will I find a computer program for matching all these possibilities? First, I will find a computer whiz to put it together."

"You can't," was the internal nagging response. "Oh yes, I can through Christ Jesus who strengthens me."

Sister began orienting the curriculum in the European style of letters and languages as the basis of degree specialties. After one and a half years of intensive basics in languages, sociology, literature, culture, history, philosophy and theology, the students would begin to specialize in areas such as economics, psychology and human relations, government, business administration, history, law, communications, the arts and cultural development; all with a world view of peace and development.

Sister finalized plans for a huge library, computer networks and newer microfilm systems. Research funding from world foundations would lighten the heavy burden for the financial department of the new University.

Such dreams and the grandeur of them staggered Sister Marta at times, as she remembered the primitive conditions with which they began in Nigeria. Only God could put this University together. She walked across the plaza of St. Peter's on the way to her office, reflecting as she often did that the building of the Basilica and its design would pale in comparison to the complexity of design for the peace university and its impact on the world. "What a presumptuous dream and adventure God had laid on us," she thought to herself.

"Marta, we hold a dream of the Holy Father in our hands, and we will have the power, funds and opportunity that come along only once in a millennium," Archbishop Gutiérrez had told her. She shivered as she thought of this, and found that it often distracted her during her prayers and disturbed her sleep. These two quiet times seemed easily invaded and so vulnerable to images more real than dreams.

The second call following the press conference came from Anna Malooff, World Wide News reporter. She called for the archbishop and asked to arrange a possible interview. She ended up speaking with Sister Helen Marie, the archbishop's American secretary, a member of the Franciscan Handmaids of the Poor. Anna Maloff explained who she was before asking for an interview with the archbishop. While describing her background, she mentioned her Georgetown graduate work. She could not see over the phone the way that Sister Helen Marie lit up as she learned the dates Anna attended Georgetown coincided with her own time at the University. It turned out they shared international relations classes almost 25 years ago. The conversation was a wonderful rediscovery and they enjoyed reliving Georgetown memories. Anna ended the call asking for an appointment with Sister Helen Marie so that they could visit further, perhaps over a cup of coffee. They agreed to get together the following morning during Sister Helen Marie's coffee break time. Anna was enthusiastic to find Sister Helen Marie shared the Georgetown experience so many years ago. Anna believed that a door to the Vatican story had opened for her. She was a step closer to developing a feature story on the Vatican's new peace initiative.

Anna Malooff had questions about the archbishop's credentials, the overview of his authority, and the extent of his responsibility for all operations. She planned to confer with Sister Helen Marie first, and then ask to interview the archbishop.

Sister Helen Marie and Anna met for coffee the next day. Anna's pen flew as she jotted notes and sipped her coffee. The conversation flipped back and forth between reminiscing about their time at Georgetown and the current peace project at the Vatican. They shared the same dormitory area as well as memories of discussion and study groups. They found friends in common. Anna's initial questions about Archbishop Gutiérrez led to questions about Monsignor Rondeau and his credentials. Did Monsignor have a friendship with the Pope or with Archbishop Gutiérrez? She collected information about the lines of authority, the scope of the archbishop's responsibility and the overall management of the university development. Anna quickly realized that one coffee date would not be enough. She and Sister Helen Marie arranged a lunch meeting for the following week, which gave Anna time to trace all the lines of responsibility and to identify the decision makers. She worked up a diagram of the operational areas of the university. It took some time but was well worth the effort. She planned to develop a major international story, through a series featuring how the university was developing. She sent her outline along with a rough draft of her plans to proceed with the story to her editors in New York. Her editors liked her ideas. They pointed out the sale would be a big part of her story. She needed more details about the arrangements to identify the pieces and the sales processes to sell the valuable treasures and properties. There was a lot to research, and it would take several weeks to lay out the story. Anna was excited about the story and looked forward to future meetings with Sister Helen Marie. Sister Helen Marie and Anna realized they were on the verge of a wonderful friendship. Sister was already more than an excellent insider source.

Following her coffee break, Sister Helen Marie took a call from the United States. "Hello, this is Cardinal O'Rourke of Los Angeles. I want to speak to Archbishop Gutiérrez," said the commanding, heavy, masculine voice.

"I'm sorry, but the archbishop is in a conference right now. May he call you back?" said Sister Helen Marie.

"Is he with the Pope?" Cardinal O'Rourke asked cryptically. "If so, then I'll call him back."

"Otherwise, I want to speak to him now, and I don't give a damn if anyone else is with him. Tell him Cardinal O'Rourke wants to speak to him. While it is early afternoon there, it is five a.m. here in Los Angeles. I did not get up at this hour because I like it! Now, please go, find him, and put him on the phone."

Helen Marie rolled her eyes. Everything she had heard about this sixty-five-year-old clerical General Patton was true. The cardinal must make everyone feel like a six-year-old. Imperious is an understatement for his manner. "Hold on, your Eminence, I'll find him."

She went down the corridor and knocked lightly on the door, opened it and went up to Archbishop Gutiérrez and whispered in his ear, as he was on the telephone. He nodded and finished his call.

"Helen Marie, don't let that old sergeant intimidate you. I said only the Pope or a death were to interrupt me. This guy is notorious for throwing his weight around, and he can be a real pain. There are going to be others like him, too, so get your script down for the future, okay?"

Sister Helen Marie thought "script, what script? I didn't know I had a script."

The Vatican was a time-honored chauvinistic hierarchy, which left women caught in the middle. Pope Francisco expressed his wish for more opportunities for Religious women, but Sister Helen Marie did not see that happening anytime soon.

"How did Mary deal with Jesus and the apostles? I wonder if the Mother of God ever felt as I do." Sister was familiar with the injustice of this male-dominated system. She was nearly fifty years old and had worked in Vatican diplomatic circles, and in missionary work for all twenty-five years of her religious life. She spoke eight languages, held two Masters Degrees, and knew most of the diplomatic corps and issues. She was aware that she did not stand a chance of moving up in the hierarchy. She jumped at the secretarial position in the proposed World

Peace Office (WPO) because it was the most creative challenge available to her in the Vatican. She hoped that new avenues would open for her through the WPO job, as well as for other religious women. She asked God for a clear strategy now that she was an insider faced with war and peace issues of her own. "I need prayer and friends to share this with," she thought as she followed the archbishop down the corridor.

"Hello, Gutiérrez here."

"Mario, I'm up very early to call you about this International Peace University business. I have an important person from the U.S. that I want you to have on the committee. He is the backbone of the Church in our country and is a multimillionaire, a Papal Knight, a Notre Dame Graduate and all that stuff. I will send you his résumé. He's just what we need, what you need, from the United States to serve on the international group."

Silence.

Mario's brain was clicking – he wondered if O'Rourke could hear it. He heard what the cardinal had to say, and then offered, "I'll take into account this recommendation. The Holy Father has not yet reviewed names. When he does, your man's name will be there." After thanking him for the call, he sat back and smiled.

Pope Francisco greeted Archbishop Gutiérrez enthusiastically, "Archbishop, did you catch any of the soccer game last night? It was terrific. Spain took Italy, two to one. I was on the edge of my seat although I only saw the last hour. Do you follow the World Cup matches? I could easily become an addict!"

Thinking, "I like his style. Yes Your Holiness, I follow the matches, but most of the time through the press. Argentina remains my sentimental favorite."

"Well, I want you to join me one of these evenings for the matches. It is a wonderful way to get our minds off the affairs of state. Now, what have we to go over?"

Archbishop Gutiérrez explained to him the ongoing explorations for a possible site location, place by place, listing the pros and cons of each. "Let me know when you have it down to the final two or three, and we'll go deeper into the details; and, by the way, be sure to review the selections with your foundation committee."

What was that? Gutiérrez looked up! Did he say a foundation committee? Gutiérrez ' face must have shown his puzzlement, which the Pontiff caught right away. "You did set up a foundation committee to work with you, didn't you? I thought I had mentioned it at the start. It is important in such a major project as this, to put together a globally recognized and well-respected group. Remember we are the Church Universal. Oh, I can see by your face that I caught you unaware."

# Chapter 2

## The Atheist

---

**V**iktor Fiderev opened the door of his six-story apartment building. The brutal winter wind slammed the door shut behind him. Leaving the extremely cold weather outside in the Moscow January twilight, he was grateful to get out of the wind and come into warmth and light. The walk home from the Kremlin was a challenge of survival on days like this. The temperature reached minus 5 degrees Celsius. The forecaster was wrong today, he predicted a warmer temperature.

He held the evening edition of *Pravda* under his arm as he emptied the contents of his mailbox. Excitedly, he tore open a letter from his daughter Alina, who worked at the research center in Vladivostok. He began the weary hike up to his fourth floor flat, his glasses steamed over with the humid heat from being indoors. His vision fogged, the letter would wait.

He entered the flat and his wife Magda glanced up from the television where she was watching the evening news. She gave a quick gesture of fingered silence while pointing to the television screen. Viktor came over and stood in front of the screen as he removed his gloves and fur hat. The newscaster was reading a news alert. The television anchor spoke about a gesture made today in the name of world peace. Listening intently, Viktor's heart began to beat with excitement and he drew the copy of *Pravda* from under his arm. He opened it and stared at the newspaper's front page. The headline startled Viktor. An unexpected proposition for world peace announced today came from an unexpected source.

Prominently featured, the news article was in the center of the page in the right-hand column, above the fold. The lead story for the day was a dramatic announcement from Vatican City in Italy. Two photos appeared – one of Pope Francisco and the other identified as the peace project's executive director, Archbishop Mario Gutiérrez. The paper reported most of the Vatican treasures as well as the excess assets of the entire Catholic Church would soon be for sale. The Vatican would negotiate with buyers through auctions and other bid processes. The proceeds of all sales would be used to establish a university dedicated to international peace.

Viktor sat down heavily in his greatcoat, unaware of the warmth of the room, or the television newscaster reporting other news. Transported to another world, the paper sagged in his hands as he gazed out on the winter twilight through his apartment window.

Viktor removed his glasses and wearily rubbed his eyes. Unbelievable, his pulse quickened as he scanned the story and visualized its possibilities. Magda listened as he softly, spoke his questions to his reflection in the windowpane: "Is this actually happening?" Do they have ulterior motives? Did they have hidden agendas?" Viktor hoped this news was genuine. If so, the possibility of peace, coupled with the right incentive, excited him. Long-hidden private dreams began to surface as hopefulness seeped into his spirit.

Viktor was not a religious man. In fact, his views were atheistic. Like his mother and grandmother, his wife belonged to the Russian Orthodox Church. The two women had been thrilled when not too long ago – the previous pope of the Roman Catholic Church and the patriarch of the Russian Orthodox Church met for the first time in centuries. The Holy See and the Moscow Patriarchate bridged the long division and took a giant step towards peacemaking. They met on mutual ground to take steps towards the healing of wounds dating back to the 11th Century. Viktor, of course, had been interested only in the creative thinking that preceded the importance the meeting had in bringing about peace between the different branches of Christianity.

Despite his understanding, respect and appreciation of the faith the women in his life had, Viktor could not make that leap of faith. He believed that there were things science and reason could not explain, but he did not believe a loving God would allow so much suffering and evil in the world.

It was Viktor's lifelong passion for peace, which led to his career in the Russian Office of Internal Negotiations, a division of the Major Office of Strategic Peace. For three decades now, following his university studies, he worked in a progressive succession of arbiter positions.

Frequently, Viktor ended up in the role of bureaucrat, an executor of orders rather than a peacemaker. He began his career filled with hope. Now, Viktor thought, "I am tired and discouraged." He tried to remember the last time his face reflected excitement about the career that once filled him with optimism.

The road to peace had been Viktor's number one goal through his work at the Kremlin's Major Office of Strategic Peace. Viktor witnessed too many futile efforts in the name of peace to count – failures in his department, his nation and the world. Distinguished leaders on fire with visions of peace burned out quickly. Budgets held promise and later deflated. Mediations failed inside and outside of the Communist Bloc. Very little progress was made towards a path to peace during his tenure.

For years, Viktor studied the complex issues involved in peace arbitrations, prowling through every library he visited. He read all the inspirational, as well as pragmatic, material available on the subject of peace negotiations. Still peace in the world seemed distant, unattainable. He witnessed the heavy investment in weapons while his own nation as well as the other power blocs of the world spent so little capital on peacemaking. Over the years, his frustration grew and grew. Viktor's work tested him to the depths of his being. Often, he and Magda spoke about this. Magda always told him he lived in a dream world. He constantly imagined miraculous solutions to the struggles for peace and believed without exception, there were resolutions to the differences among the peoples of the world. "Nothing will change," his wife told him. "This struggle between the power brokers and the powerless is endless. Viktor, this is the way of the world, built into the systems of life and history. Nothing you, your office or some institute, individual or group can do will change unrest in the world." Magda loved Viktor. Through the years, she gently tried to keep him from becoming disheartened.

Viktor took his work seriously, which caused many sleepless nights. During those nights, he smoked endlessly, paced the floor, and stared out his window studying the stars. Magda thought her husband driven by hopefulness as distant as the farthest star. She believed her husband suffered the pain of a damned soul, tormented by hope that might never come to life.

"What an idealist!" his co-workers and family members murmured behind his back, which only motivated Viktor to increase his knowledge, and skills. His superiors at the ministry office were somewhat in awe of him because of his endless questioning, the power in his words as well as his indefatigable pursuit of possible strategies for peace. Through all of the discouragement, Viktor held tightly to the dream his grandma had for him, for peace.

His words spoke power. His frame did not. He stood 5'6", with a waist to match. His metal-trimmed round glasses did not help to create an image of power and strength. However, what Viktor lacked in appearance, he more than made up for with the fluency of his words and the persuasive way he tackled questions of peace and war, with courage and perseverance.

Although from the Leningrad area, Viktor studied at Moscow University in his youth. His scholastic record was superior. He survived the devastation of the relentless Nazi attempts at occupation as a child. The senselessness of violence, killing, war, and hatred that surrounded him in his youth intensified his passion for peace. One of the greatest conundrums in his life remained his government's previous policies regarding the Berlin Wall and Afghanistan. His views about these two policies had almost cost him time in a tough Siberian prison. Despite the threats, Viktor tenaciously quarreled with his colleagues about both as well as more current military interventions.

Viktor's tireless pursuit of peace was born on a spring day many years ago.

Like so many days before, he walked from the underground cellar where he had lived with his mother since the Nazi siege of Leningrad. A quiet day filled with sunshine. Gunfire silenced. A few birds flitted from place to place among the ruins of the shattered buildings and overturned gun carriages. He noted so few signs of growth in the plants or trees. Yet, a beauty blossomed in the air, a direct result of the sunlight, its warmth, and the promise of something new and different on the horizon.

Viktor was a young child when he ran excitedly through the rubble-strewn streets on his way to his grandmother's apartment to share his feelings of springtime with her. Upon his arrival, he was surprised to find a group gathered around the solid front door. He nudged his way through the crowd trying to understand the somber mood of the people gathered there. Most of the upper stories of the structure had been destroyed, a result of shelling by the Germans during the war. His grandmother had retreated to the basement with others from the apartment building. Grandma and the neighbors spent most of their time in the cellar. This day he found Grandma on a rough bed of boards surrounded by women from the apartment building. He cried out to his beloved babushka. Her breathing was ragged and shallow. Her eyes searched for her grandson. Viktor ran up to her in disbelief. He knelt and wept as he looked at her frail, thin face, and witnessed her death.

Her death changed Viktor's life. His grandmother's dying words gave his life focus and vision. He lived his life accordingly. The last words from his dying grandmother's lips were a gift to him: "Viktor, live for peace!" Her words stayed in his memory – through his schooling, military service, marriage, career, his child, and even his advancing age. Grandma's words echoed daily in the deepest chambers of his heart. In those moments, his destiny as a peace-bringer was sealed. Grandmother's gift was a prophetic call of the spirit that so often lies hidden in a person, awaiting release in some moment of light. How it might materialize, he could not be certain, though thousands of little moments of promise came throughout the days of his life thus far. As a child, he reconciled other schoolchildren fighting on the playground. He patched up dating friends' broken relationships as a teen. Compromises whet his appetite for conflict resolution. In his own family, he spent years persuading his Uncle Mikail to speak to his son Julian, who angered Mikail by refusing to live on the family's farm. At work, he often cleared up misunderstandings between his coworkers and their ass of a supervisor, Alexandrovich. How his boss held onto his job for so many years puzzled everyone. Viktor shrugged off office politics and continued to work indefatigably to create peace and harmony in all environments.

Peace creating occupied most of his waking hours. It was a source of constant irritation at times. Yet such pleasure amid the pain! He would never be able to explain why or how he continued to hold onto hope in the face of so many dismal situations. There were times when Viktor negotiated for days over apparent irreconcilable differences in relationships. He took the people's pain as his own, while he continued to believe and work for amiable resolutions.

Moscow called Viktor to lead a team sent into an Armenian-Azerbaijani situation a year ago in February. The current conflict had roots in the Armenian-Azerbaijani war, which started the Russian Revolution. They chose Viktor because he studied the differences in cultures on his own for more than twenty years, and had an established network of countless research specialists, plus a massive amount of files and data. When Moscow brought the issues and demands to Viktor, he studied for days with team members before traveling to Baku, the capital and largest city of Azerbaijan. Baku was located on the Caspian Sea in the Caucasus region. They stayed at a waterfront hotel, located within walking distance of the sea, cafes, and fountains.

The situation was bleak. The city's population was struggling with internally displaced persons, refugees seeking sanctuary. Despite the commitment and hard work, the cessation of hostilities eluded Viktor's team.

He could not seem to put his finger on it. "What is the missing element?" He kept asking himself this question. In the end, an early morning conversation with an old Armenian grandfather brought Viktor the answer he sought.

As morning dawned, Viktor hurried to the city administration office. The people that gathered in little groups preparing to salvage something from the wrecked buildings of the recent demonstrations in Baku brought hardly a glance from him. Nor did the old fellow drinking his tea who stood back a little ways from the crowd merit his acknowledgement. The elderly man smiled watching the younger folks start work but Viktor did not see him. Viktor, in fact, almost knocked the man over. The old man reached out and grabbed Viktor's coat sleeve.

"Oh, son, how fast you are moving for such a cold morning! I thought for a brief moment a piece of concrete had fallen on me."

"Please excuse my hurry; I am off in another world."

"From your accent I believe you are from Moscow," the grandfather said. "Are you part of the relief effort here?"

"You might say that. I am part of the government's negotiating team. We're trying to negotiate a settlement to this whole mess, which is not easy when working with such stubbornness on both sides."

"You people from the bigger cities move too fast. Here, we seek slower answers, as our grandfathers did so many years ago. When a family is in a state of hate, easy or quick resolutions are hard to find. The grandfathers of our country possess a deeper wisdom. I believe age and living through pain enables us to see beyond quick answers, past our long-held feelings of hatred."

"Do you mean this hatred that exists between your people and the Muslim Azerbaijanis? Thus far, no one is willing to listen to the other side."

"Listen, son, a peaceful solution will be possible only after you gather the right people, the wise ones of each side. Both sides have seen too much blood and made too many mistakes. The wise ones, the grandfathers, will give you answers your computers or books will never provide." He sipped his tea and smiled as he said this to Viktor.

Something akin to lightning struck Viktor with those words, the "wise ones." That is it! It is not the politicians, bureaucrats or military, who bring the answers to peace. Nor do the young, eager to show their strength. Instead, I will gather the elders of each side. Both sides of this situation have historical family structures that include their elders via extended families. They are the people of experience. Both sides will listen to the wise ones and respect them and their opinions.

Viktor ignored initial suspicions from local and Moscow authorities, as he gathered the wise ones from first one side and then the other. The grandfathers from each side came on separate days to the Azerbaijan National Academy of Sciences conference hall and found their voice. They knew and respected one another. The fact that Moscow's representatives called on the grandfathers and truly listened to what they had to say honored the elders. It did not hurt that the grandfathers were surrounded by vast collections of historical documents from Roman, Byzantine, Ottoman and Soviet periods as well as other civilizations of the past.

Then, on the third day, Viktor announced meetings between the opposition elders, stressing the fact that no politicos would attend. Entering the talks, both sides were wary. The grandfathers were not a textbook solution. Yet, Viktor believed this elder resolution would work. Never would he forget the crowd of faces as he looked out on the assembly. They were two hundred strong. He focused on the intent face of the old, pipe-smoking grandfather who had spoken to him on that cold February morning. The grandfather sat among the leaders of the Armenian delegation. Viktor choked back tears looking at the deeply etched lines on the elder's face and the wisdom of years forming on his lips as he spoke. This was so much more than, a "lesson learned" for Viktor. As the grandfathers recalled all the notable figures from Baku's past – men of science, arts and other fields – they worked their way to a solution for the migrant population that pleased both sides, and restored peace. This was a winning solution, a huge victory for peace!

Through this experience, Viktor learned a new component to peacemaking. Bringing together the wisdom of local leaders and asking them to share the experience garnered over generations was brilliant. Viktor's team left Baku encouraged by this victory, and the fact the solution could be replicated.

Viktor was not alone in thinking world peace possible. Specialty institutes developed throughout the world bore witness. Established international institutes for conservation, pollution, nutrition, medical research, diplomacy, space development, and computer technology were witness. Viktor, wary of some of the newly established organizations, thought at times "these scientists will gobble us up." Their funding comes so easily from governments and foundations along with the promise of new discoveries and super technologies. Unlike his experience with the wise ones in Baku, Viktor thought some of the new inventions and discoveries exacerbated disagreements and brought about increased infighting. Peace in the world remained an abstract, primarily interpreted as disarmament.

The Vatican's recent announcement promised a peace through wisdom, understanding and sharing. Viktor envisioned the great halls, classrooms and library centers filled with students, faculty, and experts gathered from around the world focused on peace. He would apply to be a part of it. His heart overflowed with joy at the prospect.

# Chapter 3

## The Aethist and the Archbishop

Archbishop Gutiérrez wondered about the inquiry and résumé he received so quickly from the Soviet Union. He was of an age and memory that caused him to speculate that the Russian applicant might be a party "plant," a bureaucrat, or some independent thinker who would serve in no way to link up the International Peace University realistically with the central government in Moscow.

Gutiérrez made delicate inquiries of some of his contacts in the Russian Orthodox Patriarch's office. He asked them to investigate the individual who had applied to the University. The investigation found that Viktor Fiderev sounded like a character too good to be true, with credentials that the Kremlin would find difficult to hide or deny. It would take some real negotiating to bring a person of this experience from Moscow to the Pontifical University dedicated to peace. The other concern for Archbishop Gutiérrez was that he was not certain whether this man was applying for a position at the university or as a representative on the international Board. He qualified for both. This question needed more thought.

One contact of Archbishop Gutiérrez' was Father Dimitri, the Patriarch's secretary. Father Dimitri called Viktor to set up an interview on behalf of the patriarch. Father Dimitri had been the prelate's assistant for twelve years and understood the workings of the Party, the Kremlin, and the Russian religious sector. There were days when Father Dimitri could not find the top of his desk due to the amount of paperwork that passed over it.

For his part, Viktor was comfortable entering the patriarchy offices. Actually, there was a part of his soul, perhaps awakened by his grandmother, which was deeply peaceful around these strange and darkened hallways, with dimly lit icons and flickering candles. Conceivably this was the mother country's fountain of peace that his grandmother had spoken of so often.

Father Dimitri met him at the receptionist's desk and ushered him into his office. The room was dim and filled with the aroma of incense. A gentle candle illuminated the image of Christus Pantokrator.

"Good evening Viktor, we have been contacted by the Vatican to talk to you about your inquiry into the proposed Pontifical University dedicated to international peace," Father Dimitri began. "It is not unusual for us to do this, and we often act as liaisons for the Vatican in Soviet religious questions. We have enjoyed especially good working relations in recent years. They have asked us to speak with you and, of course, to check further into your credentials."

Viktor caught on right away. "Father Dimitri, let me assure you, so that you can assure them, I am not working for the state as an agent. Surely you know people in the Kremlin, the Foreign Security Service or the former KGB who can and will verify my credibility for you."

In the short silence that followed, Dimitri recalled the report from just such a check. Viktor came up as an oddity in the files. While he was no longer a Party member, he continued with a responsible position. Viktor was intelligent, experienced and dedicated to his work. The system had invested quite a bit of trust in him. Although respected by his coworkers, Viktor was a non-conformist, possibly a maverick. Dimitri was not so sure about the last point: Was he also a "wild card" who might pull this international hope to pieces with personal causes and hidden agendas. It was difficult to know from his record. He was not involved in any public issues or groups. Thus far, it seemed he was sincere and respected. The investigation would continue. Investigators will check additional references, other friends, neighbors, and associates.

"Viktor, the real problem will be after this security investigation. How will we or how will you, then, get the needed official clearance to represent the Soviet Union? What we are doing seems to be very much by the back door. What plans have you for this?"

"Absolutely none, Father. I will count on your prayers and hope for one of my wife's miracles. You know I have no standing in the Party or my directorate. I carry no weight or public image that would serve our national purposes. Have you any suggestions?"

"Prayer, as you said Viktor, and I'll see what contacts I can make through the Patriarch's offices."

Father Dimitri was impressed with Viktor's open and unpretentious ways. Viktor, a graying, honest bureaucrat, truly wanted to work for peace. The priest listened to his story, and was convinced of Viktor's ability to handle an international position like the one under consideration. Viktor would succeed, motivated by the cause of peace. Viktor's lack of self-interest surprised Father Dimitri. He was well versed and experienced when speaking of peace and previous international interventions.

Viktor was even more relaxed as their conversation progressed. He sank comfortably back into the chair as Father offered and served tea. Viktor asked the priest if he might light his pipe. Father Dimitri responded affirmatively. The meeting's atmosphere grew in trust and peace as they continued to talk.

"Viktor, this may take a miracle. In the first place, the odds are against us having you appointed for the reasons you've stated," Father Dimitri said. He leaned forward, almost consoling Viktor with a pitying look. "The Lord Christ took on all kinds of impossible situations, and He still does. I do have some influential contacts, a few debts to collect, and the Patriarch has even more. Therefore, I think it is not impossible, only difficult. Ask your family to pray, and I will pray, network and ask the Patriarch to do the same. More tea?"

Viktor had not felt this good in a long time. He ran up the stairs and entered their flat a little breathless. After leaving the cold streets, new warmth seemed to fill the room. Magda was all smiles, "Viktor, can you believe, we are going to be grandparents!" A wondrous hope came alive for him, and his spirits leapt with excitement and joy. Thoughts crowded in: He needed peace now more than ever for this promised grandchild. Life is so precious, and peace is possible for our next generations! "This child is a great sign," he said, "perhaps the first of many, of the miracles I am expecting."

Viktor put his arms around Magda before he took off his coat as he usually did first. They embraced in smiles and tears. A new age and its hope were dawning. How good it will be to sit by the window, smoke his pipe, sip a little more tea, and look out on the grayness of Moscow and the world.

The call from Father Dimitri came sooner than he had expected. In fact, it was only two weeks.

They met that evening in Father Dimitri's study, Viktor fairly tingling with anticipation. Father's first words increasing the sensation, "Viktor, the Lord Christ must want this international peace university badly. I cannot believe how easily the Patriarch was able to go through channels and deputies, but it has happened! Congratulations, Viktor! The announcement of your appointment as our nation's delegate to the Vatican in this International University peace project will happen this week. There will not be money connected with the appointment. We assume compensation will come with the work, but you will be able to leave your government work, as needed, to attend to your duties in Rome. It is unusual to be able to do this, as you know. Only a few athletes, artists and educators have been given this freedom in the past."

"I want to jump and dance, Father."

Smiling, Father Dimitri, "God is looking after you and our nation. I believe you must have some important work to do for Him."

As they sat together and peacefulness descended on them once again, Father Dimitri spoke. "The Patriarch is the cousin of the Premier's wife. She has great faith in him and they are close. I think she is a woman of prayer. The Patriarch is convinced this is a worthy cause and totally supports the Vatican's peace initiative, so he worked with haste."

"The hardest part was convincing your bureau. They are typical Party bureaucrats, afraid that you are going to move up ahead of them. I only tell you this so you will be aware of what to expect from your office. The FSB as the Foreign Security Service goes by now used some suspicious past dealings of your supervisor, Alexandrovich in the black market to leverage him. Alexandrovich does not like it. He is a bit upset that his superiors handled this. He was outmaneuvered. The FSB sometimes lacks finesse in getting a point across, so things may not be so pleasant for you at the bureau. I will pray for you about your work situation and for the peace plan in its entirety. Throughout this project, you will be reporting to your director, and to the Patriarch. Viktor, you will be learning some new international protocol with this work, so be cautious. Call me anytime if you have any uncertainty. I can always get to the Patriarch."

Viktor was anxious to tell Magda the good news about his position. When he did, her response was a knowing, loving smile. Viktor shared with her that he did not want to draw attention to his new position. He explained how the authorities wanted recognition and approval from the world, to include the Catholic Church. Magda nodded her agreement.

When Viktor returned to the Bureau the next day, he received a summons from Alexandrovich as soon as he entered the office.

When they parted the previous evening, Viktor asked Father Dimitri to pray for him to have a peaceful spirit. He sensed Father Dimitri's prayers were uplifting him as he walked toward Alexandrovich's office.

Viktor was aware of the eyes of his coworkers staring at him, following him. Some of his colleagues were sneering and shaking their heads. He smiled at the two who gave him an encouraging smile as he passed by their work areas. Viktor recognized that this meeting with his supervisor would be a true test of his newly acquired interior peace. He thought about the scene about to unfold many times during the night. How he would incur the rage of his boss, and what his response to it would be. The irony that peace did not come easily even in an office dedicated to strategic peacefulness was not wasted on him. Viktor prepared for this meeting by rehearsing his part of the conversation about to take place. He was ready as he opened the door to the office-thinking, "Ready, set, go!"

Alexandrovich was ready to explode.

He threw the official package at Viktor. "Here is your documentation. Nice move! Who do you think you are? Do you think you are the only one who understands mediation and negotiation in this office? You did this in Russia! I cannot imagine what connections bought you this choice assignment. You make me sick with this sneaky backstabbing. You are going to pay for this in ways you cannot believe, you son-of-a-bitch! You made all of us look like asses; you made me look like an ass. You think I did not have a plan for the university. I am going to follow your reports closer than Stalin followed his generals. You are going to need more than peace before I am finished with you. Be prepared for war in this peace move of yours."

Viktor stood before Alexandrovich. He waited for an opening, his chance to speak. When it came, he couched his words carefully. He did not give all the information that he had received from Father Dimitri to his supervisor. He left Father Dimitri's name out of the discussion. He used the Patriarch's name for more power. Viktor's palms were sweating. He hoped his forehead did not show the perspiration. This was definitely one of the worst moments of his professional career. Yet, it held the potential to be one of the best. He drew on his peace of mind and his honesty, not an easy combination to pull together in the face of Alexandrovich's accusation and rage. Viktor told Alexandrovich, "When they called to tell me of the government's approval to my appointment, I thought this had been processed and cleared through your authorization. I hardly believed it myself. I decided to wait until you spoke of it, so I could be sure. I apologize. I had no idea it bypassed your approval. I don't know what else to say."

Viktor held direct eye contact with Alexandrovich throughout his rehearsed performance. To eat humble pie was best in this situation.

The savage scrutiny was the price he was willing to pay for his new position. Viktor likened this to a 38th parallel situation. He knew that he could handle it. He held his ground and thought he was gaining ground with Alexandrovich.

"Alexandrovich, you will have my report every week. If, at the end of six months, you are not satisfied with my work, I will quit. Regardless of what you may think, I am trying to bring honor to our nation. I think other nations misunderstand our approach to peacemaking. I think we have the opportunity to prove we are sincere through the International Peace University. I will consult with you and the staff here. I am not out to make this some personal crusade or a one-man show. It must be a collective project, and I promise it will be. We have much experience and many skills to bring to international peacemaking. Please let's work at this together."

As Viktor offered this best and final plea, he relaxed, visibly settled down, breathed more evenly and deeply. His muscles loosened and he even felt his facial muscles begin to move in a grin. He could see by the look on Alexandrovich's face that he had gotten through with these last thoughts. Alexandrovich's sneer seemed to lessen, his brows opened, and his face relaxed and returned to normal. Alexandrovich was not about to reach out his hand or offer congratulations. Nonetheless, at least he stood facing Viktor, fingered some things on his desk, and then, with eyes down, he growled, "It had better work that way." Then he sat down behind his desk, looking out the window. He was still breathing heavily, his right fist tensed.

Finally, Alexandrovich swung around and faced Viktor, who sensed his supervisor trying to understand him. Viktor's own adrenaline continued pumping strongly, and he was certain the situation was still volatile and knew retribution would follow. Even so, he thought he had made headway with his boss about his appointment and future work.

Viktor left the office relieved. At least, Alexandrovich did not throw him out. Other thoughts came rushing into his mind: his time, now, would largely be his own. This appointment would come first, and other negotiating projects in the state would be secondary. Viktor did not have to punch the time clock first thing every morning! He was accepted. He had cleared the final hurdle. He was floating on air.

Archbishop Gutiérrez called Viktor the next week and they had a congenial conversation over the phone.

Communication flowed freely between the two men. They had command of the English language. The archbishop spoke fluent Russian.

Gutiérrez told Viktor that Italian, Spanish, French, English, Chinese, Japanese and Russian would be among languages in use at the University. He said they needed access to every major language in order to handle situations that might arise anywhere in the world. "I want our students to be bi-literate at least. To speak, write, read and reason in a minimum of two languages." A department in language communications, thought Viktor. The ability to pursue peace in every tongue was essential.

The archbishop asked Viktor to come to the Vatican the following week to meet with him, to go over some questions, and talk about plans. Viktor hoped this was the beginning of a cordial relationship. As soon as he hung up, he called the bureau's travel office for reservations to Rome and sent a memo to his supervisor and the director.

Viktor longed for the new work to begin in earnest. He would live in two worlds. No doubt, he would pay a price in each. He thought of his wife Magda, and Igor, their new grandchild.

Viktor's world was changing. It was like Columbus setting out on his voyage or the cosmonauts leaving earth. He imagined the questions and challenges that lay ahead. He smiled to himself as he closed his desk drawer for the day and thought of Father Dimitri.

Viktor Fiderev flew into Rome's Da Vinci Airport, which is also called Fiumicino International Airport. One of the flight attendants told Viktor the airport handled over 29 million passengers a year. His first thought "unbelievable!"

As the plane began its approach, the early morning haze lifted to reveal the magnificent dome of St. Peter's. The dome looked like a beacon of blessings, an omen of hope contrasted to the Kremlin's gray walls. He found the usual mess with customs, but Italian Customs was nothing, he thought, compared to customs on entering Russia. Magda had sent along some special vodka for the archbishop. He hoped the officials would not spot it. He breathed more easily as he moved on through the customs' line – vodka intact.

Sister Helen Marie spotted him without difficulty from the picture she memorized earlier, and the big smile on his face clinched the identification. His natural warmth came out in this centuries old place of creativity and romance. Viktor glowed with excitement. He looked around the terminal like a child discovering a candy store. Magda would be thrilled to be in this city with its rich history. Perhaps, one day they would come together.

Sister Helen Marie greeted him with the European double kiss and hug, as his smile grew wider. On the way to the car, they exchanged pleasantries, and the thrill increased as they entered Rome's early morning traffic. It was a beautiful winter day, clear and sunny. Although pollution blanketed the city, Viktor did not mind. He enjoyed the maze of traffic, and the way Sister handled the car. She seemed fearless to him. His driving experience included infrequent official excursions using the office Lada when permitted. Traffic in Rome was nothing compared to Moscow, where drivers spent an estimated 127 hours in traffic each year.

Driving into the Vatican entrance, past the impressive Swiss guards, the reality of Viktor's mission began to sink in. This is our dream! His grandmother's words and his life work merged. Viktor was ready for what lay ahead for him as the Russian representative at the University. His words would count. He would allay the fears and suspicions of the western world about Russia's intentions. He spent his lifetime in preparation for this assignment. Free to express his own deep thoughts and dreams without checking first with his superiors, his only instruction to report to the Russian embassy as soon as he arrived. He would report tomorrow! He relished his freedom above all in this task, and he placed his freedom in this new work with the prayers of Magda, Father Dimitri and the Patriarch. He walked excitedly on new ground in sacred places. His heart beat with joy beyond imagining. Viktor tried to contain his excitement as they walked down the dark wing of the north hall of the Vatican. His thoughts jumped from his impressive surroundings to his hopes for the dawn of a new era of world peace.

As he stepped into the study of Archbishop Gutiérrez, the scent of incense overcame the burning candle wax. Gutiérrez reached out before Viktor chanced to raise his arms, and gave him a warm abrazzo. Sister Helen Marie stood in the dim entry light and smiled at the warmth of these two men greeting one another. This is a historical moment in time. She stepped back and closed the door, caught her breath and sighed a prayer as a critical dialogue for peace began.

Viktor sat in the comfortable armchair before the fire, as the archbishop brought some tea. The hospitality was welcoming and genuine, the setting simple and homelike. The archbishop was not sitting at a desk or in an office, but before a fire with a warm drink. Perhaps all peace making and bridge building should begin in this manner, Viktor thought, instead of around conference tables, and in halls or offices.

"Viktor, do you mind if I call you 'Viktor?'" Viktor smiled and nodded agreement, as the teacup touched his lips. "Please, also, call me Mario, except in front of the pope."

"You are something of an enigma to me, Viktor. I admit complete surprise when I received your correspondence, or rather, Sister Helen Marie spotted your application among the stack of letters we get daily. Your request arrived outside of the ordinary channels by which we receive communiqués from the eastern bloc nations and without an endorsing letter or seal of inspection. To be honest, Viktor, I wondered if this was a governmental security police technique or some type of a 'plant.' I checked your credentials with the Patriarch. I spoke with Fr. Dimitri. Then, I became certain this was a new approach from Russia. You might say I had a hunch about you. I prayed over all this. I listened to God. I believe you are 'heaven-sent.' You are to be our man. You bring a refreshing view to our project. I believe we can enjoy a bit of the Divine sense of humor in you being here. I am certain someone's faith and God's guidance brought you to us. We will discover why in the months ahead."

Viktor managed a shy grin. He too underwent deep, strange feelings about being part of this gigantic dream.

"Your Excellency, I mean Mario, my grandmother, my beloved babushka, is behind my part in this. You can understand her faith far better than I can, since you are a believer in miracles. I cannot explain the dream of goodness, a love of Russia and its people she carried in her heart. Not only did she dream of peace for Russia; she wanted peace for all people, even the Germans who fought us at the time. A woman of great dreams and of great prayer, her icons lit her home. Her hands and lips spoke of caring and peace for everyone." Viktor's voice became a whisper as he said, "I cannot describe the depth of her faith..." His eyes filled with tears, and he began to weep. "Something happened to me, to Mother Russia, to the world with this new hope of peace through your university. In these last months, I realize only Grandmother envisaged such big dreams. I am lost and cannot explain how I am here except through her power and faith. I do agree that your plan to establish peace in the world is doable. Mario, I am awed to think somehow I will be a small part of this."

Near tears, Mario Gutiérrez' heart ached for the man denied his dream for so long. The two men stood together gazing into the fire. The archbishop thought about what they, men from such different backgrounds, held in their human hands.

God whispered to the archbishop about this special man and the great dream. The archbishop did not try to explain this spirit-filled insight. Convinced Viktor possessed gifts beyond his distinguished credentials, the archbishop planned to use his authority and position to appoint Viktor as the representative of Russia on the Board as well as a faculty member. The Holy Father trusted Mario's judgment. He would present the dual appointments right away. Gutiérrez would open up a requisition for a new faculty member and initiate a seat on the Board for a designated faculty representative.

Gutiérrez stood ready to fight for Viktor. He believed Viktor to be God-given. Given a chance, Viktor would prove his appointment a gift of God's hands.

# Chapter 4

## Pope's Pipe Dream Team

The next three months zoomed by for Archbishop Gutiérrez. The *Vaticanisti* tracking the Vatican's progress, dubbed the archbishop, his associates and his staff *the Pope's Pipe Dream Team*, sometimes shortened to *the Pipe Dreamers*.

Under the leadership of Archbishop Gutiérrez, *the Pipe Dreamers* grew, not only in numbers, but also in experience, wisdom and grace.

The pope's unexpected announcement about the foundation turned out to be one of many surprises for the archbishop. His office encountered a daily deluge of requests from both expected and unexpected sources. To his amazement, interested parties in the sale of Church property continued to overwhelm the Vatican switchboard. Additional operators, working 24/7 shifts, were brought onboard. The archbishop delighted in the overall success of the peace project.

One day, about six weeks into the public announcement, the pope invited Gutiérrez to his papal apartments for a meeting. While the apartment seemed an unusual place for his weekly office interview, the archbishop welcomed the privacy afforded.

They spent a great deal of time in a frank discussion of the expropriation of church property and its holdings throughout the world. One of the more sensitive issues was the Vatican rare book collection, which included parchments and manuscripts dating back to the early A.D. centuries. The Holy Father said he gave much prayer and study to these critical questions. The complications encountered in analyzing Holy Mother Church's assets could be overwhelming. The analysis would likely be astonishing as well as complicated. Gutiérrez chuckled when he thought about convincing the local leadership, the bishoprics to hand over the proceeds to the Vatican.

With nothing to divest, Gutiérrez thought the pope's directive for the third-world bishops easy to implement. However, to ask this of capitalist nations and wealthy leaders in the Church would cause real tension with the Vatican, "Lord, help us with this," thought Gutiérrez, as he dialed Oppenheim and Burke in London.

"Hello, Archbishop Gutiérrez calling for Mr. Oppenheim. Hello, Harold, how are you? Is your family well? Me? I am restless these last nights. The endless phone calls related to the holdings of local churches head the list."

"Harold, we need to bring onboard the international public relations firm you recommended. We needed them yesterday to deal with some of the more delicate issues, which wear me down. We are ready to hire the public relations firm you identified for us."

"Harold, we require the skilled personnel to deal with questions about the surrender of excess assets that we previously discussed. We also need a first-class strategy in place, a script that provides leadership that we can all follow. The potential exists for this to be a disaster for the Holy Father. We want expert advice that will protect the entire program. Harold, I realize this is a lot to ask."

Mr. Oppenheim restored the archbishop's peace. "Archbishop, I have been giving this a lot of thought. I think that you will want to use the company originally recommended by our Swiss agents, Moretti Marketing and Technology. Their marketing and public relations experience is a perfect fit with your requirements. They come highly recommended and have a proven record of accomplishment."

Harold Oppenheim explained to the archbishop that the recommended company had offices in 47 of the 193 countries recognized by the United Nations. Many of the company's clients were on the Fortune Global 500. "Mario, the company is very secure, and possesses the needed experience and wisdom in the wealthier nations where reactions, at times, run to the extremes."

Relieved, Archbishop Gutiérrez sat back into his desk chair, listening. Harold had truly grasped the nature and the scope of the problem.

Hanging up the phone, the archbishop shook his head and grinned. He thought about how the Lord cherished the Jewish people. Jewish wisdom through the ages in negotiations and business acumen served the kingdom of God beyond any historians' views. He thanked God for old, wise, and close friends like Harold. Their friendship developed and grew over the years. The Jewish people are people of great faith. He only hoped this great new institution brought about the potential in the not-too-distant future, to reach into the question of peace with Israel and the Palestinian state, which for ages now, seemed so far from any possible settlement. He prayed for a moment. "Father, please put this at the top of the peace list for our world. With you nothing seems hopeless, even when problems are beyond human wisdom."

His Holiness asked for detailed financial reports of the Church from each nation, accompanied by an outline highlighting the holdings that exceeded actual church properties in use. This information went beyond the institutions and their operational budgets, and provided a net worth statement for each diocese.

They were quite amazed to find the Church's holdings included everything from rain forest land in Brazil to factory interests in Scotland. The strangest and most disconcerting finding – the Church owned eighteen percent of a large, prosperous diamond mine in South Africa. Early reports say that revenue from the mines benefited the local South African community with economic stability, with food on the table, better living conditions, health care, and safe drinking water.

Pope Francisco asked Mario, "How did we ever accumulate all this? What would Jesus think of us?" Most of these worldwide holdings and property remained in the name of local churches, dioceses and archdioceses, and in the names of religious communities. The bulk of the Church's holdings came from estates, or gifts given to local religious communities and to religious orders. The Church did not develop many of the properties. The Vatican found itself without direct legal control over any of these resources.

The pope confided to Archbishop Gutiérrez his deep conviction about how Christ wished His church to be poor and powerless in material resources. "The riches of the Church lived in the moral attitudes and thinking of its individuals, as they dealt with daily life and decisions of this world. The investment of Jesus existed in people: their life styles and ways of living. For many centuries, the Pope said, we interpreted this investment as educational formation. We tended to the sick, poor and suffering, as always, but our investment took place in schools, universities and learning institutions. By liquidating and consolidating our excess holdings, we will be able to do more. The time has come to use our accumulated wealth to invest in the age-old elusive pursuit of peace. Because we are only using excess resources, we will still be able to provide for all of our important ministries. Our music, art, symbols, buildings and ceremonies mean nothing if we cannot show one another how to live in unity and understanding."

The Holy Father stayed impassioned. As he spoke, he held a glass of sherry in his long, thin fingers and waved his other arm at Archbishop Gutiérrez. His face seemed to glow with the inspiration of his thoughts. The flickering light of the fireplace cast a glow and shadows over his countenance. Gutiérrez wished for a pocket recorder so he would not miss a word of what the Pope said. He wanted to share this wisdom with the world.

Gutiérrez spoke gazing into the fireplace embers, "Your Holiness, a sense of urgency exists for you to write a papal encyclical on this topic. We need to proclaim peace through the Church to the world, so no one will miss our intentions or misunderstand our decisions. I think our plans for peace will ignite the action of the Church for centuries to come. The encyclical will include changing a mindset that weighed us down now for centuries, as we cared for buildings, property and institutions. Holy Father, please consider this. I think peace and poverty unlikely companions, yet peace and possessions, which exist in the more recent history of the world do not work together often for peace. Greed, consumerism and self-aggrandizement direct so many governments and even our Church interests at times." Mario, emboldened by sipping wine and the moving of the Holy Spirit, enjoyed a great moment of intimacy and inspiration. He recognized God speaking with them, through them, in some mysterious way of grace.

Oppenheim and Burke began the process for inventorying the holdings of dioceses and archdioceses around the world. At the same time, the public relations firm began their campaign to promote awareness and understanding of the Vatican's peace plans. Oppenheim's way of handling global properties proved more than satisfactory.

The Moretti Marketing and Technology firm handled all inquiries about the art and treasures in the Vatican as well as the global divestiture. They also worked out a careful plan for responding to nations and communities who demanded the return of original cultural treasures, which had somehow ended up in the Vatican Museum.

The Corporation Board selection processes gave Archbishop Gutiérrez his next headache. He met with his staff and advisors every Wednesday enabling each one to share in the briefing, and to experience firsthand the way things developed. It was important to have the right mix of skill and experience on the Board. The main divisions of work for the advisors included the museum and art sales, the worldwide divestiture of Church holdings, the site selection, the administrators of the university, faculty possibilities, curriculum development, legal affairs, finances and budget, and public relations.

Mario ultimately handled the organization of the Board based on the recommendations he gathered from the meetings. He reported his selections directly to the Holy Father, and they continued to flesh out the dream.

Most of the working areas now included space for offices, computers, and peripheral equipment. The *Pope's Pipe Dream Team* was located in the north wing of the Vatican. A clear sense of mission existed among the staff. A brief brisk walk from the Holy Father's apartments brought the Pope to the World Peace Office (WPO) for frequent chats with staff. The office grew in visibility and stature. It was still hard to realize in just a few short months such a change had taken place in the Vatican. Only the Congregation of Doctrine and Faith and the Secretariat of State employed larger staffs than the WPO.

The University's potential included the means to change the course of the Vatican, the Church, and the world. Gutiérrez could not help but compare the humble beginnings of the way Jesus lived, to the University. In the life of Jesus as well as the existence of this University, the vision of peace passed from one individual's heart and thoughts, to another, on to a group of people, and out into the world. The roots stretched as far back as Jesus and his Apostles, and reached Pope Francisco.

Organizing a new world government, one without boundaries might prove an easier task. The University offered global citizenship, complex, yet inclusive, of all people, and dealt with a new kind of bonding. A palpable excitement lived in the ancient halls of the Vatican. The WPO staff received plenty of media attention, enjoyed few budget restraints, and the Holy Father prayed with them whenever he visited. Other offices envied this favored office, its autonomy and its people. The WPO staff followed a new vision, a dream with certainty. Their commitment showed in their conversation, smiles, and dedication. The lights burned late in their offices, more often than not.

Archbishop Gutiérrez worked diligently to match the correct leaders with the important project areas. His efforts paid off. The University leadership consisted of professional, capable, international, Catholics and non-Catholics – all visionaries united in their mission.

Archbishop Gutiérrez continued to gather studies and to pray over the list of leading intellectuals, business people, and political consultants from around the world. He considered their Church background, some backgrounds of varied Christian faiths or non-Christian, and some of no particular religious background. At the heart of his consideration for each staff member was their freedom to live their heartfelt desire for peace. Gutiérrez prayed for a continued balancing and blending as he added to his staff.

Now he was on his way to visit the Holy Father! This afternoon they would sit together and go over the names of possible University Board members. Selecting these Board members came more easily than did the Corporation Board members. His team had narrowed the list to fifty names, with five in reserve, as possibilities. He incorporated all the names the Holy Father suggested, contacted them and eliminated those, which for various reasons, refused or were unable to serve. Those who remained formed an impressive group. There were some with backgrounds in politics, like Madam Katherine Moubtizou, Prime Minister of Tanzania. Others were academics with backgrounds in administration like Jacques Martine of the Sorbonne. There were business giants like Manuel Valles, of Costa Rica, one of the world's shipping magnates and a Knight of the Holy Sepulcher. Representatives came from Buddhist, Muslim, and Hindu faiths. Many women, religious sisters, nuns and government figures applied. The list held the names of persons from every continent, the Greek Orthodox Patriarch, His Holiness Maruicio Misiurka, of Constantinople, a Lutheran bishop from Norway, and two Catholic bishops. Others like Viktor and the Minister of Education from China provided a good mix.

Given the approval by the Holy Father, Archbishop Gutiérrez would release the names to the press. The release provided a double check for the Vatican. They knew that if the Vatican's background checks missed anything of importance, the press would certainly find it.

Following final selection, he would gather the confirmed Board members for four days of retreat and orientation. The Holy Father reminded him to take care about travel and political conditions for some of the Board members. Some lived in delicate, even unstable, national situations.

Gutiérrez prepared a preliminary budget for the operation of the Board for one year. This budget covered travel, accommodations and other expenses, as well as a stipend for each.

He prepared the draft agenda and reviewed the schedule with the Holy Father for each meeting. Meetings would take place four to six times annually with a provision for emergency sessions. The Honorable Rafael Prizio, the international legal consultant of Grimaldi Associates, accepted the assignment to review the final agendas and legal processes for the Board. Prizio was tasked to approve the final agenda processes.

Prizio, on behalf of the contracting corporation would also handle the legalities of contracts for all proposed peace solutions.

A big let-down might be in store for some of the Board members, those with business connections who possibly expected preferential treatment. The Board would find their involvement in the handling of Vatican and Church assets limited, above all in the disposal of the holdings to finance the University. Certain members of the Board expected to be brokers of these assets. They likely anticipated a voice in the determination of the issues, as well as the locations of peace negotiations the University would handle. Archbishop Gutiérrez intentionally neglected to put in writing the scope and powers of the Board. He left the ambiguities in the general understanding stand.

His team, still in the due diligence phase, examined documents and guidelines from other international associations, such as the United Nations, the Brookings Institute, the Swiss' Center for Freedom, and England's renowned Coalition for International Mediation in London. Gutiérrez and his team took full advantage of these, as well as other centers and institutes. Taking advantage of the vast experience and wisdom gave Mario and his team the edge they needed to apply to the cause of world peace. The *Pope's Pipe Dream Team* would touch and sift through the entire network before formulating policies for the Board of the Pontifical University. The developing by-laws contained numerous strategically placed TBDs (To Be Determined) items throughout the document. These would become clear moving forward.

The Holy Father seemed very refreshed and relaxed having come from his afternoon swim, as he entered the Papal office where Archbishop Gutiérrez waited for him.

The archbishop delineated the major projects and gave the Holy Father the status of each category: the sale of Vatican treasures, realigning the Church holdings worldwide, establishing of the international University, and setting up the independent peacemaking-contracting corporation. He brought Pope Francisco up-to-date on the incorporated Board reports, to include the treasurer's report, which defined responsibilities including oversight of policies and the millions of dollars invested on behalf of the Vatican for peace.

Setting up the separate operation and staff for the contracting and consulting corporation as a peace institute, associated with, yet separate, from the University was nearly complete. The archbishop found this was a common practice of universities throughout the world, especially those with specialized endowments.

Gutiérrez hired an international director of operations for the corporation from India, whose background and experience included the Georgetown University School of International Relations, plus ten years of staff work with the United Nations in its administrative offices. Dr. Sadha Khanna respected in international diplomatic circles and known for two popular works from the bestseller lists: "The Untold Cost Factors of International Peace" and "The Palestinian State Offer" based on the Palestinian State-Israeli history. Gutiérrez met her at a conference in Switzerland three months before. He was impressed with her reputation among the lower echelon of career diplomats, the "worker bees" of embassy hives. Well versed in peacemaking, she was fluent in several languages, possessed innumerable connections, and she would be a great help setting up the Corporation Institute. She hoped to begin work next by assembling her initial staff.

The pontiff listened to Gutiérrez, asked a few questions, and agreed with all of his recommendations. The pontiff chose Pax Internacionale Contracting Corporation for the name of the University's contracting corporation.

Mr. John Murphy flew to Switzerland, unannounced, from Los Angeles at the instigation of Cardinal O'Rourke. Shortly after Murphy's arrival, an urgent call came from a Vatican Financial Office representative in Switzerland: "Excellency, this gentleman refuses to leave our offices without speaking to you. He says he is a representative of your international Peace University Board on behalf of the United States. He is asking questions, and requesting private reports. We, of course, refuse to give him any confidential information. His stubbornness is most embarrassing and I cannot count the number of times we have explained to him the confidentiality of our business. He does not understand that our authorization is to give information only to your office. What am I to do? He is getting ruder by the minute. He refuses to leave."

The financial officer handed the phone to Mr. Murphy per the Archbishop's request. "This is Archbishop Gutiérrez. To whom am I speaking, and how may I help you?"

Archbishop Gutiérrez pictured Mr. Murphy's unsmiling face as he extended his greeting.

"Archbishop, this is Mr. John Murphy, Cardinal O'Rourke's personal representative. The cardinal asked for, but did not receive a personal review of the final names for the Board of the peace-contracting corporation. In addition, he is very upset about the inquiries made in our country, specifically about our archdiocese. These inquiries came from your office. So, he sent me here for answers." His voice grew louder and his words rushed. As he listened, Gutiérrez thought John Murphy represented a true image of O'Rourke, a bulldog type. "Things are starting to hit home," Gutiérrez thought.

"The cardinal will go over your head to the pope, if need be, and humble you before the world if the 'right balance' does not exist among these selected Board members. This means, of course, a controlling interest to the United States and the western world, respecting their power and economies. Also the cardinal says that the asset inquiry business must stop."

Mr. Murphy's miffed tone reflected the perceived insult. "I thought being on this international Peace University Board, gave us, at least, a few privileges. I represent a powerful segment of the Church, Archbishop Gutiérrez. Cardinal O'Rourke does not like the way your office is questioning our assets and the way you are limiting our representation on the corporation contracting Board."

Mario had no doubt that Murphy received the Vatican request for an inventory of all property and holdings of his archbishop.

Archbishop Gutiérrez did not equivocate. "Mr. Murphy, you are not representing the Church in the United States. The Holy Father appointed you. You represent the Holy Father and the interests of the entire Catholic Church, not a segment of the Church based in Los Angeles or the United States. Nor do you represent the laity or Cardinal O'Rourke. I hope you understand this."

"We better talk in person. Are you available tomorrow? Please catch a plane from Switzerland, and we will meet tomorrow at your convenience here in the Vatican." His meeting with Mr. Murphy would be a tough one. Gutiérrez prayed: "Lord, soften him up and give me wisdom."

"Mr. Murphy, I wish you had contacted me first, rather than go to our financial representatives in Switzerland. I could have saved you a trip. I will be glad to talk with you about your concerns. I instructed our agents in Switzerland not to release any information to anyone without my signature or the pope's authorization. They are not to deal with any diocese, bishop, or their representatives. They are people of integrity. Their job is to gather information and provide planning for us, as well as handling the sales and release of properties and holdings. They report to me, to my office, and to no one else."

"This is a delicate process in a protected area, as you can understand. The Holy Father expects the confidentiality protected. The process requires you to deal with me. Again, please fly to Rome and visit with me tomorrow."

The Archdiocese of Los Angeles was by far the wealthiest in the Catholic Church with holdings in non-church property and stocks, as well as a considerable art collection. They were uncomfortable revealing this information to other than the confidential cardinal prefect of economic audits, whose organization tracked the holdings of each diocese around the world. Although he did not say anything, Gutiérrez registered surprise Cardinal O'Rourke did not speak to the pontiff straightaway about his outrage, on behalf of the American Church.

The conversation ended. Archbishop Gutiérrez expected Mr. Murphy would report immediately to Cardinal O'Rourke. The follow-on conversation would only increase the cardinal's concerns of representation and control of the Pax Internacionale Contracting Corporation Board. Murphy had emphasized the cardinal's great displeasure of the future control of diocesan assets by the Vatican. Before the call ended, Murphy relayed that O'Rourke would be addressing the Holy Father and American bishops on this topic.

The following day, Archbishop Gutiérrez met with Mr. Murphy in the WPO conference room. An acknowledged active Catholic leader in California, he appeared to be a former athlete. Murphy, a well-known attorney in the United States, shared honest reflections of the issues involved, not only for California but also for the American and world Church. In turn, the archbishop explained the Vatican's intentions. They talked for hours. In the end, Archbishop Gutiérrez gained an American friend. Murphy came away with a better understanding of the Vatican's position. They ended their meeting with an enjoyable lunch. They parted with cordial promises of future conversations, and with kind regards and prayers for Cardinal O'Rourke. Mario acknowledged the great blessing he received, the enabling to handle this very personal encounter with wisdom and grace. "Thank you, Lord."

All institutions of life face accumulation of wealth questions with all its complications on a daily basis. Along with the bishops, the religious orders assessed their wealth, to include the trusts and investments they held. The requirements included report submissions based on operational costs, long-term educational investments and retirement care and insurance for their employees. The groups estimated the excess amount after determining the needs of their individual dioceses and religious institutions. The final figures included the excess property amounts, which were of interest to the Holy See.

The hardest part was protecting the local and more personal interests of diocesan territories and religious orders. Convincing Church leadership to reveal and to divest themselves of excess interests and holdings to address world-order questions like peace, the poor, and education, equaled the Vatican's litmus test. Mario reflected that ever since Judas kept the purse for the Apostles, accumulating and distributing assets has been subjective.

The age-old challenge presented by Judas was recorded in John 12. While Jesus was at dinner in the home of Lazarus, Mary anointed the feet of Jesus and wiped them with her hair. Judas, who was about to betray Jesus, and had charge of the moneybag voiced his opinion that the money spent on the expensive oil could have been better spent.

Today's challenge in the contemporary world was to identify Christ's thinking, understanding and approach to economics. The archbishop expected inevitable confrontational encounters to take place over this radical complex and challenge that faced the universal church.

The finance people developed a very thorough inventory form, to include an in-depth accounting of assets, and liabilities, so that the excess amounts would become obvious. They built certain checks into the process like submitting copies of the audited annual reports for the group or diocese from the last five years to provide comparison.

Amassing funds for future development and expansion of institutions and programs would be another watchdog area for this new way of monitoring finances. Archbishop Gutiérrez received warnings from those more experienced in these areas. The cautions made Mario aware of past misappropriations of funds. Pope Francisco's predecessor made reforming of the Vatican Bank a priority. Despite the poor accounting and monitoring system of the Vatican Finance Office in the past, the Vatican Bank proved necessary. Mainly because so many bishops, priests and religious orders work in countries without secure banking systems.

Historically, people found loopholes. Others employed poor record-keeping or bookkeeping practices. The inventory reporting would be an excellent start. Pope Francisco insisted all accounting practices be transparent. With tighter accounting, better reporting practices and internal controls, auditors watched for someone to establish a secret account. The system alerted them to the possibility of concealed funding hidden under a variety of cover names and projects. With the external auditors in place and involved in all phases of the processes, the archbishop expected it would take no more than one to two years to run smoothly and ensure no off-record accounts existed.

The pope depended on the integrity and honesty of his bishops. Thank God for these men, a different breed than those in ages past. These were men of integrity, administrators and leaders in the world community. Very few bishops still lived in personal opulence or amassed wealth or fortunes for themselves. The days of the church-state, prince-bishops were long past. Honesty and economic simplicity marked most of the lives of the religious leaders within the Church, a mystery of grace. Most of the men and women who controlled such wealth throughout the world still lived simple lives, without personal wealth or ostentation.

Following the Gospel, the challenge for the archbishop and his operation appeared clear. The difficulty was turning around un-Gospel-like thinking, inbred for centuries, on a global scale, from causes tolerated for centuries as acceptable: war, hatred, divisions, and exploitations.

Archbishop Gutiérrez considered little else these days. He wondered if these thoughts lived in the mind of the Pope. Daily he swam in uncharted waters. Always prayerful, the sense of leading a divine mission never left him.

Grateful for inner peace, security and confidence, he learned to call on resources and utilize consultants whenever possible. The acquired delegation skills came to him as needed, and he found this part of the plan exciting. He slept well and left each day in God's hands, or at least, as much as possible.

His awareness grew. God wanted to use his hands, mind and energy to accomplish this divine task. Moreover, he always sensed the Lord's humor and irony in this new ministry of peace. God is very tracalero or "tricky at times," remembering his own youthful calling as a priest. Mario Gutiérrez' ideas for his life, as a young man, included being a soccer star or following the family business interests, or both. That is when Christ tricked him into discovering God's beauty and greatness.

Once Christ hooked him, Mario never wanted to let go. His vocation came to him during a quiet moment, facing the death of a lifetime family friend, from cancer. He never forgot those final days at Juan's bedside with his family, or praying in the hospital chapel. Something took hold of him. God touched him in a way he never dreamed possible and God became his one direction in life.

Thinking about God's ways brought thoughts of Viktor. He rejoiced at how easily Viktor's appointment to the faculty and the University Board happened.

Mario was grateful for his part in creating this remarkable university and its supporting organization. He prayed for a wise balance of opinion and influence as he faced countless choices about his staff and consultants in the peace project. He believed himself blessed to draw from a pool of gifted people from around the world.

The staff of Lamentier in Switzerland was overwhelmed initially by the magnitude of this task – the accountability for such vast treasures! Now, the process for sorting the Vatican's treasures was methodical and moved along at a good pace. The process was much easier and efficient than the inventories of the local holdings of individual dioceses and religious orders. Under the watchful eye of Alberto Lamentier, they made real progress.

The company completed an accurate inventory of the Vatican's museum, the rare book collection, including non-religious rare manuscripts, and art pieces, as well as the inventory of the cathedrals from around the world. Many of the art pieces located in Rome were stationary and in some cases, they were a part of buildings, such as, the frescos of Michelangelo in the Sistine Chapel. Some of the buildings sold through private sales with the final dispositions awaiting settlement. The total inventory discussed at length, broke down into definitive categories. There were some remaining items scheduled for return to national museums of the countries of origin. Customer satisfaction ranked high with Archbishop Gutiérrez and the Holy Father. They were very pleased with the way the sales progressed.

Gutiérrez traveled to Switzerland to visit Lamentier's offices to examine more closely the processes the company employed to line up potential buyers and private auction outlets. The method employed a computerized network, with an electronic timetable for releasing items to the marketplace. Avoiding a market surplus made scheduling paramount. In order to determine which particular items at what specific times would bring the best prices, Lamentier, Ltd. studied art market sales around the world.

One marketing option included setting up auctions for specific types of items, such as jewels and statuary. Working with the public relations firm, Lamantier determined that certain items would sell better in the auction market than in a gallery or through a private sale approach. The vice-president of the public relations company produced announcements along with determined schedules. The schedules announced blocks of items for release. One of the more interesting facets of the marketing plan was to use international telemarketing over the Internet via a computerized network designed by the Vatican's computer specialists. The multi-faceted security protection associated with the selling of such treasures required configuration, maintenance, and ever-evolving security protection. Their security measures protected the operations procedures from threats inside and outside the operation. The requirements for the computer interfaces to be secure were paramount to operations, and protected the identities and addresses of both the bidders and the buyers.

The information technology staff's abilities, of course, were why they received a handsome twelve percent, plus salary for their part in setting up, protecting and maintaining the computer operation. These handpicked computer savvy techs ranked among the world's best, and pleased Archbishop Gutiérrez with the professionalism of their operation. The complexity of questions in the selling of such treasures required this caliber of heavy hitters from the cybersecurity world.

Alberto Lamentier arranged an auction process for medieval jewelry; the collection was valued at hundreds of millions of dollars. Bids placed from fifty-four world market centers flashed into the auction center in Switzerland. A remarkable network system, somewhat like a super video game, thought Archbishop Gutiérrez. Perhaps their operation rivaled the ultimate shopping network!

They used automated responses, notifying authorities of false or failed bids in just moments. They provided real time solutions. They also offered a chat option so that bidders with questions had access to additional information about the objects of interest to them. Gutiérrez understood the bottom line. Cyber security prevented unauthorized access. He did not understand how they did it. He simply admired the system. The programmers seemed to think of every eventuality. Mario suspected they might have been black hat hackers before working in the computer security business. They were the best in the field. The computer system analysts constantly monitored threats to the system. In addition to the routine updates, they implemented software patches to protect the system.

The Archbishop reserved two hours of the Pontiff's schedule on opening day. His Holiness would be able to witness the process firsthand.

Lamentier delivered on its promise of top dollar on all items. Their company attracted the top collectors and representatives from all around the world. The archbishop thought business conducted in the 21st century was very different from twenty centuries ago in the era of Jesus walking the earth. He recalled the Galilean villages' market places, the fishermen, tent makers and carpenters with their wares.

Mario marveled at the depth of Lamentier Ltd.'s management skills.

Protection for buyers' anonymity fell under the watchful eye of a trained editing crew.

An elaborate communication system handled international sales requests for advance information about specific items. The Archbishop tried to imagine the number of businesses using Skype and Face Time connections through i-pads, smart phones and tablets around the world. The old-fashioned mail system covering catalogue inquiries handled the smallest volume of business.

The top-of-the-line distribution system delivered items costing over $200,000 via bonded security people, following travel patterns so complex, only computer chips using GPS (Global Positioning Satellites), could track the items. Smaller items shipped insured through secure international courier services.

Archbishop Gutiérrez feared a long, drawn-out decision-making process for the campus location, but happily, he worried for nothing. The Holy Father considered all six recommended sites, and without a moment's hesitation, chose the former monastery campus of San Vicente, located twenty-five miles northeast of Rome, in the beautiful, peaceful mountains of Calabria. Surrounded by the Pollino Mountains, the nearest village was three kilometers distant and enjoyed a reputation as a sleepy, ancient community of goat herders. Pope Francisco proclaimed the site as perfect.

Selecting the site for the campus was one of those rare moments when the Pontiff knowing the decision belonged to him, chose the perfect spot. The archbishop and his staff agreed, the site was the most beautiful, economical, and logistically sound location.

The site selected, the Holy Father now named the University – Pax Dei Pontifical University. The Holy Spirit sat on the Pontiffs shoulder helping to handle things.

The site committee and staff did a great job, considering the time constraints and diversities of faculty members who made the real-estate decisions. Once the site selection was settled, they explored real estate options around the campus area to identify housing for the staff.

Interestingly, the peaceful setting for the new university happened to be located a short distance from the town of Tivoli in Lazio, an ancient Italian town, which traced its war-torn history back to 361 B.C. The last damage inflicted on Lazio happened in 1944 when Tivoli suffered heavy damage under an allied bombing.

"Hello, Mario, sorry to call unexpectedly, this is Viktor. I need to speak with you as soon as possible. It is about an urgent matter within our government."

"Well, Viktor, I hoped we would talk next Monday at the first Board meeting. However, my schedule is open for lunch tomorrow. Can you join me?" A minor miracle, thought Gutiérrez, as he looked down at his scribbled desk calendar.

Mario wanted to get away from the Vatican, the sights and sounds of traffic on what promised to be an invigorating spring day in Rome. The next day, they walked the short distance to the little Ristorante on the Piazza de la Porte, which was off the beaten path. They enjoyed a quiet, intimate and inexpensive lunch, with fine lamb and pasta.

They ate, as Viktor unfolded the developments of unrest and re-structuring going on throughout Russia. The country was trying to get a market-based economy in place. The old bureaucracy still protected its interests at the middle and lower levels. The country still needed changes in industry and consumer goods production. The tax structure continued to be a nightmare. Private overseas stakeholders invested very slowly due to concern about the future. Hope, however, was always on the horizon.

"Archbishop, my government asked me to approach you about some treasures of Russian culture and history currently housed in the Vatican. They want to make a deal. In return for the Vatican returning the Russian treasures, they will open up certain former eastern Catholic churches and dioceses and consider Jesuit staffing of several secondary schools in some major cities. To me, this seems like a big move and con-cession, and I thought I had better talk to you as soon as possible about this. They want to send students to our university and offer exchange research and classes once we are established and moving forward. The Russian students will be on a pay basis. My government empowered me to extend to you a list of the various historical treasures and manu-scripts they are requesting. I am not aware of what they may offer as far as Church property in exchange. I am to pick up lists of these from our Embassy if you are interested. What do you think? Does this plan sound all right, with nothing fishy?

Viktor's honesty caught Archbishop Gutiérrez completely by sur-prise. He gulped hard as he swallowed the harsh Chianti house wine, and lowered the glass from his lips, mesmerized as he listened to Vik-tor's words. "My God, what are you doing?" His mind grasped the mys-tery of the proposal before him. What a divine sense of humor, divine irony!

The Vatican's plan was for the Church to become poor by selling possessions and wealth, in order to market peace to the world. Now, Viktor on behalf of his country, a one-time great warring power of the world, now in great economic pain, wanted a piece of the wealth, held by the Vatican to find its roots. They wanted to trade, not guns or money or real property. Instead, they wanted to trade the faith heritage of some of their people, for those possessions. God used the Russian treasures as a bargaining chip, to re-open Russia to the faith experience, to allow its people to be touched by the mystery of God. Who would dream of such a bargain? The value of these art treasures multiplied be-yond any human calculation! Divine mathematics at work, something from nothing, a gospel creation and multiplication story. Peace and faith both financed in such a trade. What a remarkable and irresistible offer.

Gutiérrez silently prayed, "Oh Lord, let the prayer of Saint Francis be realized at the Pontifical Peace University." The Holy Father would be tickled and overwhelmed.

Gutiérrez told Viktor to bring the Russian documents to him, and he would turn them over to the proper authorities. He offered Viktor the deeper insights, which filled his mind, as they enjoyed the savory lamb. "Lamb of God," he prayed, "this is a meal to celebrate and remember. This is a moment of history, like the freeing of the Israelites from Egyptian oppression, centuries ago."

Viktor half grasped the excitement and insights Archbishop Gutiérrez offered. The only thing Viktor understood is some great resource of treasure opened up by means of his words on behalf of the Russian government.

Dialogue was so important at all levels of communication, notably peacemaking. Archbishop Gutiérrez proceeded to fill Viktor in on all the developments of the University, its Board and the sale developments. He liked the informal sounding board Viktor offered in their growing friendship. He enjoyed sharing the little insights and stories of the progress of various segments of their shared dream.

The Holy Father's schedule allowed time for only the big picture items. Although the archbishop would have liked to share the small personal stories of human interest, the Pope's calendar did not permit it. For this reason, the archbishop was even more grateful to share these stories with Viktor.

The number of applications they received from prospective students all over the world continued to surprise his staff. Scholarships were set-up by private groups of business, social leaders, governments, and universities who wanted to reserve spots for their students on the roster. Neither enrollment nor financing would be a problem. The hope of the world communities captured by this dream, led many people to invest in this vision of peace. It was thrilling to play a part. Viktor saw his own excitement mirrored in the Archbishop's eyes as they spoke of all the exciting happenings.

Archbishop Gutiérrez told Viktor the academic committee had approved the curriculum. The University planned to offer religion, along with philosophy and anthropology with an ecumenical dimension to include religious experience, to recognize God's part in all peacemaking.

An emptiness of spirit settled over Mario as he parted ways with Viktor. He craved *amor de familia*, family love. He needed to step back, as Christ did so often. The Pontiff gave Mario time off to visit his sister in Buenos Aires. "So, Mario, you are human too."

# Chapter 5

## The Agnostic

Mario flew in to the Buenos Aires, the Ezeiza International Airport, which was also known as the Ministro Pistarini International Airport. The flight found Mario entering into a world of memories. Two and one-half years had passed since his last visit to Argentina to see his family. The familiar sights and recollections filled his heart.

An excellent student, Mario enjoyed popularity as a soccer player in his school. It was during this time that he distinctly heard God's call to him, and announced his intention to become a priest. He never regretted his decision to serve God's people.

What beautiful parents blessed his life! His deeply religious, well-educated parents, now deceased, ran a successful family furniture business. They unhesitatingly encouraged him as young man to go with his dream and enter the seminary. His sister did likewise. Mario missed the family gatherings, noisy celebrations, with cousins, aunts, and uncles talking or arguing at once.

María Elena, a year younger than Mario, anchored not only her own family, but also many people in Buenos Aires with her endless supplies of faith and joy. Mario's sister married Fidel Arguello twenty-five years ago.

Her husband was a successful business executive who came from an old aristocratic family of the capital city. Fidel's reputation as a man of deep prayer included an award as a Papal honoree.

Their three children had attended quality Catholic schools. María Elena made certain that the children personally experienced working causes and hands-on need involving the sick and the poor. She brought a deep sense of Christian social responsibility to her family. The oldest, a girl, Lorenza was married with an infant son. The two boys lived in London and Madrid and visited home often.

At the airport, María Elena laughed aloud as she heartily hugged her archiepiscopal brother. Her hugs and kisses embarrassed Mario, as always. His clerical dignity and age smothered by his sister's enthusiasm. Lorenza, his niece, with her infant son, stood close by, as Fidel joined the welcome with handshaking and smiles.

"Mario, having you with us is like a dream. We planned so many things and we have so much to tell you. When you called to tell us of your visit, I called everyone."

"But, María Elena", he pled, "I told you I wanted to rest and enjoy the company of you and Fidel, so I hope relaxing time is in the schedule."

Fidel rolled his eyes. "I told her to let you make the plans, Mario, but she's a controlling lady."

It was not long after Mario gathered his bag that Fidel drove to the General Ricchieri Expressway. Once underway in the car, María Elena showed Mario her list of names, places, and experiences she scheduled for his visit. She was so proud of her priestly brother; she wanted to take him everywhere. Mario loved his sister too much to put up much of an argument.

At drinks before dinner, Mario and Fidel began to catch up on national issues. He enjoyed the warm welcome to this different world of family, school life, business and local politics.

After dinner, Mario filled María Elena and Fidel in on all the developments of the University, the Vatican, and Rome. They asked about Pope Francisco. As they sipped sherry, in the cozy family room, Fidel asked about the contracting arrangements, the scope and future of the plan for peace. The property developments of the University locale interested Fidel.

Fidel mentioned the name of Moises Leckner, one of the world's richest men, and unquestionably one of Argentina's wealthiest. The name sounded familiar. Mario recalled a magazine article that he read recently about Señor Leckner. When Mario inquired further about Señor Leckner, Fidel told him that they belonged to the same club. The club hosted prestigious golf tournaments and was quite famous for its tennis courts, all located in a spectacular setting. The mention of tennis courts peaked Mario's interest at the same time a quiet inspiration crept into his thoughts. Perhaps Moises Leckner would consider supporting the peace initiative.

The following day, Fidel finishing a match with his twice-weekly *frontón* partner, spoke about his brother-in-law's peace dream-scheme. Andres, who worked for twenty years with Leckner International, a conglomerate of vast interests, thought his boss, Señor Leckner, might be interested in such a world dream for peace. Leckner invested heavily in charities, which helped suffering, under-developed peoples to begin self-development through outside, start-up monies.

Andres said his boss was one of the five richest men in the world. Further, Señor Leckner's global vision went beyond that of governments. Andres, a member of Leckner's inner-circle was a trusted employee with the title of vice-president, advanced programs. A title Andres confided to Fidel was ambiguous on purpose. The title allowed him to venture outside of the oil industry where the vast majority of Andres' experience lay. Señor Leckner and his executives thought outside the box long before that expression became popular.

Later that evening Fidel again mentioned to his brother-in-law connecting through his friend Andres to Señor Leckner. Then, the conversation moved on to national soccer scores.

Over coffee the following morning, Mario succeeded in persuading his sister to plan a more comfortable pace of sleeping late, some tennis and increased time visiting with the family.

Mid-morning, Señor Leckner's office called Mario to ask if he and Fidel would be available for lunch later in the day. Mario accepted and asked Fidel to accompany him. Leckner's driver picked them up a half hour before lunch. Mario's mind raced as he prayed "Lord, what is this about?"

Fidel and Mario entered the offices of Leckner International, met Andres in the lobby, and exchanged the usual pleasantries. Andres showed Mario into Señor Leckner's private office. Then, Andres and Fidel headed to the private executive dining room.

Mario greeted his host with smiles and a strong handshake. Mario, impressed by Leckner's firm grip, moved next to the clarity and directness in his eyes, and found his gaze compelling.

He appeared to be a man of deep thought.

Fidel and Andres were enjoying a drink when Leckner guided the Archbishop into the elegantly furnished private dining area. Andres introduced Fidel to Señor Leckner as they took their seats.

The meal progressed with general topics of conversation. They spoke of places, travel, and world conditions. Mario tried to assess the steely mind of Leckner. His face lined and sculpted in the Greek tradition. His gray eyes reflected both confidence and friendliness. He seemed fearless and genuine. His graying hair and facial lines placed him in his fifties.

Mario explained the charter of the peacemaking university and the contracting company and the way the two worked independently, yet, towards shared goals. After wondering what to talk with Leckner about, Mario relaxed, opened up and spoke freely of the Vatican's plans for peacemaking. With the Israeli-Palestinian peace on his mind lately, he talked about the possibility of undertaking such a huge peacemaking project.

Mario mentioned the numerous attempts at peace in the 45 years dating back to the Middle East War of June 1967. For the most part the previous plans for peace called for the exchange of land. Over the years the peace accords, conferences, bridging proposal, initiatives, roadmaps and agreements all failed in the end. Mario concluded with his assessment of the most recent conflict, and the terrible sadness of all the lives lost, especially the lives of innocent children in this area of the world. Moreover, the youth who survive, spend so much of their lives in bomb shelters. Mario believed that the situation called for new thinking.

Mario shared the experience and the expertise of the corporation's Director of Operations, Sakha Khanna. Then, he surprised himself by asking Señor Leckner if he might consider spearheading an initiative, working with Pax Internacionale Corporation. Perhaps, help to fund an Israeli-Palestinian peace.

After describing himself as a searching agnostic willing to work with the Vatican, Leckner responded to the question. "Yes, your Excellency, I am very much interested. I would love to see young children on both sides of this conflict grow up in safety. The children should be provided educational opportunities, and not be restricted to playing within a few feet of bomb shelters. I will support this project; however, I would like you and Pope Francisco to take the lead. The undertaking of a peace settlement between the Palestinian State and the Israelis is important to our world. As you say, nothing worked so far. I would like to change that and support the new thinking you mention. I will pledge to you to use all the financial resources at my disposal to underwrite such a settlement. The implications of this historical peace would be far reaching. Such a project would stabilize the world economy for centuries to come. You are an infant group; yet, I see the promise, the potential. I will invest in your venture. Will you draft a preliminary proposal for me? Tell me explicitly of the cost. In order to succeed, I realize we are talking about billions. Further, please define what you see as the next steps, and provide a list of the participants needed to make this happen."

"Moises, my outline of the proposal will be in your hands in a few days."

"Mario, I will ask Andres to represent me and our corporation in all communications with you and your staff at the Vatican."

"Thank you so much, Señor, I find that I am at a loss for words."

The others at the table realized they were holding their breath, listening to and looking at Leckner. *Billions*! Most importantly, an opportunity existed to fix an unsolvable historical world ethnic problem. "What an amazing first peace project! This inaugural project fit perfectly with the charter of the peace initiative." Mario took his time letting the thought settle in his mind, his heart, and his soul.

Mario spoke, gently wiping his eyes, and taking a sip of water. In a voice husky with emotion, he said, "I would love to take the challenge. Your offer is unbelievable. I will pray, reflect and consult with the Holy Father and other key people. Yours is an extraordinarily generous offer. The credibility of our organization, our University will take a giant leap forward. Talk about answered prayer! Asking God's wisdom, let us begin the dialogue and preliminaries. This is so exciting!"

Mario considered the extensive resources needed for this project. The University and the contract corporation each operated with separate boards, budgets and staffs. Though not officially connected, they envisioned occasional resourcing support, researching operations, and assisting one another whenever feasible.

Sadha Khanna, as head of the Corporation, will be the one to handle the contracts for all personnel and material resources. The University will supply the best international negotiators the world had to offer. In addition, Señor Leckner and his group will bring vast resources to the negotiating table. The project demanded quick development of future program phases, a tentative timetable, and additional support staff.

Mario thought the first major peace project would be something smaller, with a gradual development over time. Their independent boards were still in their infancy, yet God opened wide all doors in His time.

The archbishop was barely aware of the small talk as the lunch concluded. As his heart and soul beat together as one, he thanked God. Mario could not wait to tell His Holiness of this unexpected gift. "Lord, I pray in thanksgiving that this is of you and your Holy Spirit." God's inspiration had given him a push forward on God's timetable. The Lord will provide!

Mario left the club floating above the sidewalk. Walking together to the car, Mario looked at Fidel, and asked quietly "Will he do this?"

Waiting for Señor Leckner's car, Fidel knowingly smiled. "Moises will go all the way with you. He trusts Andres, and there was a very open chemistry between you. You presented yourself well. He is as excited as you are, and he wants to invest, to help with peacemaking. He realizes the wisdom of the Church, and in a way, he will benefit from its credibility."

"In fact, Mario, I think he will follow up in a straightforward and timely manner. Look at it this way, if this project fails, he has someone notable to share the blame with him. He recognizes you as an excellent ally. Best of all, he is sincere. Leckner will furnish everything you need as far as staff and resources. I really like his style. As for you, Mario, I wonder about your other work. It seems to me this venture could end up being more than full-time work for you. On top of this enormous undertaking, the work of University management and selling the Church's treasures remain yours to handle. Are you sure you're ready for this?"

"It's in God's hands, Fidel. I shook internally as I thought of what I said at lunch, and now the added responsibility to deliver, is mine. I hope the Holy Father understands this is something the Lord will lead us through with success. I suppose this is how Peter and Paul got many things started. I keep thinking of the saying if the Lord brings you to it, He'll see you through it!"

Mario realized the remainder of his holiday time was dwindling. He did not sleep well, and during the day, he was preoccupied. María Elena listened to her brother. She continued to cut back on outside activities, and reorganized family activities. He looked tired, and she could not help commenting about this to him. He explained the meaning of a workaholic. She understood.

His last day in Buenos Aires, he slept late, and visited with María Elena. They talked about the kids as well as the state of affairs in Argentina. She shared her happiness with her marriage and her children. She wanted to show him her volunteer spot with Saint Mother Teresa's group in the Aids clinic in the barrio of Manzano, near the edge of the city. Instead, she told him of the place.

As always, her faith and love and the good works she promoted inspired Mario. One of the quiet saints of the world, he thought. Her children enjoyed the happy balance of respect and independence from their parents, which is so hard to develop and maintain in a family. The way her faith seemed to bind the family together made Mario proud.

He could not hope for a better brother-in-law. Fidel was an excellent husband and father, as well as a respected member of the community. Fidel was an Argentinean Catholic lay leader, and his most notable work was as a member of the archbishop's national peace and justice commission, which called for equality in human rights throughout Argentina.

They hugged, smiled and waved, as Tio Mario boarded the Alitalia plane for Rome. He blessed the family as they parted. He found his seat, and settled down with his breviary prayer book. After greeting the little woman in the next seat, he mentally reentered the world of the Vatican, as the sleek jet lifted them over the waters of the Atlantic, away from the South American coast. He learned via a phone call to his office that nothing much changed in the ten days of his absence. The biggest change winged its way to Rome from Argentina with him.

Archbishop Gutiérrez asked Sister Helen Marie to arrange an immediate appointment with the Pontiff, for the day after his return. He also asked her to schedule a joint emergency session for the following week with the Board of the Pax Internacionale Corporation, as well as the Board of the Pax Dei Pontifical University. The subject will be peace negotiations. Mario appreciated the name that His Holiness had chosen for the University. He believed the name would exist for centuries proclaiming the peace of God through the Gospel.

When he met with the Pope, Archbishop Gutiérrez did not hesitate with the Palestinian State-Israeli peace proposal. He believed God would inspire the negotiators. He believed the newly brokered peace would firmly establish the credibility of both the Pax Dei Pontifical University and Pax Internacionale Corporation.

Archbishop Gutiérrez registered surprise at how promptly the Pontiff responded to the proposal. The Vatican's lack of deep diplomatic relations with Israel would not affect the project. Pope Francisco told the Archbishop to bring in the Secretariat of State as part of the team addressing the initiative. An excellent in-house peacemaking move; the Archbishop recognized the value of it. He literally bounced out of the study, nodding to the Swiss Guards.

Mario's team prepared for University and Corporation Boards to move real-time to the world's center stage. While countless ceasefires in this area of the world had failed, today, it seemed a permanent ceasefire lived in the realm of possibility.

Viktor Fiderev waved goodbye as he looked up at the apartment window and glimpsed his beautiful Magda's face smiling down at him. She held their grandson Igor who waved his little hand and wore a matching smile. He dreaded checking in with Alexandrovich at times like this. In the soft light of May, flowers blossomed in the little patches of green around the city and in window boxes. Everything seemed cheery and warm. On days such as this, Viktor found it difficult to leave home.

Facing bureaucracy on a day like this seemed so unfair. His office seemed charged with electricity, with Alexandrovich at the head. He felt the anger of the top-level bureaucrats as they realized someone was escaping the system. Always faithful to the debriefing meeting each time he came from the Vatican. The authorities were aware of everything about his work in the Vatican.

In Russia, it was difficult making himself useful, getting involved in whatever assignment Alexandrovich gave to him each time he returned. The assignments usually involved research projects, which never led to traveling or to direct involvement with the negotiating groups. Viktor often struggled to keep his mind on his work for Alexandrovich.

After reporting to Alexandrovich, he called the Patriarch's office and spoke to Fr. Dimitri. Viktor had developed the habit of calling the priest after his trips to the Vatican to brief him about what happened there. Nothing official and he never put anything in writing, for the protection of all concerned. One of the noticeable characteristics of Russia communication is the absence of personal notes and memos. Such missives were subject to interception or misinterpretation by the authorities. The country still lived in a mistrust syndrome, and it was only beginning to experience confidence in personal, written communications.

Hearing Viktor's voice brought an immediate smile to Father Dimitri's face. Viktor brought Fr. Dimitri up to speed about his work. At the archbishop's request, he asked Father Dimitri to talk with the Patriarch. For Viktor, it was not the first time he mediated a sticky situation. The Russian Embassy contacted Viktor initially. They routed the request for the return of the national treasures through the Office of National Archives. Obviously, Russia wanted the national treasures held by the Vatican returned to their nation. Just as Viktor had presented his case to the archbishop, he now presented the Vatican's case to Father Dimitri, who assured Viktor the Patriarch would look into the treasures, churches and schools.

Sister Helen Marie phoned each member of both Boards to convene for a special session. Viktor and others on the Boards were quite curious about her call. Sister explained the unscheduled meeting held great importance, and expected the meeting would take two or three days. All that she would say is that an urgent issue arose, which needed the Board members immediate attention.

Viktor, flattered by the whole idea of flying-out, as an international diplomat, on what must be a very important matter, felt valued. The pressure from Alexandrovich grew even more unpleasant than usual, as he explained the emergency meeting. While it was the first time for this, Viktor thought it unlikely to be the last. Everyone will get used to it, he thought. During the flight, he experienced a great curiosity and excitement about it.

Viktor's Aeroflot flight to Rome flew over the former Eastern Bloc nations. He thought about how the realignments reshaped economies and governments in only a few years, and he wondered if the realignments would last. Some Russians believed the collapse of the U.S.S.R. was a huge tragedy of the 20th century. Viktor was not one of them. Independence and freedom were worth the struggle.

Sore points remained along with evolving governments and parties, as well as European market questions. As he looked down through the clouds from thirty-one thousand feet, he thought it was still a complicated mess.

A confirmed atheist, at times Viktor did wonder if God really existed. If so, did God keep track of everything? Would He be pleased with the way we are handling peace bringing? It was an unanswerable question, at least to Viktor. The question led Viktor to wonder if ultimately peace could ever be possible.

Viktor returned to his notes, and sipped the cognac on the little seat back table before him. He found the page he sought in the curriculum, which started in September. There it is. He smiled. He would be teaching two courses, one in the Russian historical development, and the other in ethnic group negotiation. Both topics were comfortable for him.

The joint Boards' meeting agenda promised the members a matter of global significance. The members engaged in small talk while standing around the dark wooden table in the center of the room. The atmosphere, amid the crystal chandeliers and damask walls was palpable with everyone wondering about the seemingly classified item up for discussion. The coffee and refreshments on the side bar, as well as the traditional bottles of water scattered around the table indicated a long meeting.

Viktor spoke to the Frenchman, DeVaulier, until a small bell tinkled, and the Archbishop indicated everyone should take a seat. There was no particular seating arrangement; identical portfolios were at each place.

Mario opened the meeting by graciously thanking each one for being there, speaking in English, as previously determined. It was the most common language, shared by all members. The printed materials were published in Italian, French, Spanish, as well as English. He looked at his watch, and explained that in three minutes, the Holy Father would be with them, and His Holiness would begin their session with a prayer and an explanation.

The archbishop asked the Board members to introduce themselves briefly, and mention their homeland to Pope Francisco. Mario was familiar with each of them from reviewing their dossiers, and he appreciated the opportunity to link the names, faces, and backgrounds now. A little murmur took place around the room, the members excitedly chatting about the Holy Father's visit. A moment later, everyone stood as Pope Francisco entered the conference room.

His Holiness' face was gentle and relaxed. He wore his ever-serene political smile. His white robes created a natural focus, and an air of power and presence, as he moved from chair to chair and greeted each person, with the Archbishop preceding him and presenting each member to him. He switched languages as the introductions indicated. They were still standing as he arrived at the head of the table, and invited everyone to join him in prayer. In Spanish, he asked the presence of God to inspire and guide this group in its monumental work of trying to bring peace and harmony, where there are so many differences. It seemed much like the famous "Prayer of St. Francis." At the "Amens," he opened his eyes, made the sign of the cross, and with a gesture, and invited everyone to be seated. He remained standing.

Switching to English, the Pontiff thanked them for serving and their willingness to be peacemakers, which was a rather thankless job. The Pope listened intently to each member go around the table, from chair to chair, and talk about themselves, their countries, families and their interest in being on their respective Boards. As each member spoke, the Pope responded in the member's native language. The Pope thanked each one as they finished.

The grace and charm of the Pontiff made everybody feel welcome, and they all relaxed. Everyone in the room enjoyed telling of their background and family, and their interest in peace. The Pope smiled when he described his grandmother's faith to the group, and how she cracked their heads at times growing up. He shared with the Board members how her grandchildren knelt around the fireplace, and prayed the rosary together. He mentioned they did not always pray peacefully. He charmed everyone. Viktor thought of his own grandmother's faith, which genuinely touched his life. When his turn came, he did not hesitate to mention her life, and her influence on his.

The Holy Father concluded by asking Archbishop Gutiérrez to share his background, and to explain the most important agenda item to the group for their consideration, prayers, and decisions.

The Archbishop closed his eyes in a brief moment of prayer. He explained his background. Took a deep cleansing breath, and then he addressed the serious issue, the Palestinian State-Israeli peace undertaking. He wondered how the Board members would react. He prayed interiorly.

Without exception, everyone described the peace proposal in terms of "beyond amazing." The Boards overwhelmingly supported the Israeli-Palestinian peace proposal. Viktor was 'over the moon' at this tremendous opportunity to work for peace.

They worked late into the night. The following day the subcommittees appointed by at the joint session the previous evening met to develop tasks, and allocate work order assignments for those working on the proposal for Leckner.

They estimated the proposal developmental process at three months. Once Leckner approved it, they would meet again using the proposal's statement of work to assign task managers, allocate personnel and other required resources.

As they prayerfully left the conference room, Mario reminded everyone of the professional confidentiality they needed to keep. Everyone had already signed non-disclosure agreements.

They prayed as a group before leaving and the archbishop asked for their continued prayer about the proposal as well. For Viktor and the other non-Christians, this meant quiet listening to the voice within, and hearing the wisdom spoken in the heart.

This will require a Herculean effort on the part of everyone involved, Mario thought.

Thank God, everyone involved was totally committed to the success of the proposal, and, further, to the implementation of peace in a region that was too familiar with unrest and war.

# Chapter 6

## The Woman

The Pax Dei Pontifical University prepared to sign the inaugural department heads to contracts. Monsignor Raphael Rondeau and his staff did a magnificent job. The department heads, in turn, would select and sign initial faculty staff positions to their contracts. They were ready to begin.

The faculty and the University Board members planned to meet soon to discuss and receive approval from Monsignor Rondeau and Archbishop Gutiérrez for the next steps, the process of choosing administrative assistants and teaching assistants.

Comments overheard in the hallways related to how this faculty came from every nation on earth. In fact, some said, "from the ends of the earth." Men and women, church-types, Christian and non-Christian; they represented every religious persuasion as well as non-believers. All believed in the vision of the University.

The faculty, via memos from the Board, was continuously reminded to refrain from denigrating any religious faith, or political persuasion. The Pax Dei Pontifical University was open and accepting of every conceivable culture and belief. This cross section of the world's complex society would help to establish, and to maintain global peace. A poster hung in the hallway stating peace, like charity, begins at home. The home depicted, the Pax Dei Pontifical University, of course.

The peace process included each individual's family relationships and professional experiences. Expectations were for each faculty member to have peace in their heart and mind in the workplace. The Board identified maintaining this level of harmony among the faculty members as a priority. When peace faltered among the staff, mediation, with compromise and cooperation, would begin right away.

Faculty and staff members were expected to report any friction to their supervisors in a timely manner for review and reconciliation. Transparency and honesty were vital to the international University dedicated to peace. Personal peace was always the starting point.

Prayer was crucial to providing divine wisdom, and reflective insight into peacemaking. Godlike peacemaking remained the ultimate goal. To assure fairness, a continual review of economic, and resource allocation was required, and in place. In some cases, ethnic differences might be a consideration. Understanding the applied resource processes and its interpretation by the multitude of cultures remained imperative.

Avoiding errors in essential documents and policies ranked high in importance to the archbishop. Mistakes made when participants grew weary during lengthy discussions proved costly in the past. Given the importance of the peace initiative, the archbishop thought it crucial to prevent omission errors in all procedures, especially peace making initiatives. He was grateful the university and corporation had an 'errors and omissions' insurance policy, but optimistically hoped never to use it.

Mario's staff discussed academic peacemaking at every board meeting. It was a line item, which appeared on every university Board agenda. As expected, ideological differences surfaced, and were usually resolved by the end of the meeting. The agreed upon modifications to the procedures were put in place right then. As for philosophical differences, they would always be present. Historically, heated disagreements of concept, theory, educational and personal approaches, not only happened, they were expected at higher levels of learning. The archbishop thought the battlefield of the mind was an area, which needed peace.

The initial curriculum, which included essential courses well matched to the pathway of peace, was already in place. The refinements of peace-developing specialties were in position for the ensuing years by the curriculum planning committee.

Financially, things looked good. The jewelry sale brought more revenue than expected. The cost of the university campus proved relatively inexpensive. The initial faculty contracts and operational costs came in at or under budget. After deducting the various administrative costs, and Swiss agent's expense, a multi-million dollar balance remained.

The global divestiture was not going as smoothly. The Holy Father issued several letters and instructions to some of the reluctant bishops. The bottom line was that no diocese accrued over a certain percentage based on the formula, and their size. The diocese kept one-third of the net assets for local projects of charity, service and peace, and the remaining two-thirds of the excess was sent to the Vatican, earmarked for the Pax Dei Pontifical University.

The all-new arrangement for church monies with secular management guiding it through a financial banking system was in place. The inventory, control and reporting system, international in scope, now certified secure. Regular reports were issued by every diocese and religious institution, and submitted to the Vatican's finance offices via the WPO.

Anna Maloof's current interest lay in this complex area of the Church's financing redesign. Her bosses at World Wide News encouraged Anna to find out more through the Archbishop's office. If that proved impossible, Anna planned to visit with individual dioceses or parishes as she delved into the policies implemented by the Church. She thought the national organizations of bishops could be helpful if she could find someone there willing to talk about these sensitive areas.

Anna was aware Oppenheim and Burke handled the assessment and realignment of the local churches. She had an inside source with the company who confirmed that Oppenheim and Burke had successfully implemented and tested their procedures to identify and control excessive holdings. Though she could get only limited information from her source, Anna believed the financial aspect of the Vatican's peace plan was a huge story.

To Anna, it was a bit like researching and publishing a book. She would need a financial expert to help her write this story. She consulted her New York office about whether to look for a local Italian finance professor, a lawyer or firm, or fly back to New York. On the other hand, it made more sense for someone to fly to Rome from New York to help her understand such an in-depth study.

Anna looked forward to her interviews with representative bishops from various parts of the world. She sought their advice, feedback and experiences in dealing with the papal redesign of Church financial operations. Sister Helen Marie supplied its effect on the Vatican's plans.

The University found itself inundated with applications from students around the world. Applicants, sponsored by their governments or via grants from benefactors in business, industry, or private foundations, did not worry about tuition, or living costs. All students were free to focus on their classwork. Staff members were dedicated to scholarships, endowments, and offers from benefactors. In the end, many entities sponsored students at the University. In the coming year, this office would become a standalone entity. Mario counted 7,500 students in the inaugural class. It was an elite group of selectees, chosen from more than 50,000 applicants representing over 100 countries.

Anna let her New York office know the rumors were flying about the selection of the new president for the Pax Dei Pontifical University. Anna and Sister Helen Marie conferred daily as informal reports of the selection process circulated. The adage "of those who know don't talk, and those who talk don't know" proved true around the confidentiality of the choice for the position of University President. Helen Marie mentioned it in her daily prayers.

The selection of the new president would be the concluding piece for Anna's series for World Wide News describing the various structures and the flow of the University offices and its departments. Her portrayal of the variety of staff and professional positions, as well as the many and varied backgrounds of students proved exciting and informative. She moved freely among the campus staff now as a familiar face.

Anna looked over the potential attendance lists for the dedication day of the Pax Dei Pontifical University, and began scheming about all the guests and dignitaries she would have a chance to interview. Sister Helen Marie continued to open doors for Anna. Sister appreciated the way Anna wrote favorably about the University, its peacemaking efforts and the people that Anna described as channels of peace.

Appointing the first university president proved a little more complicated than hiring professors. Prior to the nominating process, Archbishop Gutiérrez checked with the Holy Father to see if he placed higher value on any particular attributes for the position of president. The archbishop tried to hide his surprise when the Pope mentioned the possibility of a woman.

Archbishop and Monsignor Rondeau formed an "ad hoc" presidential selection committee comprised of faculty representatives, department heads, and University Board members. They handpicked a group of 12 to review the initial list of nearly 100 prescreened applicants, and that group chose 20 potential presidential candidates. They further refined the list, ranked and selected the top four candidates. The Archbishop met with the group only after they assembled their final recommendations.

The first three candidates impressed the archbishop. One Bishop came from India. There was no surprise in that selection as he expected at least two bishops. He was correct. There were two bishops, and the third candidate was a former university president. When he came to the fourth dossier, he put down his glass of sherry. He glanced at the photo of the fourth candidate.

He glimpsed a strikingly beautiful forty-five year old black woman. He noted her gleaming gentle smile, the classic high, chiseled cheekbones, and the tilt of her head. Amid the Afro halo of tight curls, he noted the glint of cleverness in her eyes. Mario recognized her.

When he knew her, everyone called her Marie Koabati. Twenty years ago, Marie, a student of political economics, enrolled for a semester in a class he taught at the Angelicum University. Her name now was Mobatumbo. Mario thought her credentials and her beauty, exceptional. Widowed for two years, her husband, a renowned international lawyer had worked for the World Bank. Her family now, three grown sons, the youngest enrolled at Oxford in England.

Marie studied at London's School of Economics and Political Science. Her doctoral work was completed at the University of Innsbruck. She spoke seven languages, including French, German, English and Spanish. Marie represented the government at the United Nations for five years, and she traveled extensively during that period. Her most recent years were spent as the Minister of Education in Tanzania, where she refused to fire several faculty members of the national university because of their pro-Palestinian State connections. Her refusal landed her in jail for six months.

Marie authored several books on political economy, from an African and developing nation's perspective. The books sold well.

She was an active Catholic lay leader, and came highly recommended by Archbishop Gregory Keytanzoe of Tanzania. His recommendation would serve her well because Archbishop Keytanzoe was a trusted friend of the Pope.

Marie became a political activist early in her life. The six months in Tanzania turned out to be her second arrest. She was arrested as a student, and jailed for demonstrating on behalf of expanded rights for women in the new government of Tanzania. Marie would be a welcome relief in the Vatican, and shine a light on the emerging leadership of women in the Church. A strong candidate, and a woman of courage and integrity, Marie was the nominee that he ranked highest. He tried to understand the committee's recommendation to rank her behind the three men. He did not understand at all, unless it was the two protest arrests.

In interviews with the final candidates, the following week, Mario included Marie as an exceptional possibility. It proved to be a charming change, from the more formal interviews with the two bishops, and the former university president.

"Your Holiness, here is a most important list with the top recommendations for the position of president of the Pax Dei Pontifical University. The committee worked diligently screening the candidates, and I prayed much over the selection process and the final choices."

Gutiérrez did quite a bit of soul-searching before this meeting. He remained nervous because the committee meeting the day before ended with a split vote on his preference. The discussion started out frank and edgy and remained in that vein for the duration of the meeting. He placed Marie Mobatumbo as his choice ahead of the other three names, and hours of discussion took place as result. The kindest way to put it, the committee wondered about the wisdom of his ranking. Not everyone on the selection committee agreed, and two members left the meeting upset. Now, he tried to convince the Holy Father about the validity of his choice. He needed honesty, and spiritual abandonment. His stomach churned and his morning coffee grew bitter. He believed strongly that Marie Mobatumbo should be the person to lead the University. He explained the discussion and dissenting views expressed at yesterday's committee meeting. He left it for the Pontiff to consider his decision in silence and prayer.

The Holy Spirit must be present, to bring such openness, and peacefulness to the hiring process. The Pontiff reflected an ease, and trust, as Gutiérrez caught the same growing sentiments within himself. This proposal to select a woman might test not only the archbishop's courage, and the Holy Father's, but also the world in light of women's emerging leadership.

"Your Holiness, we propose a qualified woman, not a nun, but a lay woman of international standing. Her name is Marie Koabati Mobatumbo of Tanzania. Here is her dossier. Her local Archbishop Gregory Keytanzoe, who you know well, gave her high marks. She is my top recommendation, though several other candidates are similarly qualified and recommended. Here are their dossiers also." He breathed hard as he handed the material to the Pontiff. He always experienced this tightness, trying to get across some special interest, or preference, in decisions with the Holy Father. He prayed, as he sat back in his chair, anxiously waiting for the Holy Father's questions.

"So, my good archbishop, you think a woman, this woman, would be formidable enough to contend with a stellar faculty, world leaders, world opinions, a peacemaking corporation, the Vatican bureaucracy, and me? She must be quite a person. Did you and your committee interview all the candidates?" "Yes, Your Holiness, we did."

"Well, no doubt, you expected I would have an unfavorable reaction to the possibility of a woman, a lay woman. I hope you are not too disappointed. If this is your final recommendation, my only advice to you is interviewing all four proposed candidates one more time. This time I will join you in prayer for wisdom and discernment. Mario, bring your final recommendation back to me. I am not afraid to appoint a laywoman, if she is the most qualified, and your number one choice. I do not want to appoint the first woman to the Curia simply to try to shock the world, or use the appointment to make an international statement. I want to choose the most qualified and inspired leader for this quest for peace. I am open to whatever the Lord presents to us. Perhaps it will be difficult to explain to the hierarchy. However, women religious around the world will cheer the choice of a woman and will counter the unease. In any case, it will be a step forward. Actually, I feel the Lord is leading us in this choice. It is for a three year contract period, is it not?"

"Yes, Your Holiness." He dared not dream the Pontiff would see the possibility with so little questioning, and without hesitation. He marveled at the ease of the discussion. He was aware that this conversation marked the first time, or one of the only times, the Pope used Mario's given name in conversation. It reflected an ease, and trust between them, he thought. The Holy Spirit brought trust and clarity to this decision.

The next steps were Mario's last round of interviews, finalizing the offer package, the Papal interview and the Holy Father's approval to announce the appointment publicly. He planned to sit back and watch the reaction to the news from Roman and world hierarchy. It would be interesting, Mario reflected. "Lord, your will be done."

Mario's resolve increased following his final interview with each of the perspective candidates. Marie Koabati Mobatumbo was his number one choice for the position.

Marie's humility and quiet confidence impressed the Pontiff in their first personal interview, also. She asked the Holy Father about his vision for the Pax Dei Pontifical University and its direction in the next ten years. It turned out to be the right question. The Pope explained his hopes for world peace via the University. He pointed out that the negotiations with Señor Leckner, the Vatican peacemakers and the Palestinian State-Israeli peace would be a litmus test for all.

Marie looked intensely into the Holy Father's eyes as they spoke. The Pope gave her a generous nod and smile, along with his personal blessing. A day later, the Pontiff, announced his concurrence to Mario. He told Mario that Archbishop Keytanzoe recommended Marie, which proved a big plus. Marie's interview confirmed it for the Pontiff. Pope Francisco asked Mario to prepare the announcement and public introduction to Marie for the media.

She was a compelling figure and possessed an engaging personality, Gutiérrez thought to himself. Marie requested that she be the one to schedule meetings with the University Board, the newly arriving faculty members, and the Board of the Pax Internacionale Corporation.

Marie met first with the Board members of the Board of Pax Internacionale Corporation in her role as President of the University and an "ex-officio" member of the Board. Then, she met with the Pax Dei Pontifical University Board.

Marie received the quietest welcoming reception from some Vatican offices. Apparently, not all Vatican offices shared the Holy Father's enthusiasm for her appointment. The lack of enthusiasm was most noticeable at the episcopal level of cardinals and bishops, who headed the various administrative offices. Notable for his displeasure was Cardinal Giuseppe Steiger, Prefect of the Offices of Seminaries and Universities. The cardinal had been displeased ever since the forming of the University bypassed the Cardinal's perceived authority. Archbishop Gutiérrez still carried fears of the Cardinal's machinations. In fact, Mario avoided various developments involving the Curia. Thus far, his plan kept the attacks upon him inconsequential.

Marie got into the business of the Pax Dei Pontifical University immediately. She took home stacks of paper to study each evening. She moved her family items from Tanzania.

The University provided a comfortable villa adjoining the campus for the president. Suitable for entertaining, the beautiful garden, complete with a fountain, and beautiful flowers to include white lilies, violets and a rose garden set amid Romanesque walls. The Mediterranean climate was perfect. Marie loved her garden. It provided an enticing setting for study and reading. Marie spent hours going over reports and documents. Her world had expanded dramatically in just a few weeks.

There was a chapel in her home. Marie would pause there in moments of tension, sit quietly, and ask for the peace and light of God. She had not prayed like this since her husband died. The Pontiff asked her, in their meeting to pray over the issues of peace they would face and to maintain her own personal peace, which her job would challenge. She realized his wisdom. She thought of what the Lord said to St. Paul in 2 Corinthians 12:9, "My grace is sufficient for you, for my power is made perfect in weakness."

In her first media interview, she fully explained the Pope's vision, his hopes for world peace. She did not mention the Palestinian State-Israeli possibilities. She responded well to the questions. She was very photogenic. The cameras captured her striking smile and her intense eyes as she spoke. The press loved her.

They hailed her appointment as a spectacular announcement, and a success among all nations and throughout international educational circles. Marie met a second time with the Pax Dei Pontifical University and the Pax Internacionale Corporation Boards. She spoke with deep humility, and yet with clarity, courage and strength, well informed on so many issues.

The University faculty continued to arrive and settle in during the summer months. The faculty graciously received Marie. Marie was kept busy seeing to their accommodations. She met weekly with the various deans and department heads, and managed to balance the demands of each department.

Marie was grateful that her assistant Father Jules Mattosha handled the renovation of classrooms and dormitories on campus. Father Jules was a Maronite Catholic priest and an over-qualified, experienced administrator on the Roman scene, and a tremendous support.

The Boards delved into architectural planning meetings for the old estate with its nineteenth century buildings, and developed plans for the new buildings, which would house a library, classrooms, and additional dormitories for the students.

The dining hall was finished. A temporary communications center was in the set up process. A professional computer engineering staff was contracted to design the latest in international satellite communications for the coming year, which would expand all of the University's satellite and computer hardware and software capabilities.

Easily one of the most appealing features on the campus was the setting of the campus gardens. The estate included five hundred acres of land. After the monastery relocated in the 1920, the Sisters of Charity of Milan took over the property and began their academy for young women. The original Academy building had two stories constructed of gray stone. The family estate of twenty acres held the administrative offices temporarily in the thirty-room mansion, of the Alessandro family, the most recent occupants. Professors shared offices in the administration section. The small lake in the center of the campus was surrounded by tree-covered lanes, gardens of various varieties, a small section of undeveloped woodland, and a three-level fountain and pool at the entry drive, beautifully maintained. A chapel that accommodated two hundred was attached to the Academy classroom building. A sense of green and coolness pervaded the place, through walkways and lanes. It was a shame some of the woodland would be sacrificed to expand parking.

The drive from Rome to the University took about forty minutes. Long enough for a person to unwind, or give fellow travelers an opportunity to get to know one another. The drive consisted of country roads, northeast of the busy Roman traffic. Beautiful trumpet gentian with their deep royal purple and indigo blue petals were abundantly scattered among the fields. The wildflowers were amazing.

The University setting boasted an atmosphere of peace, with the tree-lined entrance, and the stately campus. Pleased with it, the archbishop looked forward to the day they would bring the Holy Father, for the dedication and blessing. Gutiérrez had a small office on campus, though his staff remained at the Vatican. He frequently offered Masses for the staff and workers at both locations.

Viktor moved into his campus office early in June. Located on the second floor, with an adjoining study and bedroom, all quite small, but very satisfactory. He bounded along the hallways, inspecting the library's progress, and all of the classroom improvements. Viktor could not contain his excitement about his classes. His world was a bright and shining springtime, as if he rediscovered the meaning of life. The only cloud on the horizon was the sadness he experienced over his separation from Magda, and his daughter's family, especially Igor, his little grandson. He called home weekly. He hoped in the next year to bring them for a visit. He found the separation very difficult. He lived in two vastly different worlds and cultures. He witnessed the tremendous changes going on in Russia and the eastern nations of Europe. Perhaps he could someday relocate as an academician, with his family, to Rome and somehow manage to keep his home in Russia. He could not quite imagine an economy or income allowing such a move. He would need his pension from the State someday, or perhaps he could acquire tenure and additional income here, which would allow him to live in both places, and to travel back and forth with the family.

Viktor loved visiting the other professors, and hearing their backgrounds and stories. He became a delight among the faculty, a happy balance of seriousness and scholarship, and he was always ready to share stories and some cognac with colleagues. The Archbishop heard stories of Viktor's presence and skills, through his dealings with others among the staff.

Viktor first met Marie at the gathering of the University Board where the archbishop presented her formally to members. Her beautiful ebony face held such power mixed with fine lines and a quick and gentle smile. Her small dark eyes seemed capable of piercing your soul. She conveyed strength to the group. Viktor liked and respected her immediately.

The archbishop and his staff met weekly, at a minimum, to discuss the progress of the Vatican's ever-expanding plans for peace. With only a few problems, they were ahead of schedule in most areas. The University exceeded expectations. Of course, there are always difficult people. Staff meetings included critiques from Cardinal O'Rourke and several complaints from Mr. Yoshino, a Japanese businessperson and member of the Board.

Mr. Yoshino showed his displeasure at every opportunity. He was displeased at the way Archbishop Gutiérrez's office treated him when he made inquiries about the Vatican's sales. After numerous rejections of requests for early release of information, he finally gave up contacting the Swiss firm of Lamentier for information. Lamentier told Mr. Yoshino that they planned to release a series of catalogues featuring all sale items soon. They offered to put him on the mailing list, and explained the availability on the internet as well.

Lamentier informed Yoshino of their plans to sell certain items on an individual bid basis. They assured him they would contact him about those sales as well. He remained unsatisfied. As a result, he opened an office for his international marketing company, in downtown Rome, to be closer to the action.

Yoshino resold a number of jewelry items by this time, which he procured in one of the jewelry lots at the initial auction. He saw an opportunity to make lots of money and he sought all the insider information he could. The staff, without exception, found him unpleasant, aggressive and routinely rude. He had not been cooperative with anyone. Having given up on Lamentier in Switzerland, he worked harder on his quest to establish contacts inside the offices of Archbishop Gutiérrez in Rome.

Mr. Yoshino had little interest in the investments in local land and buildings held by the Church. The small parcel items were not worth the trouble, according to Yoshino's interests. International and local laws, and taxes would be involved in their purchase and trading, and he did not want to get involved with legal entanglements. The art treasures were the heart of his interest.

Archbishop Gutiérrez continued to challenge the Pontiff to write an encyclical letter addressing peacemaking, and his plans and goals for the International Pax Dei Pontifical University and Pax Internacionale Corporation. Mario smiled broadly when the Pope took his suggestion.

His Holiness recruited a team of three theologians from the Gregorian University to meet and suggest outlines for him and to be available to provide additional research as needed. The research of the few key theologians, working in close collaboration with the Pope, was genius and critical.

Encyclicals presented difficulties. For formal statements like this one to take on meaning in the reality of complex global questions, it needed open-endedness. Archbishop Gutiérrez, a part of the encyclical team, spent a lot of time reading the drafts. He read in the chapel with its dark, quiet, reflective atmosphere. As he read, he prayed and questioned. He asked for the Light of God's Spirit. He prayed to understand the reality of complex global situations.

Archbishop Gutiérrez believed the Pope's message of peace to be transcultural and multi-generational.

He was certain the Holy Father reviewed and rewrote the drafts while on his knees in the papal chapel. In the past, God built great understandings from small lives and the insights of a few people. These persons would humbly rather be elsewhere, like Moses with Pharaoh, before the Exodus, or the signers of the Declaration of Independence of the United States before the Revolutionary War.

The encyclical grew into quite a project, as the Holy Father began to outline his thoughts and to meet with the theology team. An encyclical could be an intricate creation, involving the historical and contemporary thinking on a situation, with theological basis, such as Saint John XXIII's, "Peace on Earth" or, Pope Paul VI's "Progress of Peoples." They spoke to world interdependence, as did a later encyclical by Saint John Paul II, on the world economic system, in relation to the Gospel. They were eloquent documents, which summarized and crystallized Christian thinking on complex issues. The most famous and numerous encyclicals composed were presented by Saint John Paul II.

The encyclical team fell into a rhythm of review. The Holy Father would bring drafts of his peace document to Archbishop Gutiérrez for his review. At which time, they would sit and discuss certain points, remove ambiguity. It was difficult to compose such a comprehensive document with such broad scope.

The encyclical traced the Gospel teachings of peace, from the New Testament, referencing Jesus and His Apostles. Next, the efforts at peacemaking and peacekeeping cited from notable moments of history attested to the efforts of the United Nations today. Law and legal entities, noted as necessary systems in a complex society, which helped maintain peace. The encyclical team sought and explored peace solutions in the workplace, among communities and with neighbors. The most deplorable peacemaking efforts were clearly a peace obtained through force or fear.

The encyclical outlined many causes, which rob an individual and the world of peace. It called out world peace among nations. The Holy Father wrote about a need for an awareness of these structures and systems, and the exploration of the imbalances involved. Justice is central to establishing the balance of peace, freedom and human rights.

The Church itself faced a struggle of war and peace, over the control of assets, among bishops, and religious communities. The peace encyclical brought the calming insight of Jesus, to resolve this unrest in the Church universal.

The Gospel of mutuality and sharing, of being poor and trusting, is almost as difficult to get across as the gospel of interdependence and cooperation, and of dying to vested interests, in favor of the community of the common good. Society and the Church internalized much of Jesus' Gospel.

The Pax Dei Pontifical University supported the methodologies, and mediation at all levels, advocating compromise and cooperation always.

Archbishop Gutiérrez looked on the global inventories as a game of wits. He thought about it, as "Ecclesial Monopoly." He found that the Archdiocese of Los Angeles contributed more to the Vatican coffers yearly, than asked of them. Now he was in the process of tracking the trading, bargaining, and shifting. The process should be the envy of Wall Street.

However, Cardinal O'Rourke had his own ideas. He was certain that the dream of international peace could be financed in ways other than the ones presented by the Vatican, thus far.

# Chapter 7

## The University

September brought the official opening of the Pax Dei Pontifical University. The invited guests were amazed at the beauty of the campus. Amid towering pines and cedars were dazzling zinnias, bougainvillea, oleanders, dahlias and buttercups, bordered with variegated greenery. People crowded the campus, strolled pathways, and walked through the buildings opened to inspection. Proudly displaying the University logo on their blazers, student monitors ushered the visitors, took photos for them, and answered questions on this special day.

Of all the attractions offered by opening day, the longest wait time was to meet the Pontiff. His Holiness went early to the soccer fields where he planned to celebrate an outdoor Mass and officially dedicate the University later in the day. The papal line from Saint Peter to Pope Francisco, an unbroken line of saints and sinners, made Mario wonder how many other popes generated this much excitement. The atmosphere around him was best described as electric. Celebrated as the people's Pope, the crowds followed him as if he were a rock star.

The press, who presented the university to the world, headquartered in tents throughout the grounds except for the dozen or so who were assigned to the Pope.

The President of Italy, Salvatore Guardini, accepted the University's invitation to be the keynote speaker. Archbishop Gutiérrez' office took special pains to invite representatives from all nations, which according to the United Nations totaled 195, more if you counted states partially recognized by the U.N. Hosting as many representatives as possible was more important than the level of officials who attended.

Worldwide recognition of the University was crucial. Building credibility and establishing networks for the University in its infancy would
take time.

One or two generations of graduates would establish the alumni
necessary to strengthen connections for the University throughout the
world. The Archbishop scripted the day's communications and ensured
his public relations group was prepared for this special kick off day.

Anna Malooff took advantage of her newfound friendliness with
the faculty. She roamed the grounds freely interviewing the international personalities. She talked with the President of Italy, the first-year
students from Russian and Asian countries, like Vietnam. Iran's two
undergrads ranked the most popular with all the members of the press.

Viktor radiated joy! He formed a special team to escort the Eastern European nations' representatives through the day. He beamed his
biggest smile as he energetically grasped hands, and made introductions
with a gentle bow. Viktor shared with his colleagues his only regret on
this special day was that Magda, his beloved wife, was not with him.

Marie moved with grace and charm among the dignitaries. Her
command of languages, and her United Nations connections made
her the center of attention. Previously, she had organized the expected
guests into manageable groupings. The groups were escorted by faculty
and students. Everyone was included. Her sense of hospitality awed
the more protocol-and-formal-minded Archbishop. God gifted Marie
abundantly, he reflected.

A lot of attention was focused on the Board of the Pax Dei Pontifical University, as well as the Pax Internacionale Corporation Board.
Marie had prepared them for the recognition, and recommended the
Board members serve as escorts to the representatives of the national
bishops' conferences from around the world, along with the major Religious Order superiors.

The Holy Father personally invited each nation with a bishop's
conference to send an official representative to the dedication. He
intended to meet with them the following day in a group audience.
The Holy Father planned to ask the National Conference of Bishops,
to sponsor at least one scholarship for a talented student each year.
He hoped the University would offer rotating scholarships among the
poorer countries of non-Christian traditions. The scholarship recipients
would insure the diversity of the University, and provide a steady input
and distribution of alumni all over the world. Thereby, creating a corps
of leaders dedicated to peace from all countries.

The outpouring of financial support, prior to the opening to the official opening of the University, surprised everyone. Donations for the Corporation as well as the University came from international corporations, small businesses, governments, foundations, and wealthy donors all over the world.

The Holy Father cautioned all recipients to be grateful, yet aware of any strings attached. All gifts must be transparent. It would take time for the Corporation to establish its credentials, to prove its value. Adherence to guidelines meant acceptance of any donation met the highest ethical standards.

Archbishop Gutiérrez wanted the corporation to remain independent. His vision for Pax Internationale included negotiating settlements even if the parties could not afford mediation, as in the under-developed nations. There were funds earmarked for these nations. They were at the top of the list for donation distribution.

Lamentier Ltd. sent several representatives to the opening day ceremonies. The Lamentier team explained how the company managed the sale of Vatican holdings, and maintained the inventory. They talked to the press about how money involved in all transactions, receipts or expenses went through Oppenheim and Burke, the Vatican's brokers in London. They handled the funds, which financed the operations of the Pax Dei Pontifical University and the Pax Contracting Corporation. The team assigned to work with the press, also answered questions for Oppenheim and Burke. They provided an annual audited accounting of all ordinary accounts and expenses of the two institutions. While they also provided audits of the Vatican accounts, the accounts remained separated always. The University, the Contracting Corporation Board, and the Pontiff all held strict oversight of their respective accounting systems. The annual audited financial reports were independent, and not linked together in any way, except by association.

The sale of holdings and treasures of the universal Church remained the major funding source for the University. The Holy Father, Archbishop Gutiérrez and his staff relied on this funding to finance the day-to-day operations of both the University, and to a lesser extent, the Corporation, which would soon pass the break-even point and be self-supporting. They offered countless explanations to dignitaries and the press on this special day.

As the Holy Father prepared to leave, following the Mass and formal dedication ceremony, he leaned over to get into his car. Marie could not help but lean toward him and give him a fatherly kiss on the cheek. He glanced back over his shoulder at her and gave her a knowing smile and wink, as if to say, "You're wonderful too; keep up the excellent work." A kind of unspoken appreciation existed between them, a language of the heart.

Archbishop Gutiérrez witnessed the small exchange. He often described Marie as a leader with a heart, a rare individual. She bridged the politics through her personal charisma. Mario found her to be genuine, sincere and loving.

As the limousine drove away, Marie and Archbishop Gutiérrez turned to walk back to the reception where they were separated. Most of the dignitaries would be leaving since the Pontiff made his exit. Marie and Mario moved among them, bidding farewells, and extending invitations for further communications. Adrenalin continued to run high. The day was declared an absolute success.

After the majority of visitors departed, Marie walked back to the administration building, and Archbishop Gutiérrez met her on the path near the entrance. He seemed anxious as she approached. He invited her to walk with him on the pathways around the building to the quieter tree-lined driveway. The Archbishop shared his concern about not seeing Señor Leckner, or his representative at the opening. He asked Marie if she received any word from Leckner's office. The Archbishop, understandably troubled, wondered what happened.

Marie allayed Mario's concerns. Señor Leckner had arrived the day before, and was holding private conferences in the guest quarters or at other times in Marie's private office. He saw an opportunity to talk to a large group of perspective international investors at one time, and took full advantage of it. Marie relayed Leckner as saying, "The right people at the right time, the right venue, in this setting make this a very special opportunity." Mario smiled and nodded his understanding as he decided to catch up with Señor Leckner later.

Mario dreaded it when he saw Mr. Yoshino in an intense, animated conversation with Cardinal O'Rourke late that afternoon.

Dampening his mood further, Mr. Yoshino cornered Archbishop Gutiérrez before leaving in his limousine. He emphatically conveyed to the archbishop his dissatisfaction with the way the Vatican and its agents handled the art and historical treasure sales. He threatened to call a press conference complaining about the deliberate plot to tie his hands, to prevent him from moving forward with his plans as an entitled member of the Board. "Sorry about the ultimatum and the way this will hurt the Church, its image and sales. Nonetheless, unless things change, the only recourse left to me is to go to the press." Waiting for the limousine, Yoshino promised to keep in touch through his legal representatives. Archbishop Gutiérrez stood flabbergasted at the intensity of Mr. Yoshino's threat. "Let's talk further about this issue," was all that the archbishop managed to say.

As Archbishop Gutiérrez relayed his concerns to Marie, she mentioned her awareness of the situation with Mr. Yoshino. One of the guests, as well as a student monitor, mentioned an earlier heated discussion to Marie. The visitor said Cardinal O'Rourke and Mr. Yoshino loudly discussed some failing point about the University Board. The discussion proved lengthy, but remained exclusive. Thinking this discussion did not concern her and might be too private to join, the visitor simply walked past them. Yet, when she ran into Marie, what she witnessed bothered her enough to mention it. The cardinal and the business executive walked off, shaking hands as they went in different directions. Because the curiousness of the scene stood out, the student observer also reported the event to Marie.

Marie relayed that the student intentionally listened to some of the discussion. The student monitor's preparation for today's activities included security and safety precautions. The student guide overheard Mr. Yoshino's interest in buying some Los Angeles properties tied to some investment interests in the area. The student eavesdropped on the real estate conversation long enough to realize it did not pose a security threat. Then, he moved on.

As they walked along, Marie took note of Archbishop Gutiérrez' wrinkled brow, gentle shaking of his head, and the concern in his lean face. There was evidently more going on than she understood. A voice called to them across the path, from a building behind them. They stopped and waited for Viktor to join them. All smiles, Viktor appeared to be on a high from the wonderful experience of the day. He spent most of the day directing student ushers, and escorting the Russian delegation around the campus. He breathed heavily as he began to walk with them. The delegates told him of exciting changes taking place in Russia.

"Archbishop, you will please excuse me. I share news from home." He was even more excited about his news, than the success of the day's dedication. "Mario, I mean Archbishop, the security police withdrew from our offices, and old party members are out. My boss, Alexandrovich is gone. The whole operation changed, opened up. Is this not wonderful news?" Marie reached out with a big hug, "Viktor, I am so happy for you."

The archbishop looked a little embarrassed at the emotions, and with a nod and smile, gave Viktor a reserved pat on the shoulder, as to an excited child, echoing, "How wonderful," though less animated than

Marie's affirmation.

Marie invited Archbishop Gutiérrez to her residence, as Viktor departed. Time to unwind and share their observations and conversations of the day, and sharing a little Campari sounded good.

The archbishop followed Marie into the cozy sitting room of her turn-of-the century country home, nestled in the gardens and arbors of the estate. A small area with warm décor, it looked comfortable and inviting. They shared Mario's impressions, which provided a diplomatic viewpoint, and Marie's remembrances that were more personal. Together, they produced a complete picture of this special day.

"Marie, what might you suggest about how to handle this situation with Eiho Yoshino? His tunnel vision irks me. I would like to drop him from the Board. People of such blatant self-interest are difficult. Yet, I do not want my personal feeling to get in the way of the value Mr. Yoshino brings to the Board."

"Archbishop, you will find your way to peace about this situation. I am sure of this. I will pray for you."

The hour wore on into dusk. They enjoyed the relief of talking quietly and being able to come down after an adrenalin-filled day. He relaxed, as he thought Marie is a graced listener. She offered something to eat from the kitchen, but the weariness set in for both and they agreed to call the day "officially over." She walked him to his car, which was parked nearby. He gave her a warm clasp of the hand, with an added special squeeze. He thanked her, and seemed to want to reach out in an "abrazo" of appreciation but hesitated and did not. She sensed his embarrassment in his rather flustered words, standing by the open car door, as he got into the front seat, with a sheepish smile, "Ciao" and a wave.

Marie was a little confused by the Archbishop's boyish goodbye, elated at the success of the day and relaxed by the warmth of their sharing-time. Today, as they exchanged feelings and impressions of the day's excitement, Marie found more personalness in him than ever before. Unsure of the meaning or its depth, they bonded in a new, deeper way. Oh, well, he is a deep and yet boyishly handsome person. She turned back in the direction of her home.

Marie and her team plunged headlong into the day-by-day operations of the Pax Dei Pontifical University. Dr. James Whitney, an experienced administrator from Oxford, filled the position of the University's Executive Vice-President. He directed the staff and handled the usual daily business questions. The weekly faculty and staff meeting held each Tuesday morning kept Marie informed, and helped to establish needed policy formulations. Marie spent a lot of time dealing with the public relations, communications and developmental aspects of University. The requests by the media to report on the Pax Dei increased following the opening day activities.

Delegations from around the world wanted to tour the facilities and discuss the future of the University. Corporations and governments continued to request information. Marie spoke once or twice weekly with Archbishop Gutiérrez. She kept him informed of all important discussions, policies and decisions.

Classes got into full swing the following week. The press still followed the faculty around the campus and dropped in on sessions to audit classes and to interview professors and students. The novelty swept everyone along in an air of elation. Only minor problems were reported. The faculty, students and staff were all in good spirits, excited by the school year.

The University had been forced to place a cap on enrollment and had accepted only a realistic number of undergraduates. Some sponsoring governments and international leaders did not like the decision because their protégés did not make the cut for the first year. Those students were moved to the waiting list for the following semester.

The completed curriculum did please everyone, to include the areas of study and disciplines established. The basic college areas included languages, mathematics, history, computer science, religious studies, sciences, sociological and cultural studies, psychology and philosophy, business and other university-required studies, which provided the foundation for the specialty fields to develop later.

Specialized areas included the history of peacemaking; treaties and document sources on peacebuilding; cultural handling of mediation in ethnic groups; the psychology of violence, arbitration and peacemaking; heroic figures and writings around peacebuilding; economics of peacemaking; psychology of mediation and negotiating; building peace in the family and community; pacifisms and terrorism studies; the processes of intervention; institutions related to peacemaking. Eventually, through a virtual classroom, these courses would be broadcast in partnership with libraries, as well as public and private peace institutions operating around the world. Related issues such as population growth, religious studies, economic development, cultural understanding, psychology and anthropology, demographics, and diplomatic history, would also be included in the course work.

The philosophy of peace was central. The faculty recognized the gifting of an endowed chair as a hallmark of a great university. The endowed chair came from one of Germany's wealthiest families. They were recognized for their strong Catholic heritage.

One surprise that came from the Pax Dei Pontifical University's development was the compilation of a worldwide list of wealthy Catholic families. Before the list could be generated, some of the families stepped forward offering help. Other names popped up in various discussions as a list quickly came together. Many donors were associated with corporations. Still others managed inherited wealth. The lists for individual bishops covering their local areas was collected and put into a master directory. The directory formed an interesting register, a sort of a *Who's Who of Catholic Wealth*. The Vatican did not solicit the names from the dioceses, rather they surfaced in a variety of indirect ways and the archbishop identified the potential major donors for future reference. Mario believed God gave wealth to enable good works, to include developing the vulnerable. This simple Gospel understanding is an important part of the long-taught teaching of Christ and the Church.

Viktor set up plans for field research teams' next summer at Marie's request. They expected to send groups from the University out for project study in the processes of peace negotiation. The University planned to provide on the job experience for the students and their faculty advisors. Viktor's task included finding the funding, identifying resources and making all needed arrangements, to field as many student teams as possible.

He and the archbishop seemed to be on different paths of late, given the busy routines of an operational University, the contracting office, and the established World Peace Office. They both missed the personalness of their friendship. Life moved too fast not only for them, but also for everyone around them these days.

They finally managed to get together on a beautiful, clear October day at Il Napoli on the Via Veneto. The restaurant was a favorite of the archbishop. He had frequented the small restaurant since his days as a student in Rome. Viktor told Mario all about his new experiences. He bubbled with words and energy.

"Archbishop, I am thrilled to be involved in so many things, especially my work with the students. I love everything about the Pax Dei Pontifical University. If God does exist, I give Him all my thanks, for arranging this wonderful opportunity for me, and to you I also give thanks."

Gutiérrez likened listening to Viktor today to a child's enthusiasm on his return from a first trip to the amusement park. Viktor fascinated him with his energy, the flow of conversation. All of his expressions were so alive and graphic. Viktor cited name after name. He spoke of his impressions of the administration and faculty, without hesitation. How blessed to listen to this fluid and creative stream, like sitting beside a country brook on a beautiful spring day in the warm sunshine, and absorbing sounds. As he sipped his sherry, Mario asked, "How is your family back in Russia, Viktor? Are you planning to visit soon?"

"Mario, I am planning more than a visit. However, I am concerned about the close relationship of my grandson Igor and my wife Magda. Inseparable, they go everywhere together. She is teaching him much at such an early age, which is good. Even as they stand in lines for food or banking, she is working with him. We have never been so economically well off. Now, she can buy him all kinds of food and toys. I want to bring Magda here to live with me, for at least for part of the year. My fear is that it will be a difficult separation for Magda and Igor. I hope that my grandson can come to visit often."

"I will help you, Viktor. This is an excellent idea." The Russian embodied for the archbishop, all the best of the University. Mario wanted to bring happiness to Viktor by helping to reunite his family.

Mario wished also that he could give his friend the gift of a Christian faith. They often talked about religion, about God on many occasions. Viktor struggled to find a way to reconcile all the tragedy in life with a loving God. Still, Viktor's deep natural faith gladdened Mario's heart. Viktor personalized the best hopes of peace, and speaking with him always encouraged Archbishop Gutiérrez.

The Archbishop, in his good-bye, repeated his offer to help Viktor relocate his wife as soon as possible. They returned to their respective offices after lunch.

Viktor left humming, as he bounced along the sidewalk to the parking area. Viktor, the seventh owner of the Saab he recently acquired was unaware of the numerous dents and dings. The car was a dream come true for Viktor, and he drove it with the reckless abandon of a Russian cab driver in New York City. The traffic in the eternal city did not frighten him at all.

Archbishop Gutiérrez was flooded with mixed emotions as he entered the dim hallways of his offices to face some wearisome and complex situations, namely a Japanese business executive and a United States cardinal.

He knew Pope Francisco had not escaped Cardinal O'Rourke who insisted on a private papal audience at the University's dedication. Mr. Yoshino would likely be next on the Pontiff's schedule. Mario reported on both men earlier in the week via the Pontiff's weekly status report. He thought of St. Paul's thorn in the flesh, which God would not remove. These two men were twin splinters, if not giant thorns. He prayed for them and asked for the Lord's wisdom as well as the patience of a saint to negotiate with them. "Lord, allow these men to realize we are all dedicated peacemakers, not enemies." Ironic, in a global peace-making venture like this one, peace among men remained elusive on this basic, personal level in his life and work. A humbling irony, Mario thought.

He set up luncheon appointments on two separate days for Cardinal O'Rourke and Mr. Yoshino. He entered the solitude of his private chapel, with pad and pen in hand. After deep listening prayer, he outlined his strategy, hoping his ideas lined up with the Lord's plan.

Mario identified the problems of the warring men by reviewing each of their agendas. Giving up the extra monies that his archdiocese had accrued over the years proved difficult for Cardinal O'Rourke. There was no way that he wanted to share so much with the Vatican.

As for Mr. Yoshino, the archbishop had disrupted his manipulative efforts. His entry into insider acquisition of Vatican art and treasures had been blocked, which left him hurt and frustrated. Yoshino expected certain entitlements as a member of the Board.

With motivations so indelicate, neither man would openly reveal this to the other in their planning and conversations. Instead, they bonded as allies citing Archbishop Gutiérrez's general handling of things, and eagerly expressed their mutual dissatisfaction to the Pontiff. This situation was reminiscent of the time that Herod and Pilate became reluctant allies, as the Gospel relates, over Jesus at the time of His trial and crucifixion.

Archbishop Gutiérrez discussed his strategy in detail with his support staff. He wanted to get their thoughts and keep them informed in case of any fallout. He did not look forward to either luncheon appointment, and prayed mightily on both counts. He reviewed his notes and plans with the Lord. He smiled thinking this a bit theatrical, like rehearsing for a trial. Mario believed resolving the conflict was critical, not so much for himself, as for the Board and the Holy Father. "Lord please be with me in this day of testing" was his final prayer as he left the chapel, adrenalin pumping.

Cardinal O'Rourke, a "fast riser" in the Church, was not familiar with Vatican politics, as he had only attended seminary there. He took his priestly vows in Los Angeles, and following ordination, his promotions came in quick succession. His appointment to chancellor for the Archdiocese of Los Angeles gave O'Rourke the opportunity to work with the bishops' state conference, as well as the national bishops' conference. He was soon appointed auxiliary bishop, and then Archbishop of the Archdiocese of Los Angeles. He remained Archbishop of the Archdiocese of Las Angeles, even though he currently wore the red hat of a cardinal. His archdiocese covered 8,762 square miles, and nearly 300 parishes.

A hands-on American political type, the cardinal moved easily among his people, his priests, bishops and cardinals, and close to 4.5 million faithful. His highly extroverted personality made him a natural leader of the Church. His constituents welcomed his knowledge of social-political systems, and appreciated his ability to represent them in all arenas. O'Rourke tackled the difficult issues from abortion to unions, to women's rights. Most recently, he dealt with the anti-environmental Californian interests. Intelligent, outspoken and none too subtle, he never hesitated about where he wanted the Church to go in the future.

Mario chose the Vatican's private dining area as the setting for the luncheons, a setting, reserved at special request for dignitaries. A little wine never hurt, he thought. Jesus accomplished much over food, during His lifetime, to include influencing people. Why not follow the Master's plan, he mused. Step number one in peacemaking.

The cardinal brought his secretary, a sharp, young Roman-educated Canon lawyer, Father Robert Cole. Two-to-one should mitigate the home court advantage. Archbishop Gutiérrez moved into the substance of their differences as the waiter cleared their table. He had carefully studied the financial questions of the Los Angeles Archdiocese and the Church in the United States.

"Your Eminence," Mario began, "I have offended you in some way by not consulting you about some of the arrangements by my office, specifically handling international diocesan finances. Am I correct in this?"

The Cardinal, sipping his coffee, nearly choked. Apparently, he expected an indirect approach to their discussion. This tactic disarmed him. He gulped a mouthful of water.

"Well, Your Excellency, you are direct. Yes, you've hit the nail on the head. I admire your straightforwardness. I am a direct person myself. I believe that I speak on behalf of our American bishops when I say we perceived your approach as high-handed in asking us so casually to relinquish years of assets, which we believe are needed to run our dioceses. Ours are not like the dioceses of most of the world, you understand." He leaned his heavy chin forward, looking candidly into the Archbishop's face. There was no mincing of words here.

"Your Eminence, you are very perceptive. Lately, when assessing the progress of the operation, I try to put myself into your shoes. In doing so, I begin to understand why you are questioning." He ate a good bit of crow. He abandoned an adversarial position, not easily done in the face of such a confronting presence. Mario needed a delicate balance of admissions, rather than concessions. What he said next would be important. His adrenalin surged and his palms became sweaty. He tried to sit back with a relaxed countenance, hoping to ease his own personal tension. After a taking a sip of coffee, he placed the cup down, and continued. Looking right into the Cardinal's unwavering stare, he asked, "How might the operation change, so as to be more accommodating to the American Church experience?"

Gutiérrez braced for the coming diatribe. He prepared to listen as the Cardinal preached.

It was the cardinal's turn to shock Mario. O'Rourke had a plan. He quickly agreed to turn over excess holdings and assets to the Vatican, with a caveat that one third of the assets be set aside, held in reserve by the Vatican in an escrow account for twenty years. His reasoning covered the possibility of refund to the original diocese in cases of proven need. He also asked that the dioceses receive interest on all holdings turned over to the Vatican for a period of five years or until such time as the assets were liquidated by Rome. This plan allowed a transition period to adjust the local church's budget while in compliance with releasing the investments. O'Rourke had talked to a number of American bishops and this would be agreeable to all.

Father Cole sat like an expert spectator at a tennis match, watching the back and forth of the play. He witnessed tense, careful and exciting negotiating. He nodded his head in concurrence. As a final point, the cardinal asked the priest to write up the arrangement, to refine their concessions so that the archbishop could incorporate their agreement into the financial processes. The final agreement would be reviewed and approved by both men.

Cardinal O'Rourke, a prince of the Church, taught Mario a lesson in humility. When the cardinal spoke of reaching out, Mario realized that he failed to do so. Neither Mario, nor his staff conferred with the hierarchy, which left him ill prepared to address the complexities of the U.S. dioceses.

Mario had under-estimated the cardinal. Now, he understood the Holy Father's reservations about O'Rourke during their previous discussions. The Pontiff respected O'Rourke as an influential friend, independent of the Roman way of doing things. This was definitely an 'aha moment' for Mario.

They lingered over coffee, wrapped up the final points, and Mario recognized God arranged a good order for his luncheons. He thought he would enlist the cardinal's influence to reach and bring peace to Mr. Yoshino.

He decided to test the waters. "Your Eminence, I face another problem where I need your advice and experience." Nothing like eating a second serving of humble pie for lunch, I might as well make the meal complete. Jesus will be proud of my humbling, Gutiérrez thought. If possible, this was even more painful and delicate.

"Your Eminence, I believe you are acquainted with Mr. Yoshino and are familiar with his requests for special favors. Forgive me, Cardinal O'Rourke, but he expects insider privileges because he serves on the Board. He comes across as blatantly self-interested; and is rather offensive at times. I tried repeatedly and honestly to remind him of his position and perception. I voiced how the appearance of his requests looked to other people on the Board, but he does not grasp the idea. Perhaps I am missing something. I do not want to create an embarrassing public situation. Because it is an internal peacekeeping problem, I spoke with the Japanese Apostolic Nuncio and asked for some suggestions, but nothing came from it. It is my hope that you can provide some insight. Cardinal O'Rourke, I have lunch tomorrow with Eiho Yoshino."

The cardinal smiled knowingly. "My dear Archbishop, I will be most happy to speak with Mr. Yoshino. I have listened to him, especially these last few days, and I understand his points and self-interest. I will approach him. I will invite him to dine with Father Cole and me this evening." Thinking the cardinal's "alliance" with Mr. Yoshino might persuade Mr. Yoshino to see the Board's position. Mario felt it best to leave it to the cardinal and his creativity.

The lunch with the cardinal and Father Cole was one the most intense meals he had ever shared and it left him drained. He could recall nothing of the food. He thought of Jesus eating in much the same circumstances and recalled some of the fierce mealtime confrontations the Gospels record.

The archbishop did not sleep well that night. His prayer the following morning was distracted. After the morning phone call to O'Rourke, he spent some time reviewing notes, readying for lunch. As the archbishop readied for the blatant aggressive personality of his luncheon guest, the cardinal took the edge off by providing insight, and needed tools to work with Mr. Yoshino.

Cardinal O'Rourke advised the archbishop to come across as an

enlightened Christian, yet somewhat forceful, too. Following the soft-
ening up of Mr. Yoshino by Cardinal O'Rourke, Mario was advised to
take the onus off himself and his staff, and to place the responsibility for
Mr. Yoshino squarely with the Corporation Board. The Board would be
the proper avenue to consider insider requests in advance of any sales.
This took the matter completely out of his hands and put it into an
unbiased open forum.

The Board members might be open to lobbying by Mr. Yoshino,
but Mario believed their basic impartiality and fairness would serve as a
checks and balance for any unrealistic demands. Jesus arranged a similar approach in the first Jerusalem Council, as the Acts of the Apostles
recorded when they dealt with particular interests in receiving gentile
neophytes.

Mario planned to suggest an amendment to the by-laws. The
amendment would move the Board into self-governing with regard to
monitoring its own privileges. This included insider knowledge on advance sales. While the policy change did not single out Mr. Yoshino, the
amendment would take care of the problem.

Over lunch, Mr. Yoshino told the archbishop of his confidence in
his ability to maneuver the Board, to manipulate them to his advantage.
Mr. Yoshino had a big ego, and strongly believed in his own entitlement
to extraordinary Board privileges. Archbishop Gutiérrez placed his faith
in the Board to control all self-interest questions. The group would be
able to handle Mr. Yoshino's overtures.

Mario believed above all God provided this opportunity for him
to face his own fearfulness when faced with aggressive personalities.

# Chapter 8

## Christmas in Rome

The weather was chilly but clear blue skies prevailed the week of Christmas. Temperatures ranged between 6 and 10 degrees C, so a little cooler than normal, but still a pleasant time in the temperate subtropical climate. Most of the students left the campus to travel Europe while they had the opportunity. Some went home to spend time with their families. Still others stayed in their dorms at the University.

December was a fascinating time to be in Rome. The city's Catholic religious legacy shines in the Eternal City during the Christmas holidays. Many restaurants and shops closed on the holidays, but not all. There were half dozen restaurants open for Christmas and New Year's Eve. Outdoor cafes served mulled wine and hot chocolate. Most of Rome's sights and attractions remained open. For the students, the University cafeteria would remain open both days with limited holiday menus, and a volunteer skeletal staff. Archbishop Gutiérrez along with all the faculty and staff looked forward to the break from the University and the Board meetings.

The next Board meetings scheduled for the Pax Internacionale Corporation and the Pax Dei Pontifical University were after the holidays. The Board members would return from holiday to face heavy agendas. The item weighted heaviest would be the critical study sponsored by Señor Leckner. The study titled, *Hope for Peace,* occupied a full, all-day session on the agenda. Many members were as excited to be a part of this as they were about the holidays.

Reports and policies arrived beforehand so that Board members were able to better prepare for the meetings. The financial reports for the University and the contracting corporation were slated for review with their Swiss representatives, as well as reports on the status and policies for projected property and museum sales.

The University Board planned to review the plans for growth, to include expansion of dormitories, curriculum development, and a presentation about how to direct their studies for world needs. The presenting group would be offering symposium-type papers from international scholars on the direction and development of world peace issues.

Members of the Board experienced a heady time. They approached the holiday filled with excitement and hope for the future.

Viktor and Magda looked forward to Christmas dinner with the Archbishop and Marie. They were happy to accept Marie's invitation, as they were a little unsure about holiday traditions in this part of the world. Viktor knew all about Father Frost, and the Russian customs, which the government had substituted for the Orthodox celebration in his homeland. Viktor told a toddler's version of Ded Moroz to Igor. The image took its final shape in the USSR where Frost became the main symbol of the New Year's holiday, which replaced Christmas as the favorite holiday in pre-revolutionary Russia.

Grandfather Frost dressed in a red caftan, edged with snow-white fluff, a red cap, and white mittens. He sported a luxuriant snow-white beard, a ruddy nose and cheeks, and a friendly smile. Grandfather Frost carried a huge red sack with gifts for kids. He was often accompanied by his fair granddaughter, Snegurochka, the Snow Maiden who plays with children and presents the gifts to them. She wears pure white garments with a silver and pearl decorated crown. Viktor told Igor that none of Grandfather Frost's foreign colleagues had such a cute companion.

While, traditions were important, the most important thing to Viktor was having Magda by his side.

Viktor visited the representative in the Embassy of the Russian Federation in Rome every week working towards a permanent relocation for Magda. Her Christmas travel proved no problem at all. Magda's month long stay started when she and the Igor arrived on 20 December. Oh how Viktor would miss them when they left after the holidays. He would not think about that now.

The archbishop planned to concelebrate Mass with the Pope and other members of the papal staff and hierarchy. They followed a tradition of the Holy Father to celebrate midnight Mass at St. Peter's on Christmas Eve. Following Mass, the small intimate group of the Curia leaders and staff joined in a light meal and reception with the Pontiff in his apartments. The Holy Father presented them with some small personal Christmas remembrances such as an art print or statue.

The archbishop's personal holiday patterns had changed this year, which enabled him to accept Marie's invitation. Christmases past, Mario spent the holiday with his oldest school classmate and his family, Hector Anchondo, who had been the Deputy Argentinean Ambassador to Rome. Things changed two months ago when Hector received and accepted his appointment as Ambassador to United States, quite a distinguished achievement. Hector and his family's move left a big gap in the Archbishop's friendships and traditions. Mario would miss the lovely family warmth, which had provided a real touch of home for him.

Viktor enjoyed everything about the University, his classroom teaching most of all. His seats on the faculty committee, and the Pax Dei Pontifical University Board excited him as well. Seeing the workings firsthand of these representative bodies gave Viktor a new depth of experience, which opened up the world for him in a new way. The directness of the Board members at the meetings surprised Viktor, who always thought the Church, much like Russia was a hierarchal monolith. A quick study, he found the people in discussion, and sharing their values, an inspiring process. These frank and open sharing of experiences did not enter into the one-party system, which ruled Russian life for so long. Viktor hoped for change like this to take place in Russia, too.

The caring and openness of the Holy Father impressed him. The pontiff and the archbishop possessed amazing imagination and talent.

The students brought great joy to Viktor. One of the few individuals able to enjoy the day-by-day experience of firsthand contact with the students, Viktor loved to see their unbridled enthusiasm. He grew to know the faculty well, and to witness the inner workings of the administration, as well as the visions and directions of the University and the Contracting Corporation. He sat in a rare seat, appreciating and marveling at being part of it. No one on the faculty enjoyed a similar position. Viktor did not mind the demands. There was relief at being free of the oppressive shadow that had haunted his work in Russia, and he could not believe the freedom and initiative he enjoyed at the University. No one ever looked over his shoulder. His only regret was the lack of time to do serious research work, as a scholar and for his classes.

Viktor thought all parts of the student lives were important to their education. Aware of the students from the Eastern Bloc countries enrolled at the University, he scrutinized their dossiers, and easily identified hardline Communists. The majority came from socialist or democratic backgrounds. Viktor's concern extended to reclusive Chinese, Cuban and Albanian students as well. His vision was to bring all students into the mainstream. Viktor spoke to the archbishop about his concern that the students acquire a forum, a safe place, to discuss their national interests and concerns.

Viktor's rationale – these scholars represented the future of their nations. Their university experience, critical to sculpting world peace, would equip them with needed leadership skills to settle differences with neighbors, some disagreements included old, historical animosities, which reached back thousands of years. Mario liked the idea of the students having a network in place when they graduated from the University. He gently reminded Viktor to gain Marie's support for his idea before proceeding.

The two Israeli students and the twenty or so Arabic students were among the most difficult relationships presented by the student population in the beginning. These students did not grow up as "normal children." They lived through rocket attacks, stabbings, bombings and the nightmares that followed. Given some time in the peaceful environment of the Pax Dei Pontifical University campus, the students' attitudes began to soften, to change. They began to understand the cycle of violence could stop with them so that their own children would not grow up in an environment of hatred. Viktor who was most aware of this brought the matter to the forefront in faculty and boardroom discussions. He reminded everyone Pax Dei was an unusual University, chartered to work at peacemaking and harmony. The faculty noticed the students change in attitude through classroom discussions and committee conversations. Through dialogue in both arenas, the students revealed the beginning of new, shared dreams for their countries. The young people expressed a deep-seated desire to move away from the pervasiveness of war in their daily lives. They wanted to live free of air raid sirens and bombings perpetrated on their families for generations. Many young people emerged who wanted to take an active role in bringing peace to their nations. The students asked why youth around the world could live in comfort and safety while they, both sides of the conflict, lived with death and destruction.

Viktor brought the students' desires to the attention of Archbishop Gutiérrez, who, in turn, made a suggestion to the Pax Internacionale Contracting Corporation. Following the archbishop's suggestion, the contracting corporation established student intern positions within the Board of Directors. The four students selected were the first interns to sit on the Board. Along with a seat on the Board, these students were given a voice, which gave them a chance to make a difference in peacemaking for their nations.

Deep differences existed between some of the African tribal students. Much dissimilarity was based on religion, and other differences attributed to tribal histories and recent ethnic clashes. The University needed to put its own peacemaking endeavors and strategies in place.

The students of the Pax Dei Pontifical University lived in a mini-cosmos laboratory for getting along, among many clashing cultures, religions, ethnic and political differences. Viktor brought this to the forefront in faculty and boardroom discussions. He reminded everyone what the extraordinary University exemplified. He stressed the importance of working Pax Dei's own peacemaking and harmony. Evidenced by the efforts of the Israeli and Arab students, the dream for peace lived on despite multi-generational, deep-rooted conflict. This ongoing effort took constant attention, attitude, and work. Viktor believed the more exposure to living in the peaceful environs of the University, the more the deep-seated desire for peace would take root in the hearts of the students. Viktor willingly became an unofficial advocate for the students.

Viktor's spoke often in front of the Board, and the Archbishop listened closely to this inspired professor speak of the University's image, and the living of peacemaking together, on campus. Archbishop Gutiérrez greatly admired Viktor's giftedness. Although, at times, the archbishop grew uncomfortable as he listened to Viktor's motivational reminders at their gatherings. The Archbishop realized that his discomfort came from his own inability to verbalize his convictions towards peace from Christ and the Gospel. Viktor's conviction humbled Mario, and provided a divine spark to all.

There was no hesitation at any level, to bring in this peace-bringing perspective, whether among students, in the dorms, in classes, at faculty meetings, even when the Pope was present. Like a prophetic voice sounding out in the village square, Viktor prompted the Board members to return to the primary commitment. Everything he did and said reminded others of their mission of peace-formation. No matter what issue the members raised, Viktor had the uncanny gift to bring any topic full circle, back to their mission of peace.

Viktor's remarks often helped Archbishop Gutiérrez bring in the thinking of Christ and the Gospels, to back up Viktor and to show the way to peace. Viktor's fluency and grace seemed to roll from his consciousness into his remarks. With the archbishop, it seemed to be more of a reflecting and recalling process, as he would search for a Christian remark, or associative statement or image relating to peace. The archbishop was a studied searcher for peace. Viktor was a person of nature and grace, alive with insights, principles and a deep understanding of peace. Viktor had a special grace, a gift from God, which struck the Archbishop at their first meeting, and at which he never ceased to marvel.

On the other hand, some of the staff members found Viktor a little tedious, at times. Their focus was on their individual disciplines, not related to peace, but rather more towards academic accomplishment. Viktor related the varied study areas with a focus, and relationship toward peace. Professors wanted to present math, psychology, history, language, economics, computer science and such, as standalone subjects. Viktor would not allow them to forget the link to peace. Viktor called everyone to focus on peace, and forced everyone to think in unfamiliar ways and to carry peace forward into all areas of teaching.

Christmas Eve proved an exciting time for Viktor. He and Magda were excited about celebrating Christmas at Marie's residence on campus. No sooner had Magda and Igor unpacked from the trip, when Magda set to work baking Russian Christmas goodies for Marie's Christmas dinner. She reminded her husband of the differences between this and the Russian Christmas and calendar. Viktor's rental kitchen became a workshop as he played and danced with little Igor to Russian Christmas music in the background. An atmosphere of freedom and happiness surrounded Magda, who radiated joy.

They looked forward to attending midnight Mass at St. Peter's and going to Marie's home the next day. While Magda worked in their kitchen, Marie worked in her kitchen. She transformed her housekeeper into an assistant chef, and they worked side-by-side in the well-appointed kitchen. The experience was exhilarating and left little time for thoughts of University business.

Marie planned to attend midnight Mass at St. Peter's, along with her son and his wife who flew in from London for the holidays. Her son Rene, at 30, enjoyed a successful career as an international banker. His wife Eugenie, a French woman, was devoted to their three-year old son, Jacob. The toddler proved to be a joy to everyone. Marie carefully planned the Christmas gathering, with Viktor and Magda, Archbishop Gutiérrez, and her family. The archbishop offered to bring the wine, which was always his "go-to" host gift.

Mario was pleased that this holiday would not be a lonely time for him. In the past, he spent too many holidays alone. A non-Italian, Vatican bureaucrat not affiliated with a religious or parish community occasioned a lot of time spent alone. This year would be different.

Midnight Christmas Mass never failed to capture the heart of

Catholic Rome and the Vatican spirit. Mass capsulized, in a mysterious way, the lives of dedicated Church people, in the formal, ancient, yet warm celebration, with its clouds of incense. The chanting, the immense cold and dark stone corners, and ceilings of St. Peter's added to the commemoration. A mystique of faith gripped everyone, as television cameras from many nations, ground away, transmitting the scene around the world in innumerable languages. A history of lives and peoples seemed to stand at the altar, as the Pontiff raised his eyes and hands in prayer. Pope Francisco's voice echoed from hearts, which carried centuries of faith from all directions of the globe.

The Holy Father nodded to Viktor and Magda on his way to the altar, as they stood holding Igor in the throng of worshippers. A presence of God from history, from the memory of millions of worshippers over thousands of years, gathered in this spot, to acknowledge the order of peace and goodness, which ought to be at work in the world. A tremendous connecting of lives took place, from past ages, in the huge, dark, cold, incense-filled atmosphere, amid the lined and attentive faces, and the haunting songs. God reached out, through all this, into lives today just as Jesus reached out to anoint Peter "the Rock" on which He built His Church. Viktor shuddered with a chill, and wondered what gripped him as he took note of some of the students and faculty among those present.

A clear Christmas afternoon with the dull winter light of the shortened day, and the usual haze of smog covered the Roman environment. The fire crackled in the fireplace of Marie's spacious 19th century living room. The Christmas tree in the corner glittered with ornaments, many of African tradition. Rene's wife Eugenie and son Jacob spent the afternoon before Christmas, putting the decorations in place.

Later when Viktor and his family arrived, they gave Marie a handmade Khokhloma Samovar Christmas ornament, which Jacob and Igor hung on the tree.

The Archbishop arrived shortly thereafter.

The gentle, hazy afternoon sunlight lengthened the shadows around the campus. The house filled with wonderful aromas, to include the fireplace, the Christmas tree, candles, and the kitchen. The warmth brought back memories to each person. The Archbishop wore his cassock, the perennial garb of the clergy around the Vatican. He appeared relaxed, even if the others thought his apparel too formal.

Marie wondered if he ever traveled in sport or casual clothes as she hung up his coat. Surely, he dresses comfortably when he visits his family.

They prayed the blessing together over a bountiful feast. Viktor and Magda amazed at all the dishes. The other guests were in awe of Magda's "Herring under the Winter Coat" salad. It was made for those who enjoy herring and beets. While that particular dish enjoyed mixed reviews, her Knish was a hit with everyone.

Viktor translated most of Magda's observations. Her observations amused him, and he stopped short of translating her thoughts about how many rubles everything cost. The archbishop, of course, understood the entire conversation, and winked occasionally at Viktor. Magda chattered on through the evening.

After the hours of food and conversation, they retired to the living room, with cordials and after-dinner coffees. Gathered around the huge fireplace, they enjoyed its warmth as well as the warmth of growing friendships. Jacob grew drowsy on Eugenie's lap. Little Igor slept too as he lay in Magda's lap.

Archbishop Gutiérrez entertained everyone with tales of Vatican and Argentinean personalities and lore. Marie shared her stories of Africa and the family. Viktor in a mellow mood shared his own quiet memories of the Russia of old, and the hardships they endured for many years. He listened with a quieter, thankful spirit, as the others talked. When Viktor grew tired of translating, the archbishop stepped in to help Magda, whose energy never ran low. This visit by the fire was a pleasant conclusion to the warm gathering. Content, Viktor thought was the best descriptor in any language. He leaned into Magda as the gentle music of Christmas choirs and hymns floated throughout the house as the music played away.

Viktor and Magda excused themselves as the evening, concluded. Perhaps the drinks contributed to the drowsiness. Famous for their capacity for alcohol, still Russians, like everyone else, became less coherent as they drank. Viktor carried Igor, who yawned a lot and gave a sleepy wave goodbye. Then, Rene and his wife excused themselves as they carried their small, sleepy son upstairs, mirroring the family of Joseph, Mary and Jesus, by their quiet presence and family caring.

The Archbishop started to excuse himself, even though he found it difficult to leave such a beautiful setting. As he and Marie returned to the fireplace and the warmth of the glow of the fire, with the soft light of the Christmas tree in the corner of the room, Marie insisted that he sit down and finish his brandy.

Mario sat in the large sofa positioned before the fire, and she sat on the floor cushion leaning against the sofa, facing the fire, absorbing the warmth. They savored a glow from within, as they enjoyed the hominess of the setting. They had appreciated the day, reflecting on Christmases past. Marie spoke of this reflection and of the beauty of the day. She treasured the stories Archbishop Mario told about his family. The stories of Marie's marriage, and their young family in Africa, as well as the struggles to keep the family going, as a single widowed woman, touched the archbishop.

"You know those memories from my life; they all seemed to gather up in this evening. I did not realize so much passed in me, until I shared my memories tonight. Do you have that same sense? About your remembrances, I mean. I seemed to bring the feelings of everyone's past Christmases into my heart, and memories, this evening."

"Yes, Marie, I do feel that way. Strange, so many memories I never spoke about, came to me tonight, and other memories too, which I treasure but did not share. The memories we shared tonight reminded me of going through an old trunk in the attic, finding and sharing the discoveries with everyone. I found it amazing to discover despite the differences in our cultures we share so much in common."

The Archbishop, standing to leave, mentioned he would be flying to Zurich in a day or two. Marie reached for his hand, and offered a gentle respectful kiss of his hand, just as she had kissed the hand of the Holy Father. Mario heard his heart, and breathing, above the crackling of the fire. An awkward, embarrassing and confused moment for the archbishop as he realized kissing of the clergy's hand had disappeared as a cultural gesture of respect. Marie spoke. "Mario, I thank God that He gave us a wonderful priest in you. You shepherd so many of us."

"Marie, I thank you for a full and a rich day." He tried not to show the mix of impressions rushing within him. She caught him off guard, and he wanted to back away from the whole scene. Fear, anxiety, guilt, confusion all seemed to jumble up within him. Mario was like the little boy caught with his hand near the cookie jar. He stepped out into the night air, afraid to look back at Marie in the doorway. He was afraid her beauty, and that a new vision of her attractiveness, would overtake him.

He half-turned at the bottom of the steps, and waved. "I had a wonderful time. Thanks again for today, Marie. *Benedizioni di Natale*!"

Marie closed her front door, and leaned up against the inside with a sigh of relief. "Oh God, how could I be so flirtatious with the archbishop, my boss? What must he think of me?" A huge sigh escaped and she shook her head at herself, as if denying the whole thing. "Why did I feel so compelled to kiss the hand of the archbishop?" Walking back to the fire, Marie picked up her brandy, and stood gazing into the gentle flames for a long, long time.

The following day, at morning meditation, Mario tried to focus on the Lord, but his mind kept jumping back to the previous evening. He fell asleep in weariness and woke up in the same state. "Thank God, today is Saturday." He needed time to breathe and think. Mario was never so distracted during meditation. He tried to explain to the Lord. "God, I feel awful, this morning."

"I am all over the place in this prayer. Please, Jesus, excuse me and help me to gather my thoughts. Last night's intimate kiss of my hand by Marie has now exhausted me. Forgive me. I did not realize how attracted I am to her. She is a beautiful woman, and my heart wishes to be in her company, to be near her, Lord. So many feelings, and I weary with the struggle. Lord Jesus, this is like having a splinter, I cannot find, or get out. Help me Lord, to deal with this! God, I am like a foolish schoolboy."

On and on, he prayed. His words tumbled out mixed with the jumble in his heart and feelings. All through the day, he tried to read or review some reports, but imaginings of Marie kept creeping into his thoughts.

Sunday dawned. He hoped to feel differently today, and was sorely disappointed when his feelings had not changed. Mario helped with Masses at St. John Lateran parish, the feast of the Holy Family.

That night, he spoke aloud with the Lord. "God, I'm supposed to be a man of control, mature! Why do You allow me to be distracted, to suffer like this? This is for a young man. I need to rest." "Please, Lord," he complained out loud, "this is upsetting."

He put on his robe and got a glass of water, and sat in the reading chair, in silence, listening, to himself, and speaking out to God. This must be like the wrestling of Jacob with the angel in Genesis.

"All my turmoil and feelings are like a jungle. I cannot shake these thoughts. I should let go of these feelings. I am a mature celibate, dealing with a staff person, who is attractive. We covered this many times before, sweet Jesus. I want control and things as they should be, but I want to explore this attraction too. I am like primitive man, discovering the mystery of fire. Lord, I need your help to let go of this."

The next morning, as he drank his coffee, strong and black, in his large wingback chair, he picked up his pad and pen and began a letter to Jesus. Mario often did this, when trying to handle involved complex issues over the years. Writing brought in the perspective of another person, and the insights of this other person, as well as the Lord's feelings. He began telling the Lord that he had never faced anything this draining, intimate, or emotional before. Torn apart by a simple encounter with a very special woman, and overcome by the feelings of years. Mario had lived at a distance from his maleness for so long, and now suddenly found it ignited. He wrote all this in his letter to Christ. Finally, Christ began calming his feelings and conclusions.

Mario's peace returned as he wrote and he began to experience clarity of emotion and thinking. Breathing eased. The muscles in his hands and arms grew less tense, as he wrote, and Jesus seemed to be sitting across from him, and hearing each word as he wrote. Mario continued for forty-five minutes. He poured everything out into his writing, his turmoil, temptation and trauma. He prayed as he put down the pencil, asking Christ to take all this, and to direct his feelings. At the Lord's urging, he would take a few days of retreat, after his trip to Switzerland. He picked up the phone and placed a call to the Benedictine monastery outside of Zurich. He made a reservation for the day after his business in the city.

Mario boarded the flight to Zurich Monday afternoon at the Rome airport. Glad he checked with his office and pleased to find out the trip and all his arrangements were finalized. He watched through the window as the plane climbed in the afternoon clouds and the Adriatic Sea fell away.

Coffee in hand, he reviewed briefcase notes, he wondered how so many people go through these kinds of inner struggles day-by-day or week-by-week in their lives. He thought about what obsession and fantasizing about another person can do. He marveled at how compulsions and obsessions take over a person's mind and energy, and lead to all kinds of problems as they take over that person's interior spaces. Mario gained insight into others' lives as he realized how people fell into crime, violence, cheating and abuses in sexuality. How temptations tear people up; drag them in all kinds of directions. Thinking about his experiences over the last few days frightened him. All the ideal and spiritual motivations of his life tested. Mario had the sense that he had traveled to the gates of hell and back. Then, God somehow released him of this testing. Beyond exhausted, he settled back into the window seat and let the drone of the jet lull him into sleep.

# Chapter 9

# Peace Plan in Motion

---

Mario arrived in Switzerland, and spent the afternoon with the project managers who handled the sale of the art and museum treasures. The following morning he planned to meet with the investment people for the Vatican sales. The art and treasure sales continued to exceed expectations. Another catalogue dedicated to the pieces of sculpture would be published soon. Museums and institutions showed a lot of interest in the bidding processes for these items. Negotiations continued with national groups and some countries with regard to returning items of particular cultural significance whose provenance the Vatican questioned. This issue turned out not to be as sensitive as they originally expected, their office worked easily with many of the institutions and governments involved in this. The company employed several full-time staff members who negotiated on behalf of the Vatican.

Tracking inventory and negotiable assets for each of the dioceses around the world remained the greatest challenge. Archbishop Gutiérrez wondered what Jesus thought of this global interpretation of the Gospel. St. Paul addressed one community sharing and helping another community from needy areas in his letters. In fact, it was a recurring theme in his writings. Still, there were individuals portrayed in Acts, who managed to salt away holdings from this communitarian sharing.

This plan to finance peace proved a new experience for the Church in the wealthier areas of the world. What the Holy Father revealed in his encyclical letter was the encouraged sharing of income, holdings, and wealth of richer parishes with the poorer parishes in a city or local area. Until now, wealthy parish communities built up their holdings and savings, while a neighboring parish might struggle, perhaps in a poor ghetto area. In other words, a mile away one church enjoys a flourishing school, air conditioning, and heating, with padded seats and kneelers, while a second parish is without any of these. The Vatican's plan changed the way all local parishes worked to share their money, facilities and resources with neighboring needy parishes.

The Pope tried to educate the parish system on the ways to share their wealth and resources. He tried to implement the same plan with the Bishops and their dioceses. Though not an easy task, the plan remained consistent. The Vatican's plan was gaining recognition as being even-handed throughout the world. Combining resources proved effective for all involved. The poor mission parishes brought additional people resources. Even the poorest of the poor were able to contribute.

The encyclical challenged traditional thinking and the handling of monies by local churches, and the Vatican. The taxation system or "cathedraticum" came from a yearly payment, taken from the Sunday collections to support the Vatican and the local Bishop. Cathedraticum was according to the official Canon Law. Canon Law did not examine limiting the accumulation of wealth, or sharing among poorer, needy places, other than on a donation basis.

The Pope based his management style of the Church on Gospel principles, which were mentioned in the Gospel but not necessarily in practice today. Prior to Pope Francisco's strategic plan for peace implementation, the Church's sharing of wealth resided with a missionary donation system. As economies developed, and the disparity grew naturally between the "haves" and the "have-nots," the system became accepted by most everyone.

The Church had developed along the lines of capitalism, and Christian socialism was absent in the minds of most Catholics. Archbishop Gutiérrez thought rearranging the financial dealings of the Church was an easy task when compared to the Pontiff's task of rearranging the mind-set of most Catholics. Mario's prayer was for Pope Francisco's encyclical to lead a return to Gospel-like teaching and a deeper understanding of Jesus' ways.

Anna wanted to report the work on the encyclical, but decided to save the papal letter for what she hoped would be a key moment, a personal interview with the Pope. Sister Helen Marie was working on her friend Anna's list of interview requests. Anna's plans included seeking first an interview with Dr. Marie Mobatumbo, Pax Dei Pontifical University President; followed by a private interview with Archbishop Gutiérrez; and finally, an exclusive interview with Pope Francisco.

Anna had no way to know that Archbishop Gutiérrez' latest dream was to establish a second University dedicated to dealing with poverty and all of its implications. He imagined awarding degrees for eliminating poverty, and breaking free of the cycle of poverty. Is there a way for such thinking to be taught, he asked himself, or is possessiveness innate in most of us?

Gutiérrez dreamed of a University established for the impoverished around the world. They would gather students from only the poor, who would receive special studies and degrees in understanding, and handling the situations of the vulnerable: health, education, psychology, family life, culture, languages, economics, history, and all the other disciplines, all based upon the lifestyles, experiences, and viewpoints of the poor. People not exposed to dire poverty did not understand. Whereas, middle-income families worried about budgets, stretching funds to buy groceries, the poor worried if they would have food for the next meal.

The University assembled a small ad hoc committee with the specific focus of supporting the Corporation's design for a proposal that could serve as a model. This was a direct request of Señor Leckner who wanted the ability to replicate the Israeli and Palestinian peace proposal in future endeavors.

Archbishop Gutiérrez discussed this innovative effort in detail with the Holy Father. Both men saw the merit of Leckner's request. Pope Francisco recommended that the Archbishop hire a trusted expert in this area. At the same time, the Holy Father relieved Mario's fears of escalating costs incurred simply preparing for the peace summit. Following his meeting with the Pope, Mario turned to their Swiss financial agent for suggestions. Acting on the recommendation, Mario hired an American contracting consultant.

John Lowery was an alumnus from Georgetown and Harvard with a degree in international law who divided his time between Washington D.C. and New York. At 50, his experience included all types of negotiating and proposal situations, most with the United Nations, where he had served as General Counsel for the past few years. Besides English, he spoke French, German and Italian. He told Mario he was a widower and available to travel as needed. The Archbishop counted finding him, as a real blessing. In addition to his accreditation and expertise, he was an outstanding lay-leader of the Church in United States.

"Archbishop, my staff and I completed the contract and we have reviewed it with your Pax Internacionale Corporation Board." No mincing words or special diplomacy for Lowery, he got right to the point. In three months of working together, they now had an operational prototype for the peace contract, as Lowery had promised they would. His staff of six consisted of élite international attorneys, all with backgrounds in diplomatic contractual work. All were well aware of the criticality of their work. The next step was to expand the handpicked staff to include representative leaders of both the Palestinian State and Jewish people as they moved forward to begin the real work of hammering out the details of settlement possibilities.

"Mr. Lowery, you and I will meet this afternoon with the Holy Father. Can you please bring a copy of the contract with the main points highlighted, so we can discuss this with His Holiness? He does want to be informed of all the salient points involved."

"Will do, your Excellency, what time do you want me at your office?"

"I would like to be briefed by you prior to our meeting, so let's say one o'clock. Afterwards, we will go together to see the Holy Father. Thanks, John."

At four o'clock, they sat in the Papal apartments, waiting for one of the visiting ambassadors to leave. They were ushered into the office of Pope Francisco just as the ambassador left by the other door, which saved papal visitors from the need to identify themselves to one another. The Pontiff stood to shake both their hands and gave them his usual warm greeting.

"Mr. Lowery, I heard good things about you from our Apostolic Nuncio to the United States, Archbishop Runaba. He says you are a daily communicant and an active alumnus of "Notre Dame.""

"I am sorry, Your Holiness, it is Georgetown, not Notre Dame."

The Pope chuckled: "Ah, a little good Jesuit theology, in your background, I see. Well, Archbishop, where are we with this contract, and our Argentinean friend. Please be seated."

"Your Holiness, financing for this project will not be a concern. Nor will the staffing and traveling be a problem. We will be in touch with many of the power brokers of the world, both politicos and economists. Señor Leckner will add his connections, too. The toughest part of the problem will be our relations with Israel, as you know. We are unable to gain easy access to them. The Palestinian States will, of course, be cautious of us on a religious basis, and likely view us as inexperienced."

"Archbishop, I anticipated this. While I am not sure how it will sit with our Palestinian State friends, I am thinking about how we might expand diplomatic relations with Israel. What do you think? Does Se-

ñor Leckner suggest ways to bring the parties together?" Lowery, whose
ears pricked up at the issue, waited for the Archbishop to reply.

"Your Holiness, there are no big trade items or financial assets to
offer Israel to open the door to negotiations. We can however begin to
gather world opinion and future investors, as a lobbying block. We can
line-up allies and investment possibilities with caution and also bring
in live representatives to convince Israel that it will be well worth their
time to sit down with us in this venture."

Lowery spoke. "We do need to offer diplomatic recognition to the
Israelis, plus a lot of visibility, financial possibilities, and goodwill above
all. I believe the Palestinians will understand that we are sympathetic
to their causes. We need that same understanding from Israel. My team
will prepare a participants' list as well as an economic stakes list. The list
of incentives needs to be extremely tempting and visible. We will detail
the initial agenda steps for the sides to consider." Lowery moved forward and sat on the edge of his chair in intensity. His first time to speak
with a Pope, his palms were moist.

Together, they reviewed the contract highlights, made minor
changes and the two men left the papal chambers breathing easier.
They smiled with delight because the Pontiff accepted and wholly en-
dorsed their proposed contract. The next hurdle, travel to Argentina
in two days. They faxed the approved, advanced document for Señor
Leckner to study. They expected the Argentinian meeting to raise more
questions. The success or failure of their first venture into the arena of
international peace would stand or fall on this. For some reason, the
archbishop thought of the early Christians battling the lions in the
Coliseum.

Archbishop Gutiérrez' flight to Argentina always reminded him of
going into a time machine, as he entered another world of people with
different styles, values, and time. He leaned into the window to enjoy
the feathery white clouds against the beautiful blue, sunlit sky as they
flew west.

The Archbishop and Mr. Lowery stayed with Señor Leckner as his
guests. Mario hoped to visit his sister when they concluded their business in Argentina.

Señor Leckner's guest accommodations, and the way his villa sat
above the city, were exquisite. Mario commented to John Lowery that
they had definitely entered a different world, one unlike historical Europe, and the timelessness of Rome.

"Archbishop, my people tell me there is a fine working document
with which to start our project. I am most happy to sign it," Leckner

got right down to business. "Mr. Lowery, I understand you played a key role in accomplishing this. Congratulations. The main point I am curious about is what kind of a team, and agenda, we will use to draw the Israelis into the discussion."

"Right to the heart of things," thought Gutiérrez. "God, guide us in this."

"Señor Leckner, one of the Holy Father's assurances relates to Israel's desire for recognition. It is not in the contract. However, we believe this is one way that we can begin negotiations. What are your ideas, suggestions about how to approach this? We believe most of the Israeli initiatives will upset the Palestinian States initially, but the Holy Father believes they will still work with us. With little to lose, we hope the Palestinians will listen to world opinion urging them to sit down and negotiate. There is little Israel needs, with such strong support from United States. In fact, I am not sure they even have need of our diplomatic activity in any form. What do you think?"

Leckner smiled, like a knowing cat, "Well, I think I can sweeten the pot, by offering to bring in several billions of dollars in industrial development. We would like to save development dollars as a trump card that we can play later. It will take some arranging to gather the investors to do this, but there are many chits to collect around the world. Leave that action to me. Please, tell the Holy Father to go ahead. I think his initiative will start the process, and we'll see where things go."

The Archbishop felt a little silly and naive as he sipped his Perrier, and glanced at Lowery who still said nothing. Gutiérrez thought this discussion, thus far, could have been handled in a phone conversation. It seemed to be the way of international diplomacy, delicate and subtle decisions called for a face-to-face. What about human conditions made personal presence such an imperative, he wondered. Mario dealt in the area of spiritual presence, and God-reality, and the intangibles of life. In the spiritual realm, he found it easy to transcend distance, place and settings, in prayer and speaking with God. Dealing with our human condition, trust did not come so effortlessly. In the world, humans required verifying, certifying and credentialing, he thought. The phrase, "trust but verify" came unbidden to his mind. We are not divine, or God-like in many ways. In fact, we are far removed from God-respect with one another.

"Mr. Lowery, I am told of your experience with all types of international legal negotiations. I am happy to see you on the staff in this venture. How do you see the big picture?" asked Señor Leckner. Lowery felt patronized by the tone of Leckner's voice.

He replied. "I enjoy my work, and over the years put together a varied portfolio, Señor Leckner. Is there a specific part of my background of interest to you?" It seemed like a rather direct conversation for people who just met, thought Gutiérrez.

"I understand your wife was Brazilian, Mr. Lowery, which should give you an edge in understanding our thinking here. What family was she from?" Again, a certain tone present in the question, which took Lowery and the Archbishop aback. Señor Leckner, in an abrupt manner, plunged into the personal life of a minor program deputy. The Archbishop and Lowery each took note of the surprise in one another's eyes, and they wondered about Leckner's point. He had claimed familiarity with Lowery's background earlier. Señor Leckner must be aware the late Mrs. Lowery was the daughter of Brazil's former Minister of Finance, Adolph Ruedo. Leckner's many business dealings with Ruedo over the years would make him aware of the family and the fact that Estella Lowery was the oldest of Ruedo's daughters. Ruedo's daughters were distinguished in society circles for their style, sophistication and beauty, as well as their superior educations. John's wife Estella attended Harvard, the London School of Finance, and worked in Switzerland's financial world. She met John at Harvard. They married, and together they raised three children.

Señor Leckner struck a sensitive chord. A bewildered John searched for mental connections and memories to understand how his deceased wife's family connected to Leckner. Nothing came to mind, yet Leckner continued to push him for some reason, which left John Lowery clueless.

The archbishop, unimpressed by the little Leckner-Lowery exchange, moved to conclude their reviews and plans. Leckner appeared to enjoy his little mystery about the Ruedo family and Lowery's relationship to it. Mario wondered what connection this mystery had with their business. Other than that one incident, the visit went well.

Mario was lucky to fit in a dinner with María Elena and Fidel before he and John departed Buenos Aires.

The archbishop and John Lowery stopped overnight in Rio de Janeiro on their way back to Rome, to visit the Ruedo in-laws.

Archbishop Gutiérrez and John Lowery spent an evening with the Ruedo family. John seemed to enjoy his educated and sophisticated in-laws. The Ruedos welcomed John and the archbishop in a warm, open and loving way. John belonged, and during dinner, he moved the conversation away from his more formal law background as well as the protocol used by church and state business.

The archbishop was a spectator, in the midst of the family dinner-repartee, the memories and familial exchanges. He thought about his own sister, María Elena and their family gatherings. He always treasured their special family times as sacrosanct moments, almost too special to allow outsiders, and now he was an outsider with the Ruedo family.

He experienced a twinge of loneliness, as he laughed at remarks during the family banter. Did Jesus share this same kind of distance, as he sat in homes, and listened, and shared with families? Did Jesus feel a part of all families, yet belonging to none? There was sadness in it all that settled in his heart. These feelings contributed to a strange evening, this hearing and viewing of his inner self. An outsider, not a part of the lives around him, and yet welcomed, respected and accepted.

He was fully aware that his celibacy and being a stranger caused him a sacred loneliness. He thought he was more of an onlooker than a true guest, as he listened, smiled, laughed, and reacted. The Ruedo family enjoyed John's visit. They brought to life the love and memories of Estella and other family members no longer present.

The archbishop's witness produced a strange mix of feelings. He felt special and blessed even as a stranger who participated in an intimate family time. It would be the same experience regardless of the family's economic or educational standing for an observer like himself. It caused sadness in him, and awe, and a desire to weep, as they shared their caring love and memories. He did not understand his feelings of exclusion. When and why had he lost his sense of intimacy and belonging?

John explained some of the tension that surfaced about the family connection from the Leckner meeting on the flight home. His father-in-law reminded him that Señor Leckner had married, and then, divorced Estella's sister, one of Ruedo's daughters. The marriage took place a long time ago, and did not last long. Lowery told the archbishop despite the divorce, he believed Leckner expected Adolfo Ruedo to invest in the peace proposal.

John, pleased with the consulting contract's terms saw the Archbishop shared his satisfaction with Señor Leckner's acceptance of their work. Their team in the Vatican could proceed with the next step, and hire the consultants they needed.

Leckner's generosity gave the corporation autonomy as well as financial flexibility to pay expenses, hire consultants, and expand resources. The team assembled an impressive list of the world's leading experts in the Palestinian State-Israeli situation.

Archbishop Gutiérrez reviewed the status of the corporation with the Holy Father. The Pontiff reminded the archbishop of the "prayer and fasting" technique called for by Jesus, in certain situations. Gutiérrez appreciated the reminder, and took it to heart.

The archbishop could not recall a contemplative prayer community with a charism to pray for peace. The Carmelites, Poor Clares, Carthusians, or Trappists would consider it. He prayed and asked God to shine a light in this area, to show him how to go about securing this lifetime prayer-dedication for peace.

Mario called Viktor because he missed the genuine conversations they shared. The Archbishop noted that he walked the halls of the Pax Dei Pontifical University less and less, as administrative tasks got busier and busier. He hated the idea of losing touch with the people closest to him. Viktor represented the humanity of the institutional world to him.

Viktor was genuinely pleased to take the call from the archbishop. The spring semester was at an end. Viktor, a leader of the faculty-student group, dove into the student's plans for the summer break. He matched students to summer opportunities, which would place the students into experiences and employment situations where they had the chance to experience living in peace-seeking environments.

The archbishop eagerly accepted Viktor's dinner invitation. He loved visiting the off-campus apartment that Viktor and Magda now shared. The new apartment was one of the benefits of moving Magda to Rome. As he walked the last half mile to Viktor's, he nodded and smiled at all the other people enjoying an evening passeggiata too. He enjoyed the gentle stroll before dinner, and mentally prepared for the staircase climb that lay ahead for him.

It was a fourth story walk up, which reminded Viktor of his apartment in Moscow. This apartment included the usual shared patio in the rear center of the building. A lovely, green community garden of flowers smiled up at the surrounding families as they opened their balcony doors onto a beautiful deck where they enjoyed the Roman sunlight, breeze or smog, depending on the day's local weather conditions. Tonight, the weather was perfect with a gentle breeze.

Archbishop Gutiérrez brought wine, as always.

"Viktor, I am a little out of breath after the steepness of the four flights of stairs." Viktor hugged Mario as only a Russian can do, and gave him the traditional welcoming kisses. It felt like a homecoming. They had attended a meeting together only two weeks ago, but it seemed longer.

Mario reached out the wine, and shared another Russian hug with Magda. She told him he looked thinner and she worried about his poor

coloring. He agreed with her assessment and explained due to the busy-
ness of recent days, he was sleeping less and always eating on the run.
They joked about the good potatoes and cabbage they would share tonight. Mario asked if she mastered the art of serving pasta, with a broad
grin. Viktor shared Magda's attempt at making cacao e pepe, pasta made
with cheese and pepper. She reported the dish was easier for her to
make than to pronounce, as she laughed and hugged him again.

He enjoyed Magda's conversation. A woman of insight and energy,
and love, Magda's smile and womanly Russian strength brightened any
room.

Viktor, Magda and the archbishop sat on the little patio, over-
looking the garden below. Some of the other apartment dwellers did the
same. They resembled the audience in an opera house, only instead of
experiencing La Bohème or Tosca; they watched the sun begin to set.
The cool of an early May evening, relaxing with friends, away from the
concerns of the Vatican, made him happy. Mario wished he had taken
the time for a siesta earlier in the day as he was getting a little drowsy
with the wine and cool breeze. The fragrance of Magda's potted Jasmine
added to his relaxation with such good friends. They spoke of the family in Russia, and the changes, still happening there. Viktor and Magda
would be back in Moscow for four weeks in August, visiting family and
friends.

As Viktor poured the after-dinner cognac, the Archbishop asked
Viktor for his thoughts about the Pope's concern about the importance
of prayer over the peace situations they faced. "Viktor, do you think we
should add a course on peace prayer or meditation to the curriculum?"

Viktor, drinking his cognac, stopped with the glass at his lips,
smiled, put the glass down. Viktor looked at Magda. Magda was never
at a loss for words, and responded with great gusto as she leaned into
the Archbishop.

Mario, a little taken aback by her response to his question, was no
longer drowsy and instantly alert. The archbishop always valued Viktor's thoughts, and now witnessing the deference shown Magda by her
husband, he realized how much Viktor respected and valued Magda's
thinking in much the same way. His question struck a chord with
Magda. She released a torrent of conversation, an obvious flood of feeling and ideas came forth. Her discourse, more vibrant and effusive than
usual, Mario listened carefully.

The archbishop normally did not need a translator for Russian.
However, as Magda spoke so hurriedly, Viktor began to translate her
conversation in certain places. She spoke rapid fire so that Gutiérrez

could tell Viktor too struggled to keep up. Viktor gave Magda a hand signal to slow down, gesturing toward the archbishop. Magda nodded, took a breath and continued to speak as rapidly and ardently, passionately as before.

Magda spoke of her Grandfather Dimitri who was an Orthodox priest that spent the final years of his life in prison. Sentenced by Stalinists, he was accused of being a pacifist because he spoke out against military build-up. The most dramatic part of the story turned out to be that the priest grew up with Stalin. They came from the same village. The two went through school together and developed a friendship as well as a mutual respect. Stalin, as well as her grandfather treasured their friendship, but Stalin could not tolerate his old friend speaking against the State.

Her grandfather served 14 years at Lubyanka Prison, much of it spent in solitary confinement. She remembered going with her grandmother and mother to visit him, and bringing some bread and other items the prison allowed. She cried every time. His face aged each time in a different way, wrinkles growing, and beard graying. His hands grew narrow and bony. Yet, his eyes held a gentleness and light she found hard to describe. The wrinkles at the edges of his eyes spoke of an inner peace beyond believing. His hair and tremendous beard grew longer, each time she saw him. He never spoke in bitterness or anger, only in love, toward the police, the Army, Stalin, and other possible enemies. He said Jesus called him to this place and gave him a mission to offer his life and silence, and prayer in peace, for Russia, which he loved, and for the world, to include Germany. Magda, a confused youngster, did not understand his imprisonment. Most of all, she did not understand his peace about his life in solitude or the way he prayed. Each time she left the prison visiting area, she left in tears of anger and confusion, toward Stalin, and her grandfather. She believed God, and the government conspired to allow such waste of a loving life.

Her young life of peace turned to bitterness. Magda refused the last year and a half of his life to visit her grandfather. His heart disease resulted in his death in the prison. Broken hearted over her own hatred and lack of peace, she stubbornly refused to visit. She loved her grandfather from infancy, and remembered so well his hugs as his huge beard surrounded and tickled her. A martyr and holy man, he died in 1949. He was only one of the thousands of innocent victims falsely imprisoned by Stalin.

The passion with which Magda spoke held the Archbishop spellbound. Poor Viktor tried to slow her down, but shrugged every once in a while, to show the hopelessness of his efforts.

Magda's daily prayers with her mother and grandmother for her Grandfather's release went unanswered. She lived in an inner war every time she thought of him, and found no peace in his situation. She hated the government. She recalled his funeral as a large one for those days and his economic circumstances. Word of his death spread around Moscow. Many people of all lifestyles attended his simple Orthodox service, which the government allowed. At the funeral, people called her grandfather a sainted man who died for the cause of peace. They pledged to remember him always. Still, Magda found no inner peace. Confusion and anger raged inside her. As they lowered him into the ground on a cold, gray, November day, she wept more for her own lack of peace than for her grandfather. What peace did he bring? All Magda saw was that he brought death for himself and their hearts.

Her prayer life was shaken and her faith in God empty. Her life of peacefulness was shattered by her grandfather's experience.

Then, she met Viktor. While she much preferred to hear sweet nothings in her ear, this young, bold crusader spoke to her of peace as they sat on park benches and held hands. Excitedly, he recited all the peace initiatives going on in the world. This dreamer of peace caused an inner war to rage within Magda. What a bumpkin, she would think, as she listened to his peace litanies. She wearied of hearing him, so she began asking God to help her to understand Viktor. Magda recognized a definite attraction between them, but their hearts spoke different languages. Viktor spoke about peace, while she, restless, experienced nothing but war and the inner turmoil within her.

Magda continued to pray to understand Viktor, and her attraction to him. She prayed most of all to her grandfather, as her closest intercessor saint, to bring her understanding of herself, and this young, peace-speaking idealist, and her attraction to him. Magda wrestled with her memories, hatreds, fears and angers, in daily prayer sessions.

She prayed to God through her intercessor Grandfather Dimitri that God would teach her Viktor's way of thinking about peace. The war within her subsided over time. She surrendered more and more of her life to peace. Praying as she walked to the University, to meet Viktor, or, to the library, home, or anywhere and everywhere. She discovered a surrounding presence of God, and genuine peace, which grew deeper day by day. Magda's exchanges with Viktor no longer seemed to be one-sided, or skirmishes with protection of her warring feelings. Instead, Magda was open to loving, in a way she never thought possible. She came through the weariness of reflection and prayer over her life, and the world around her. Like a soldier walking from the battlefield, she returned home with a new vision of peace and order, feelings that she had almost forgotten existed.

God brought Magda into wholeness through her daily prayers for personal peace. She discovered a relationship with God and Grandfather Dimitri through her need of personal peace and her askance of it in daily prayer. Her face glowed as she shared all this.

Magda lived and prayed in meditation daily, communing with God and her grandfather, over the peace needs of her life and family, and of the world.

God clearly spoke through this excited, energetic woman of faith. Magda was a vivid reminder of the presence of God in and among us.

Mario listened to Magda relay her adventure of prayer for peace, and he wondered how he missed the scope and importance of such a key element like prayer. He thanked God it was possible to incorporate prayer so thoroughly into the peace institutions.

Magda had asked God for peace, through prayer, sacrifice and fasting. God responded affirmatively to her prayer request.

Viktor told Mario about how he always brought his problems to Magda. He consistently asked for her prayer and advice, and her insights most often brought the solution he sought. She prayed over the issues Viktor discussed with her, and brought back to him any words or insights of the Lord. Viktor said he received all of the credit in his career. However, too many times to count, Magda supplied the insight. Together, they found answers. They formed a peace team. She brought the mystical, spiritual insight of God into every circumstance.

Mario knew prayer was an ideal way to approach the complex peace issues of life, whether family, city, government, nations or businesses. He would appoint someone, perhaps a group to pray for intercession over the issues of world peace, and to listen for deeper insight and wisdom, while the active negotiators spoke with one another. The prayer team would become spiritual support for the negotiators. An interesting possibility, Mario knew of religious orders dedicated to pray for ecumenism, the conversion of pagans, the sick, and for foreign missions. He was unable to identify a group dedicated to intercessory prayer for peace issues.

Intercessory prayer raised a myriad of questions for Gutiérrez, as he tried to attend to Magda and Viktor in their excited explanations, while his own mind exploded with ideas and possibilities. The Lord dropped something akin to an atomic bomb within his brain, and fallout spun around in his thoughts. Mario wanted to stop, so he might jot down his ideas. Instead, he listened intently, and prayed he would remember all his thoughts later.

The evening turned to darkness, as the apartment lights around the little patio garden grew brighter, and the noises from family kitchens and balconies drummed, with occasional shouts, or laughter. Magda topped off the cognac and brought coffee to the table. Exhaustion hit all of them, Gutiérrez' tiredness came from listening and thinking so intently, and Viktor and Magda's weariness from speaking so passionately. A wonderful, peaceful companionable silence fell over them. They listened to the crickets below for a time.

Mario silently thanked God for the gentleness, the tenderness of this evening shared with two beautiful souls living in such a tough, unyielding world. He experienced the pain of humility in his heart at the privilege of looking into someone's deepest yearning soul. At the same time, he was overjoyed at this vision of prayer and hope. This evening turned out to be unlike anything he ever dreamed. God used these two simple people as His prophetic instruments.

Mario took his leave knowing that the Holy Father would endorse incorporating prayer into the University, the Corporation and their activities.

Gutiérrez gave Magda and Viktor big Russian hugs as he left. The night air so enjoyable, he walked part of the way before hailing a passing cab, his thoughts still racing.

He arrived at his apartment, and immediately went to the chapel, put his head in his hands and wept, uncertain as to why the tears. Exhausted, not only from the night, but from so many possibilities and people over these last months, he needed to cry and cry, and to ultimately rest in God's presence. There were so many people and experiences of peace, his own efforts so weak and small!

"Humble me, Lord!" Mario prayed in his crying exhaustion.

The *Pope's Pipe Dream Team* working alongside their Swiss teammates immersed themselves in the sale of art, statuary, paintings and artifacts. All parts of the program reported in on time, or ahead of schedule. Brisk sales led to predictions of a sellout. Pope Francisco approved a revision to the brochure.

Items listed began at a base initial offer. The public emailed, faxed, or called in bids through the 24/7 processing center. The system took advantage of all the latest computer and electronic linking without excluding those lacking access to the latest technology. The system enabled inclusivity for all.

A first-rate British security protection company surveilled every phase of operations. The process used to screen the bidders began with their login. The connection with security agencies around the world provided investigations into the names of companies and individuals in a matter of minutes. The computer program denied and deleted undesirable and fraudulent offers as soon as their bids were screened. If an immediate determination could not be made, they were put in a "research" category, which proceeded to an examination of their business standing in their stated country of origin. The latter process took a little more time, and sometimes required follow-up. In the end, the screening eliminated poor financial risks or suspect bidders. The security team monitored the initial transaction to the final accounting and delivery of the items. To describe the Swiss efficiency as impressive was an understatement.

Art collectors went wild over the unique, one-of-a-kind pieces up for bid. The new catalogue contained pieces not seen before. The number of museums and exhibitors proffering bids on the listed antiquities surprised everyone. The items interested universities and museums, especially archeology and anthropological collectors.

As time went on, the team received fewer claims from countries and ethnic tribes for the art items. Archeological and cultural plundering went on for centuries under flags of all nations. The team realized they could not repair old "wrongs" in every case. They realized a 90% plus return rate. The ongoing national and cultural recovery process proved successful for the most part.

The artifact recovery process identified the owner country, and often times traced ownership to the individual owner. The owners, most of them, museums, filed claims for missing pieces that should be returned. The legal procedures engendered all kinds of research and time. However, with cooperation, especially with regard to claims of public ownership, the returns were processed without complications.

In the area of private sales, Mr. Eiho Yoshino continued to submit his bids early, and he persisted with his false expectation that his offers should be handled in a more favorable manner than the other offers. His name, on approach had become a byword of warning to the Swiss agents, and familiar to the international bidding community. His crassness embarrassed the Vatican and Catholic officialdom.

The other area meeting with some resistance was the divestiture of church property by the wealthier dioceses around the world. The agreement with Cardinal O'Rourke helped; however, this area continued to experience a slowdown. The archbishop considered Cardinal O'Rourke a somewhat reluctant ally. Despite their earlier truce, the cardinal continued to stir the pot among the United States Bishops. O'Rourke continued to bring up all kinds of questions about the assets of the wealthy dioceses in his nation. Mario admitted the finances involved in the United States Church included more legality, tax and insurances questions than most other nations. Yet, he wanted to remove this gridlock from their plans.

The Vatican encountered many variables, most notable, the human elements of the individual bishop's character and of the bishops' national conferences in each country. Other factors in the divestiture process included the developmental needs of each diocese, its country's status, and the size of its Catholic population.

Despite the problem areas, Lamentier managed to complete the global inventory ahead of schedule. The company estimated it would take two to three years to get a valid working inventory system in place. It would take longer to finalize the liquidation of all the holdings, and property, and the final transference of those assets to the Vatican.

The reality of recording these chapters of Church history proved difficult in some areas. There were nations and their bishops who proved similar to the governments of the world. They spoke often of transparency, but reluctantly, if at all, made their records public. The divestiture process became more painful than necessary, at times. Some dioceses begrudgingly turned over their excess assets. There were times when the laity joined in protests, not wanting "their money" to go to outside causes, and not wanting to relinquish control. This proved a decisive test of belief versus practice.

In contrast, many wonderful and forthright actions took place during this time. More than a few bishops, who understood the Church's need, explained the Vatican's requirements to their people and priests, and complied in a timely manner by reporting their excess assets directly to the Vatican.

Keeping all processes transparent created quite a legal structure. They set up holding accounts in each nation in accordance with national laws, which dispersed properties, investments, and cash to the Vatican. The procedure encompassed a gigantic inventory and control process; the handover complicated by international laws.

Liquidation of assets, such as property, stocks, and other sales fell to the individual dioceses. The individual dioceses sent the money to a London account earmarked for their specific country, and the funds became available for the use of the corporation or the University by way of Oppenheim and Burke, as needed. The published reports were located in the public domain. The hope was that one bishop or diocese would inspire others to take these steps, to follow the procedure guidelines.

The plan formulated in the Vatican included a cap for each diocese to limit assets. Each diocese established an individual limit to allow retention of their savings for specific projects, such as building a new church or school. The assets were scheduled for review every five years, and reports forwarded through the National Conference of Bishops in each country, to the Vatican. Special needs, disasters and catastrophic events would always receive special consideration.

The Vatican worked out a formula for the dioceses in which certain assets could be accumulated and retained. The Holy See studied a variety of formulations. Through the study of varied situations, they came up with a workable formula, one left open to revision in the future.

Mario and the team of *Pipe Dreamers* learned the world of international economics in a crash course experience. In the end, the Vatican depended on the national Bishops' conferences from around the world for follow-up and support.

The Vatican's management of the use of and redistribution of national resources, and excesses from wealthier dioceses, to help poorer dioceses in each country became official policy. It did not make sense to send money to the Vatican when dramatic needs existed in the countries themselves. The Christian ideal described in the Acts of the Apostles about shared resources, applied now to all dioceses, down to the parish-level. This ideal was considered more a call of justice, than simple charity.

As Catholic parishes and dioceses grew larger, it was customary to keep resources and finances, for their own use. Crises or emergencies arose, like, floods, fires, starvation or other disasters, and churches responded by gathering contributions to share with those in need. Each parish community or individual diocesan populace handled these situations independently. Yet, in some instances, the gospel of the poor had become the gospel of feeding the bureaucracy.

Jesus' style seemed rather distant from the affluence of the modern world. Pope Francisco sought to reverse this mindset. The Holy Father asked the Church to invest in peace, to the degree that they were able. The Pontiff's thinking, like Jesus in the Gospels, met with much resistance. The peacekeepers found the hardened attitude of the parishes difficult to reverse after so many centuries.

Controversy arose among the bishops of national conferences in a number of countries. The audit process brought out much of what parishes considered private information in the past. The poorer Bishops called for a more even distribution of assets among the dioceses in each of the countries. A healthy self-examination went on globally, which in some cases, led to a sense of antagonism. A lot of self-policing took place in the national Bishop's groups. A new honesty called for genuine concern for the poorer areas of the world. Grace at work!

The Pax Dei Pontifical University flourished in its second year of operations. Viktor went full tilt in everything he did. He and Magda were able to afford twice-yearly trips back to Moscow. Each time the officials asked less questions and expected fewer reports from Viktor. His reputation as a skilled researcher and negotiator spread beyond Russia and the University. International magazine articles frequently mentioned Viktor by name. He spoke to and joined peacemaking teams in all categories of business and political conflicts.

This happened not only with Viktor, but with other members of the faculty as well. The University professors were in demand as the world-renowned peacekeeping experts they had become.

This recognition brought about an unforeseen blessing. The Pax Dei Pontifical University professors found themselves in demand for peacekeeping assignments as expected. The surprise was they were also in demand for public speaking engagements about the University, peacekeeping and peace initiatives. The recognition of the University's success in peacemaking gave the professors spin-off work. With this newfound recognition came additional income for the professors who welcomed the supplement to their teaching salaries. The University defined contract policies with individual staff members as opposed to contracts with departments, or teams, or the University as the contracting entity.

The idea that peace had a price tag did not seem as far-fetched as before. Jesus would gulp a few times at the money changing hands over this idea. In the modern world skills, training and results, without investment, proved elusive, nearly impossible. People willingly invested in peacemaking. It became a high priority commodity. The peacekeeping team established a new type of contracting area; models set up by the University and supported by the associated Contracting Corporation benefited many businesses, government and institutions around the world.

New businesses sprang up in the peace arena. These businesses marketed freedom from anxiety and fear, from tensions and reprisal, with a little justice sprinkled into the mix. Peace became a commodity financed by affluence and education. A new branding of peace, stability, tranquility and order came with price tags.

The pontiff and the archbishop discussed competitors at some length, and decided any genuine peace effort would not go too far afield. Competition is always healthy. The discriminator was that the competing companies lacked the added faith dimension as well as the spiritual perspective offered by a Vatican-related operation.

Viktor called the archbishop on the evening prior to the Pax Dei Pontifical University Board meeting, and asked to meet for breakfast the next day. The two dear friends greeted the new morning together over coffee. "Mario, I am worried about you. You are tired. Magda says that I am a high-energy person, yet your schedule would drain me. Mario, I admire the way you manage to live under so many restraints. I never realized being part of the Church and working for the Pope could be such a strain. Are you happy? With all this pressure on you, you don't smile as much as when we first met." Viktor always found the way to penetrate his mind and heart. Archbishop Gutiérrez felt naked. Am I so obvious? Honestly, he was not certain what he was feeling. Relieved one moment, and in the next, he felt more like screaming or crying. Mario was certain of one thing; he did treasure his friendship with Viktor.

God knew we all need a friend like this, even though this level of perception proved painful at times. Most people avoided friends who are so direct and insightful.

"Viktor, I love to sit and talk with you. You pierce my soul with your observations. You disarm me," said the archbishop as he glanced up with a wry, gentle smile, from his coffee. "Viktor, I'm not sure how or why God brought us together. I do appreciate the way you call me to an illumination and honesty. At times, I would rather not acknowledge such honesty in myself." He smiled again.

"Listen Mario, I care about you and I worry about you. Why did God bring us into friendship? You ask an easy question. To use your manner of speaking, our friendship is a priceless miracle. It was you who brought me to freedom and to a work, and people I cherish. My dear friend, I want to bring you to slowing down, to enjoy life, enjoy friends and family, and continue to help me to find faith."

"Mario, what I say to you is true. You carry the university, the corporation, the Argentinians, the peace contracts, and the other demands of Pope Francisco, to include the treasures for sale. You carry all this around in your head, and you open your heart to deal with all kinds of people. This work is difficult for you, no?"

Gutiérrez rotated the cup with his thumb and forefinger, looking into his coffee as if the drink might turn into a crystal ball. He did not raise his eyes as he began to speak. "Viktor, you are very observant. The truth is many times my work is like dealing with a bowl of spaghetti, all loose ends. A friend like you is precious to me. You keep me honest. The Holy Father is the same way, though ours is more a fraternal working relationship. I guess the deepest friend, through all this, the One who is aware of my sighs and weeping in the nights, and lonely moments is the Lord Jesus. I struggle to find the exact words, Viktor. Jesus is my closest supporting companion through all this. There are many times that I have not listened, or liked what He has shown me. Yet, with His help, I am free to be myself. The times when I do not listen are the worst times. Jesus calls us to rest. I am listening to you, Viktor. I will work on making time to be still, and to incorporate leisure activities into my schedule. Sounds funny, I guess. The greatest gift God gives to me is His inner peace, and calm. We are doing His work, and He is walking beside us all the way. I work on the fringe, or outside, and He does the heavy lifting. Makes sense, right?"

Viktor smiled, a little puzzled. "Mario, I think you are giving the Lord, your God, too much credit. You did much of the work, my dear comrade, whether you admit to this or not. Credit God, if you wish, but I witness your work. I see you, like all religious people, give God the credit, yet, you do a lot of inspired work, from my viewpoint."

"Thanks, Viktor, for your support. Tell me, are you getting rich on those consulting fees floating around the faculty these days? I have heard good things. I am going to let you buy the lunch next time."

Viktor shook his head no, and grinned. "I will buy our next lunch, if you agree to rest. You know few from Russia or the Eastern Bloc can afford my skills. The rest of the world is becoming familiar with me through the writing of the reporter Anna Malooff. Anna's interviews with the staff exposed and promoted all our professors to the rest of the world. Thus far, I have not had time to publish for the journals. I continue to develop subtle and team building skills, which will add to my negotiating talents. I continue to love our students, our work, the University. Magda says that we are abundantly blessed."

Mario concurred, "We are indeed blessed, my friend" as he and Viktor rose to leave.

Señor Leckner flew in with his staff the following week for an intensive briefing on the status of the Middle East peace plan. Archbishop Gutiérrez found that he eagerly anticipated seeing Leckner again. He was an interesting and charismatic individual.

They scheduled an audience with the Pontiff. The archbishop searched, but did not find a record of Leckner receiving the sacrament of Baptism in the Catholic faith. Señor Leckner did not appear to be a part of the Jewish faith. Mario could not find any indication that he had actively practiced any specific religion at any time in his life.

The press publicized the importance of the powerful meeting between the Pope and Señor Leckner. Sister Helen Marie, always a part of planning for the press, assured her dear friend Anna Malooff of a good seat for the press conference following the meeting.

Señor Leckner would enjoy the *Castello*, one of Italy's finest hotels. Señor Leckner would enjoy the hotel's spa, wine cellar and acclaimed menus.

The Corporation staff handled the meeting rooms, press credentials, communications, and other details. Only those with "a need to know" status possessed copies for the finalized contracts and details for the visit. The meetings would be held at the Vatican.

Gutiérrez and two of his associate directors briefed Pope Francisco early the morning of the meeting. The meetings with Señor Leckner and his staff would be important. Everyone was a little anxious, wishing the meeting would be a success. Together, the Pope, the Archbishop and a few members of his lay staff prayed for guidance. His Holiness prayed aloud, guiding their prayers. He asked the Lord to inspire Señor Leckner, and the Israeli and Palestinian leaders. He asked for this proposal to lead the world in new directions of goodwill and peace. Their prayer concluded, the Pontiff smiled and suggested "Archbishop, Monsignors, and staff members, you may now relax and leave this in the good Lord's hands. He will guide us. Remember, we share belief in one God with our Jewish and Islamic brothers and sisters."

Leckner was briefed by his staff in Rome as well as Archbishop Gutiérrez. An air of efficiency accompanied by genuine hope hovered over this meeting.

The papal library served as the main meeting room. Attendees included four of Leckner's key people, Pope Francisco, and Archbishop Gutiérrez with his two Monsignors. Most everyone met earlier at Señor Leckner's briefing and so only the Holy Father needed to be introduced to Leckner's staff people. No media were invited to this meeting.

They debated everything, to include, how to extend the invitations, what overtures to make and which allies to enlist. Which, if any, part of the negotiations to make public? Finally, the peacekeepers discussed ways to make participation in the process attractive.

The Pontiff asked prayer of all involved, and for the Church be a continuous voice of justice, human rights, and historic peace.

The peacekeeping team debated the lack of economic sanctions for participating nations, which might be used in the negotiations. The church would only issue the very few sanctions available, and then, only with extreme reluctance.

Church sponsored sanctions were limited. The Church could suggest discontinuing religious tours and pilgrimages, which might result in economic consequence. They could send a message about the need for global justice. It was possible that the Church could withdraw ambassadorial representatives of the Vatican from Jerusalem or expel the ambassador's staff from Vatican City. Absolutely, no one wanted to extract Catholic assistance programs from either nation. Few Islamic government representations involved the Vatican. Bottom line was that none of these options appealed to the archbishop.

The most complex questions included economics and trade with Israel and the Palestinian State. The Vatican held minimal advantage in this area. To be a convener and gatherer of the economic possibilities was the best the Vatican could offer. The group noted that the United Nations maintained neutrality without voice or realistic sanctions.

It seemed only right for the people paying the bills, Pope Francisco and Señor Leckner, to make the final decisions about critical points. Those who understood the consequences answered the big questions.

It was during a quiet refreshment break that the Holy Father discretely asked Señor Leckner about the possibility of Jewish heritage. Leckner, surprised, considered this direct question about his ancestry.

"Why do you ask, Holy Father? Does my heritage show, or did the Vatican ask for background checks on me? Few people ask such direct questions of me."

Pope Francisco studied him; ready to apologize, if his question proved too personal. Leckner put the Holy Father at ease. "I am Jewish on my paternal grandparent's side. Expatriates from Prussia, we lost our Jewish roots in one generation. With my parents' early deaths, I became an orphan and an unbeliever. I never discovered God, or faith, or any tie of spirit of heart to religion, though I did some research and studied various faiths to some degree over the years. Does this make sense? Or, am I marked in some other way?"

"You are marked by faith and belief, Señor Leckner. The work you started here and its costs are not in the realm of natural thinking. You are unusual beyond what people perceive of you as a man of vision and faith. God is with you, and I thank Him for you."

"Holy Father, my mother used to quote Golda Meir, 'there will be peace in the Middle East only when the Arabs love their children as much as they hate Israel.' It seems to me the reverse is also true."

This little intimate exchange seemed to spark the eyes of each man; they acknowledged something deeper in one another than was seen by the others. Leckner's fiftyish face, showed a hardened man with features sharpened by his years in the business world, and a consciousness of the image of strength he projected. The other face, less intense, showed the loosened muscles of seventy years, with crows' feet in the eye corners, from countless smiles bestowed upon life's pilgrims. Both men possessed piercing eyes, which cut through to the heart of people. These men were accustomed to delving deep into the issues around them and into the depths of life's mysteries.

The Holy Father and Señor Leckner nodded their heads in some type of agreement. Their eyes seemed to be speaking to one another, unknown to the rest of the group. Gentle lips seemed ready to speak, in affirmation. They had no need to verbalize.

They reached a faith understanding, of life-to-life, heart to heart, an accord struck between the two men, of such different beliefs and backgrounds. In a short time, the two men endeavored, and bridged their differences.

The discussions went on for several hours, with breaks for refreshments of coffee, tea, wine, and sweets. Accords were reached, and details delegated to their respective staff members to work out.

Leckner eloquently explained to the Holy Father. "Your Holiness, a fair percentage of this budget will go to enticing economic interests, such as the private sector of the United States, to invest in research and development, marketing, and consultation. Promotional dollars are earmarked for establishing and maintaining this peace for years to come. Peace cannot take root by itself or grow from good will. A percentage of every dollar will go to marketing the peace project. We will bring in new investors through promotion."

At the conclusion of the session, the Holy Father suggested they end with prayer. Fatigued, his voice reflected his tiredness. Those present, who shared in the intense few hours, experienced a drained elation. In simple words, straight from his heart, the Pontiff offered a closing prayer asking the Holy Spirit to move upon Israel and the Palestinian State, and the negotiators who would bring them together. Pope Francisco lifted up Señor Leckner and his interests. Archbishop Gutiérrez thought about the background and faith of the billionaire, as he witnessed the way the prayer touched Leckner. Until today, Mario did not realize Leckner's interest involved more than just worldly interests. That realization came to him during prayer. It dawned on Mario that as this peace project touched people's lives; it left them forever changed. Not only would the accord impact the Israeli and Palestinian people, but also those who worked with the developments of the hopes, dreams and details of this "impossible dream."

With each line written in job descriptions, contracts and reports, people expressed their deepest personal selves, whether secretaries, technicians, or policy planners. Everyone possessed a personal stake in all the developments. No one involved thought of himself or herself as only an employee. Instead, they, too, became self-described dreamers in pursuit of the dream.

Señor Leckner, accustomed to taking risks, called this investment in peace the biggest risk of his career. Mario believed the Lord allowed Leckner to accumulate such enormous wealth to bring about this opportunity for peace, which would bring blessing to this rich man and with the grace of God to warring peoples with centuries of hatred between them.

The Norway site selection was agreed upon for the peace talks. A villa was rented and the location kept secret. They set the time for the first meeting. Invitations were extended to all involved parties. The initial circulation of invitations took two weeks. The team planned to collect menu options along with the RSVPs. All possible interested third parties were consulted and asked for their diplomatic help.

Telephone lines buzzed, priority mail, e-mail, and faxes went out in a flurry. Excitement ran high in Gutiérrez' office, as the months of work paid off. Finally, the big day arrived.

The quickness with which both sides agreed to convene in Norway surprised the Archbishop.

The press releases from the office were intentionally written with ambiguity by Gutiérrez. The articles referred simply to overtures in a reconciliation process, by Pax Internacionale Corporation and the Vatican. Journalists searched for leaks and insider sources.

Preliminary reports, to include a full listing of proposal ideas, were circulated to all with "a need to know." Instructions spelled out explicitly that revelations to anyone outside the approved group would not be tolerated. Señor Leckner's staff was cautioned along with the *Pope's Pipe Dreamers* and all associated contractors and other members of the team. Only the Vatican would issue statements, and then, only when approved by Archbishop Gutiérrez. These instructions contained no delicacy or diplomacy.

Archbishop Gutiérrez, distracted a lot these days, tried to spend as much of his time in prayer as possible, asking the Lord to bring all invited participants, without incident, to the negotiation table.

The Jewish and Palestinian delegations were led by Abraham

Steiner and Omar Haddad respectively.

Overall, things progressed with positive responses from the team members. Pax Internacionale Corporation representatives, plus two from Leckner's office, and agents representing the United Nations, participated as well.

The peace summit budget covered all related expenses, and included paying representatives a stipend, which proved an enormous help.

The total cost of the package to be offered to the Israelis and Palestinians was estimated to be billions of dollars. Continual revision and negotiation requirements would provide the bottom-line guarantees, as well as motivation for the peace settlement.

The Archbishop's representatives, already in Norway, kept in touch with him twice daily by phone, and indicated all was well, and going as planned. His staff had role-played the expected scenarios many times, in preparation for this huge encounter. They prayed for few unexpected developments. The team employed a skilled and wise strategy, which Pax Internacionale Corporation's contributors put together. Despite the team's preparedness, they realized that this was indeed a baptism by fire.

The international interest in the peace talks from Norway had a positive impact on other peace making initiatives. The Pax Internacionale Corporation had received many other intervention opportunities during the past few months. The news of the Israeli-Palestinian peace talks became a new tool in peacemaking processes. The reality of what they offered opened a myriad of peace possibilities.

The business aspect of peacemaking grew complex quickly. Additional staff and processes for handling the many requests came in to play. *The Pipe Dreamers* sifted through and set-up operations for designated groups to handle the varied types of inquiries, such as those of government civil disputes, business, and public institutions like schools and hospitals, as well as family interventions. The staff streamlined the front office in order to establish a new intake department, which would allow them to take on as many cases as possible given the current structural limitations of the organization.

It was at that time *the Pipe Dreamers* came up with a way to ease the struggle to keep up with the demand. *The Pipe Dreamers* put forth a plan to expand their outreach around the world by establishing regional satellite peacekeeping centers in the geographic areas with most need. The plan made the best use of the WPO's resources. They capitalized on the buildup of professional experience, as well as the fact that they were in a financial position to grow. The regional peace hubs would employ the very same plans, policies and procedures in use by the Vatican's WPO. They would start with consistency of service, and efficiently handle many more requests for intervention and peacemaking.

The timing was right.

# Chapter 10

## American Bishops

---

The American Bishops issued a letter on world money matters, and used the sharing characterized in the early Church found in the New Testament as a model.

The Vatican noted that a strong movement toward downsizing in life was growing in the United States. Pope Francisco held a huge mirror on consumption up to the American bishops using the divestiture movement as an ideal. That modeling of the individual ideal extended to individual personal lifestyles came as a pleasant surprise.

The majority of the American Church hierarchy cooperated with the plan to turn over their excess assets to the Vatican. The opinion polls showed many of the nation's Catholics did not understand the financial system of the Church; yet, they trusted their leaders. The plan provided a crash course in economics for many in the Church.

Catholic consciousness was raised because of this new movement, which asked the question should all Catholics profess a restricted lifestyle with regard to the way they utilized their finances and goods.

American Christians examined and discussed whether Christ called them to live in poverty. Catholic communities, from small country parishes to large religious institutions like Notre Dame, Georgetown and Gonzaga Universities began to question the Gospel's call to live a simple life. In earlier times, Saint John Paul II spoke about a "preferential option for the poor," in a move toward aiding the needy and vulnerable of the world.

They talked about depletable resources and ecology, as well as money matters. More people took up the debate than ever before in history; ordinary, everyday people, lay Catholics, as well as vowed priests and religious sisters and brothers.

Other Christians became part of the discourse. They examined the ethic of work and rewards, and individual enterprise and wealth.

The Jewish population questioned their system of God blessing wealth. A hard realization came to all of the world via the new public directions of the Vatican, and this dramatic move of divestiture.

Deliberation took place in world circles. The United Nations debated the goals of Pax Dei Pontifical University and work of the dedicated Pax Internacionale Contracting Corporation. The Congress of the United States mentioned the Vatican divestiture plan, as a means of simplifying life in the country. They compared this simplification to the ways of Mother Theresa, and her work among the poor. Wall Street and Madison Avenue eyed the art market; reviewed the Vatican treasures listed. The late night talk shows used the debate for endless spoofs and jokes. Publicity stirred, far beyond anything the Pope imagined. Mario found the attention given to the peace plan incredible. Pope Francisco likened the way God used the media to awaken the desire for peace throughout the world to His mysterious ways.

Archbishop Gutiérrez reminded his staff and all Board members how God used them for arbitration in the world, and compared that concept to the Gospel story of the rich man building new barns, and to the poor beggar Lazarus, seeking scraps, at the rich man's table. Pope Francisco told the world that the Lord invited all His people to reflect on simplicity of their lifestyles. Archbishop Gutiérrez and his staff prayed about this daily. *The Pope's Pipe Dream Team* asked the Holy Spirit to enlighten them and help them to understand their part of this prophetic call from God, which went out to the world, to repent, as Jonah told the people of Nineveh.

The world reflection on divestiture surprised the archbishop. He had not foreseen this spinoff of the Vatican's plans. That some of the American Church cried out in protest did not surprise Mario. His discussions with Cardinal O'Rourke helped him realize that the stakes were higher for them as the U.S. dioceses held the most assets. Divine humor was at work bringing about so many unexpected and surprising results of the peace initiative. This thought brought a little chuckle to Gutiérrez, as he sat in his chapel. Mario realized the Pontiff must chuckle as well in his quiet moments of reflection about the mysterious, tricky and humorous ways of God.

"Yes, Cardinal O'Rourke," Mario asked for patience while he prepared to listen to this fifth call this month from O'Rourke. O'Rourke extolled his Archdiocese's generosity. The Los Angeles Archdiocese gave forty-five million dollars this year to the peace project. O'Rourke insisted Archbishop Gutiérrez come to the U.S. to speak to the American bishops at their November meeting. The bishops needed answers and their issues resolved. Mario found that he agreed. The trip was a good idea. The Church in the U.S. merited his personal attention.

The archbishop last traveled to the United States of America ten years ago. He planned to take advantage of this trip to visit his old friends in the Washington D.C. area. The American Church deserved kudos. The Holy Father would agree. The Pontiff received continual questions from the American hierarchy. Their most recent questions came from their scheduled ad Limina quinquennial visits. These visits with the bishops and the Apostolic See resulted in questions, which Pope Francisco referred directly to Gutiérrez office as they referred to disclosing and releasing funds.

The business end of the peace initiative tested the honesty of the highest level of hierarchy. Pope Francisco and Archbishop Gutiérrez became aware of most self-interest issues. They found some protected the interests of the local church by using loopholes. So much circumvention kept everyone involved busily rewriting and adding sections to the governing procedures. They agreed that the Church loses its spiritual identity when caught up in disagreements, jealousy, power games, and pettiness. They prayed together the passage of St. Paul in 1 Corinthians 12: 24-25, "God has composed the body so that greater dignity is given to the parts which were without it, and so that there may not be disagreements inside the body but each part may be equally concerned for all the other."

The Canon lawyers answered all the inquiries not envisioned when the new Code was promulgated in the 1980s. This new proclamation of economics from the Gospel took many by surprise, and a balancing act happened at all levels of Church bureaucracy.

Archbishop Gutiérrez wished everyone involved understood that the Vatican based its peace plans on Christians' treatment of sensitivity to the needs of neighbor. Catholic social teaching provided a pathway irrevocably linked to Pope Francisco's plans for peace. Mario believed that true peace was much more than the absence of war. Peace was God-given and it was built on justice. The peace plan bound the Christian faithful to assist the poor using their own resources. A pastor was to seek out the poor with particular diligence. Religious institutes were to provide sustenance for the poor. The poor were not to be deprived of fitting funerals. Richer dioceses were to provide for the poorer ones.

The corporal and spiritual works of mercy have long been part of the Catholic Christian tradition.

St. John Paul II reminded the church of its responsibility to safeguard the rights of the individual, to be a strong defender of the human person, respecting their dignity always at the core of the protection of human rights, while promoting and protecting the common good.

All appeared quiet on the Japanese front. The art world absorbed the latest release of Vatican fine art works. Eiho Yoshino called Archbishop Gutiérrez to congratulate him on the revised catalogue, and thanked him for purchases he made in recent months for clients in Hong Kong.

Archbishop Gutiérrez studied the issues involved in preparation for the U. S. Bishops' meeting. Mario asked the Lord for a deeper understanding of their complex, democratic, capitalistic society and theology.

Marie did a superb job with the expansion of the University. The University enrollment grew ahead of schedule. The budget remained healthy. The faculty grew more diverse in nationality and background. The growing esteem of the Pax Dei Pontifical University attracted a high caliber of professors. The professors would not grow rich on the University salary and paid benefits. The intangible compensation was the prestige of taking the lead in rethinking peace.

Many in academia drew hope from this updated concept of peace. The University explored communitarian theories with the concept of studying peacemaking and its unlimited effect in the world. One of the published professors compared the pursuit to undiscovered gold in his first book.

In the world, peace moved to the forefront, and remained there. Activists supported it, churches prayed for it, governments called for it, soldiers were willing to fight for it, and musicians sang about it. People toasted peace, hippies greeted one another with it, and children symbolized it.

Peace accompanied by respect came to troubled marriages, family life, to employment and workplace tensions. The peace concepts brought harmony and accord into judicial proceedings, law enforcement, and classroom life. The awareness level rose in institutions and industry as they too realized initiating peace plans make a difference. Mario's staff set up standard operating procedures for peacemaking to mirror orientation and training processes. The beneficial boost to employee morale came from the knowledge their employer cared about a peaceful work environment and valued their employees.

The world awakened to the realization of how they spent emotional and psychic energy. How it was wasted at times on unneeded tension among people and their communities. The peace investment realized by families, nations, businesses, industry and institutions grew at a rapid pace. The peace dividend equaled growth and order in individual cases and family development. It was much easier to promote when peace was believed not only possible, but also sustainable.

The world needed peace and order in the environmental arena, a centuries old battleground. One battleground included rights over specific water resources, or firewood, or hunting areas, or fields. People who abused nature were another battlefield. The ecological environment is an explosive, complicated area, made personal when you when you consider the needs of the people of developing nations. Nature's battles included daily depletions, scarring, wastes, and illegal dumping. Animosity developed into accusations over fishing, the ozone layer, and rain forests. The world needed to restore balance. Conflicts over environment and resources arose. This was a new type of warfare, using different calculations and emotions with regard to depletion of resources, eco-dumping and abuse, consumption and controls. Ecological warfare of business versus government, consumers versus producers, national interests versus special interest groups and world interests moved to the forefront of peacemaking. The one thing everyone agreed upon, the future of our world is at risk.

Other important areas of study included the theology of ecology, global warming and resource consumption, which they included in the University's peace-building studies.

The study of violence syndromes of societal life remained in the early stages of examination. Violence ingrained in the human psyche was an early finding. Working with the World Health Organization they found one of the greatest challenges was to understand whether violent traits are a part of genetic makeup, or an environmental factor. The World Health Organization reported overwhelming global statistics from every socio-economic status.

As the archbishop flew to the United States, his thoughts were focused on the question, who would not want peace? His first thought was that power does not like peace. There will always be world leaders whose pride will respond to the temptation of power. Power hungers, craving more control, more domination, and selfish pleasure. Not for the first time, Mario thought that Jesus sets the model for peaceful negotiating and sharing in life issues.

The clear, cold November day bright with sunlight sharpened the historic shadows of Washington. "His Holiness appreciates you, and the economic rearranging work of the American church." It was the first greeting from Archbishop Gutiérrez to Cardinal O'Rourke as they met at Washington's Reagan National Airport. "Well, why didn't he call and say so himself," an unsmiling O'Rourke snidely replied, as they shook hands in a stiff formal manner.

"I hope you are well." Not waiting for a response, Gutiérrez continued, as they entered the baggage area. "All the news reports indicate the Bishops' Conference is going well this week." Mario shivered with the inner cold as he struggled to try to find a warm conversation spot. "God help me with this man," his silent prayer. "I thought we were past all of this."

The unease of dealing with O'Rourke, settled in. Gutiérrez disliked being tough and hard, which stressed his character and soul. Yet tough talk appeared to be the only language O'Rourke spoke. In the United States, they called this playing hardball. Mario hoped he would not need to play, instead, he trusted God to show him, His way.

The archbishop and the cardinal sat back in the limousine, as the driver pulled away from the terminal.

"Archbishop, we realize you are here to check up on some of us, and to calm others," O'Rourke barked. "The Vatican still does not understand the economic complexities here in the United States. This is not a picnic as I told you and the Holy Father so many times before." "We call your plan taxation without representation."

"Cardinal O'Rourke, I don't understand your stress. This specific policy is exactly what the Church has practiced for years, under Canon Law, with the cathedraticum tax. This is an application of an age-old system in the Church. We have simply linked it to the Vatican's peace plan."

"Gutiérrez, pat answers for all the complaints about our assets going to Rome will not work. The way you characterize your plan does not matter. I do not care. This plan is a pain in the butt, and unfair to our people, and to the development of our local churches. We understand that we need to help the poor, missionary, and developing churches around the world, and we have helped the vulnerable for years, with mission collections. This plan is unbalancing the budgets of our American, and I am sure other countries, local churches. I don't care what the formula states, to me this is robbing Peter to pay Paul, and we want to thoroughly reexamine this plan of yours."

O'Rourke stared straight ahead, red-faced, neck veins pulsating around his priestly collar, as the driver sped into the Washington DC airport traffic. Archbishop Gutiérrez glanced over at him, trying to think how to bring peace to the Cardinal, and to his own heart in the next few days. Mario prayed as they drove on in a petulant silence, each looking out the windows on their side of the car.

Mario second-guessed his decision to travel alone to the United States, given the welcome he received. As he imagined Daniel going into the lions' den, he thought he should have brought backup, moral support.

That evening in his room at the four-star hotel on Connecticut Avenue, he made a list of the friends he counted on for backing. Thoughts of old friends from his seminary days and Rome cheered him. His dear friend Hector Anchondo, whose Ambassadorial position brought him to D.C., headed his list.

Mario added up the networks of his geographical friendships, and he began to place some strategic calls. Before leaving Rome, he had placed calls to a few of the friendlier archbishops, bishops, and cardinals. Yes, this is the time for some more personal lobbying, and honest feedback from trusted friends.

He made lunch and breakfast arrangements for the following day with four or five of the more notable hierarchy of the United States. Mario hoped to get their opinions on how to best approach the conference gathering, and to garner a more personal, and friendly sense, of what to expect.

Archbishop Gutiérrez knelt over his bed to pray. The loud street noises below made for a distracted and somewhat fearful time of prayer. He tried to unite with Jesus in the garden of Gethsemane, praying the night before his crucifixion. Mario thought of all the agony the Lord went through the night before His passion and death. He recalled all the other sacrifices and pressures of the recent years, which led Mario to this point. Not knowing what to expect over these next few days made things difficult for him. He continued to pray, and, then, the Archbishop heard, "Mario, be anxious for nothing, but in thanksgiving, make your requests."

At breakfast, Mario met with the Cardinals of Boston, Philadelphia, and Detroit. Familiar with "power lunches," Mario thought this would be a "power breakfast." He was well aware of the power of these three churchmen. The beauty of the meal was when the power of God's Holy Spirit took over the breakfast conversation. The Spirit moved the three cardinals from their initial position of marginal support to an enthusiastic position for the Vatican's peace plans.

As Mario became more comfortable, he shared that his lunch

plans included the cardinals from Chicago and New York. He did not say that he thought the luncheon group might prove difficult. As the cardinals moved to a supportive posture, they offered tips on how to approach the other men Mario would deal with later in the day. Mario found himself overwhelmed by the reaction of these prestigious leaders.

They went up to their rooms on the elevator, Cardinal Schwarz of Detroit and Archbishop Gutiérrez exited the elevator last. The Cardinal offered Mario one last piece of advice. Walking down the hallway to their rooms, Cardinal Schwarz suggested Mario talk first to Cardinal Braun of Chicago, in private. Braun would be pivotal and would require special attention from Archbishop Gutiérrez in his role of representing the Vatican. Mario thanked him for the insight as he continued on to his room.

Mario smiled as he entered his hotel room. What a victory, he thought. He wanted to jump into the air, with elation. He threw up his hands as if at a soccer match, glanced up to the heavens and shouted his thankfulness. Mario fell to his knees, and emotion swept him up in joy as he thanked God for the peace and solution with the three powerful people he faced over breakfast. What a victory! He kept repeating, "For You Lord, You made this happen!" This must be what it is like to win the World Cup!

The Bishops' Conference was scheduled to start that evening in the main conference room of the hotel with Mario giving the keynote address. He read the keynote address one more time. Mario had practiced the highlights of his speech with Pope Francisco before leaving Rome. He took a little time to prepare for questions he expected from the conference, which was due to open in a matter of hours.

The luncheon meeting was in the hotel restaurant. Despite the excellent customer service, his lunch with the Cardinal Archbishops of Chicago and New York started out apprehensively. Cardinal Kline of St. Louis joined the group for lunch. Cardinal Kline was a strong ally, and he helped to ease the situation by telling a few jokes. The American Church enjoyed a global reputation of inclusiveness, yet, these men had a need to protect their dioceses' interests too. Mario, a pastor early in his vocation, understood the dilemma. They were torn by the idea of sharing Gospel-style with the needy, and skeptical of supporting the new, unfamiliar Pontifical University, in Rome. They had the pressure of local interests, including local parishes and pastors, who did not want to part with any monies, to include any excess funds. Parishes formed local parochial interest groups, and worried about giving up any assets.

The cardinals felt pressured by other clergy, boards and other groups. As hard as closing schools and parishes in poorer areas was for the Church, having to share with unknown others across the seas seemed even less tangible, and more difficult. The peacemaking challenge of returning to Gospel-sharing shook the whole system of the American Church, to include thoughts of capitalism and parochialism. The Pope tried to explain his requests in a gentle manner through his Peace Encyclical and the University's vision and teachings. Some recognized this new approach as a reversal of hundreds of years of self-interest. Many said this change would be difficult to absorb in just one generation. Most held hope for their own situation to be the exception, or to be considered a special case.

The poorer dioceses of the world grasped the principle. They worried less, as they possessed very little.

Archbishop Gutiérrez finished his lunch, and thanked the cardinals for their encouragement on behalf of the Holy Father. He empathized with them and told them so.

Mario would state the same to the media later in the day. He went up to his room to return calls. He had a message from Pope Francisco telling him that he had spoken to the cardinals from St. Louis and Cincinnati, and that they were true supporters of the Vatican's plans.

Mario did a double take as he came to the entrance of the conference room, the bishops' meeting place for the evening. There was a small group of what appeared to be aging hippies. They carried signs reminiscent of the 1960s peace rallies in the United States. Some of the posters read, "Give peace a chance." Others had the image of the familiar sign of peace and one read, "Peace, hippies still believe in it." Mario smiled, as he began to relax.

The atmosphere at the meeting turned out to be much less tense than he expected. Cardinal O'Rourke held his own press conference, prior to the one scheduled by the bishops for Mario, and gave his expected address and position.

Mario's press conference proved to be a customary one with more aggressive questioning by the free-world press. Mario was accustomed to, and comfortable with the pressure. The press brought up all the sensitive reactions of the U.S. Churchmen. The archbishop received the usual offers for CNN, Good Morning America, Today Show, Worldwide News and others. He accepted most of the offers, declining only those that conflicted with his schedule.

Archbishop Gutiérrez acknowledged the one friendly face, which stood out among the American press. Like a ray of sunshine, Anna Malooff with her World Wide News credentials sat upfront and smiled encouragingly at him even during his most stressful moments.

In much of the questioning, news people drew parallels to the American taxation system. Few of the press had actually read any of the Holy Father's documents on the peace process and so they approached their questions from the democratic, capitalistic thinking. Archbishop Gutiérrez enjoyed reminding everyone when his or her specific questioning was not of the Church or the Gospel. He answered affirmatively about the ongoing historical process to remake the Church's finances. He cited the more even-handed distribution of resources first seen in the Acts of the Apostles, among the early Church.

Many of the questions asked in this news conference, were questions asked in previous press conferences. One reporter stood and simply made a statement about the United States establishing diplomatic relationships with the Vatican in the 1980's. Mario thought the statement to be a prelude to questions. However, the reporter sat down and said no more.

Afterwards, Anna requested and received a few rare moments with the archbishop away from the other members of the press. Anna thanked him for the special consideration, and the proper press credentials, which gave her additional access to the USA National Conference of Bishops. She asked the Archbishop to relay her gratitude to her dear friend Sister Helen Marie.

Anna went on to interview bishops from all over the country. She welcomed their reactions to the peace initiative. Anna's current interest lay in personal experiences dealing with the papal redesign of Church.

Many interviews took place, and feature stories developed around the Church's new approach to finance. The interest in the selling of Vatican treasures took second place when compared with the new methods of processing the wealth of the Church. Archbishop Gutiérrez found himself a little bit disappointed because the press asked so few questions about the Pax Dei Pontifical University, the Contracting Corporation, and the endeavor with Israel and other peacemaking operations. Mario thought Americans somewhat removed from the current peace negotiations. With the exception of the September 11 attacks on their soil, they had enjoyed the benefits of peaceful living for many years. Perhaps it is different for them. Other places in the world still struggled for their share of political and economic peace. The emphasis was different for the United States. Mario admired the Americans and their system so much.

"God bless America, this generous and sensitive people, who are so aware of themselves, and who freely share so many of their blessings," he prayed, "they do not realize how generous they are. God, always stay close to them."

Mario's tension left him completely as the conference of bishops wound down. He planned dinner with Hector and his family at the ambassador's residence. He called Pope Francisco to give a firsthand report. The Pontiff, following the news reports also discerned a lack of interest by the press in the University, corporation, and its efforts. His Holiness thanked God that Mario was able to reassure the US Bishops, and that the commotion had abated. The Pope planned to travel next year to the United States for a pastoral visit.

In a final farewell gesture, the archbishop called Cardinal O'Rourke, to ask his opinion about the conference and the tenor of the talk. Mario got the expected earful. This time however their conversation took a different track. O'Rourke's conversation held a new edge of respect, which surprised him. The cardinal no longer talked down to him like a little boy. Neither did he patronize Mario. The archbishop thought somehow he might have finally gained a new friend, and reached an understanding despite the reluctance of the past. The other cardinals and bishops responded in affirmative ways to him. Mario experienced firsthand the intensive politicking he expected in Washington in keeping with their reputation for this type of intrigue. He would return home a gentle winner from his encounter.

Mario planned to spend the last day of his trip with his former classmate, Bishop John O'Donovan. They did some quick sightseeing before lunch. John asked how things went at the meeting. Mario realized he hoped for a friendly opinion from his former classmate.

O'Donovan's round Irish face, squinted and smiled, with happy crow's feet beside each twinkling eye, as they sat over lunch at the Union Station eatery. "Mario, I wouldn't want your job for the world, getting crap from every corner. Yet, my friend, you handle everything with ease. I loved watching O'Rourke and his suffragan bishops calm down. They paced and squirmed as the majority stood and applauded your talk. This is an exciting victory for the Gospel of Jesus. I think Jesus is proud of us, for the change with the humbling of our wealth, and changing our high and mighty approach to how the Gospel should be lived. My people in Providence are accepting the plan in a noble way. So don't be dismayed, Mario, you're doing honorable work, pretty thankless though."

"John, when I took this job on a few years back, I had no way of knowing the peace plan would endorse such radical thinking, and cause so much stir. Initially, I found myself caught up in the idea of peace making. We realized selling the Vatican's treasures would be touchy. We were not as well prepared for the redistribution of Church holdings and wealth. Consequently, this issue crept up on Pope Francisco and our team. I think this brought us back to the Gospel, which is wonderful. His old friend and classmate smiled as he listened to the English roll from Mario's tongue. O'Donovan struggled with Italian when they studied together at the Gregorian, and Mario helped him. In exchange, O'Donovan taught Mario the nuances of the English language. Mario's dear friend spoke in "internationalese," rather than in Spanish or Italian thought patterns. Their lunch brought about an enjoyable exchange, a wonderful time with his dear friend.

Gutiérrez surprised himself at how well he now conversed in the English idiom. With an accent, always, but he was not afraid to let the words flow. His international reading kept him current with English colloquialisms. Mario liked the directness of English.

"We crossed one big hurdle. We released the statuary and the historical artifacts from the museums and historical archives. The sales will go on for two years more, but the income expected is astounding. John, it was a big surprise for me that not one question was asked by the press as to how much income the Vatican brought in thus far."

Mario's visit to United States ended with this pleasant personal confirmation. The Lord's voice had said not to be anxious, and to trust Him. Mario, left the United States blessed by the reassurance of heavenly as well as human lips, the high-tension situation defused.

Certain the Holy Father followed the press and news reports, Mario believed the Pontiff would be satisfied as well. "Thank you, Lord, for victories, big and small, and for your Hand easing our concerns," he prayed as the plane headed for his Vatican home.

He slept on the flight in an effort to regain drained energy.

Mario returned to Rome, and he kept his appointment with the Holy Father. His trip summaries ready to review as he entered the Pope's office. He found the Pontiff standing. Pope Francisco walked toward Mario with a big abrazo and smile, as he closed the door. The Pope's warm embrace and welcoming smile surprised Mario. His Holiness' usual custom was to wait until people approached him. His smile was always ready, but he held the abrazo in reserve for special moments. Mario was certain Pope Francisco was joy-filled because of his U.S. trip.

Pope Francisco ushered Mario to the sofa, rather than the chairs around his desk. The fire glowed in the fireplace. The Pope took the high wingback opposite the sofa, and smiled, again.

"Mario, I think you suffered enough for the Lord in the difficult jobs I have assigned to you. Jesus said to me, as I read the press releases from the U.S., "Go easier on the boy." "How do I do this Lord?" I thought the Lord would say, give him an affluent archdiocese somewhere, or let him run one of the Vatican offices. No, the Lord spoke in a clear voice: "Make him a Cardinal!" I jumped up from my kneeling bench. That is wonderful, Lord! That is a terrific idea! To be a cardinal will bless Mario and his work. My heart overflowed and I wept before the Lord for such a wonderful and uplifting inspiration." The Pope smiled like a child.

Mario sat stunned. A handful of his reports rested lightly on the sofa. The Holy Father's news caught him off guard. Unsure how to react, his thinking still caught up in his untouched reports. Confused by the turn their conversation took, he held his body tight as he sat upright on the sofa. His breathing slowed and became shallow.

After some time, his chest sunk, and he breathed normally again. He released the tension in his back and torso, and when he moved his lips and facial muscles, he managed a little smile.

"Holy Father, words fail me. I am shocked and surprised. What can I say? Appointed a cardinal is an honor, yet in no way a concept that I am able to grasp, at this time. It is the furthest thought from my mind. I am still wound up with information from the United States conference. Please forgive me; I cannot comprehend what you're saying."

The Pope appeared to be a little disappointed as he sat upright in his chair with his left arm on the back upper part of the wingback. His Holiness gazed into the fire.

"Mario, I want to tell you the other part of the inspiration, and sense God gave me in this. This was a clear message from our loving Lord, not only for me but also for the Church. Perhaps, as time goes by, we may discuss this further because the revelation does pertain to you. In any case, I understand. I will name other Cardinals in the next consistory to bring the number up to about one-hundred and twenty. We need some new men, younger men, as you, no doubt, agree."

Pope Francisco's obvious interest lay in his inspired plan for new cardinals. Mario realized that he craved silence; he wanted to pay attention to his own heart.

They went on to speak of trivial things. Citing fatigue, Archbishop Gutiérrez finally asked the Holy Father to excuse him. He thanked Pope Francisco as he left, for the honor. Mario shared with the Pope that he wanted to pray about the cardinal designation.

He reached his chapel and knelt back on his heels. He wept, in total release and relief. The archbishop wearied of everything "Church." He recalled the Scripture, "Be still and know I am God." Mario wrapped himself in this deep, calming stillness.

Viktor called the next day and asked for a lunch date. Marie had already asked for an appointment to brief him about the faculty meeting. Mario asked his staff for a current report from the Pax Internacionale Corporation, along with the status of the Israel-Palestinian State contract. Their Swiss operative reported everything was running on schedule. Mario experienced a little pressure. However, in comparison to the shock of the Pope's revelation following the United States Bishops' conference, everything else paled in comparison.

The Israeli-Palestinian peace initiative remained the number one initiative. The talks had a tendency to bog down more often than not based on their lengthy history and deep-seated feelings. Changing the focus from eradicating one another to a two-state peaceful solution was not an easy task. In fact, the past problems went a long way to explain why so many past efforts towards peace led nowhere.

Mario sat quietly in the Pax Internacionale Corporation's conference room. He thought of his own lack of experience in the hot seat of a negotiator. He truly appreciated the people gathered around the table in the corporation's boardroom that had a broad range of experience and negotiating skills.

The Palestinian-Israeli negotiators sent a team to report the news, and to examine critical questions about the peace talks. The Pax Internacionale Corporation committee took an active part in the peace settlements. Mario depended on the team leader, Monsignor Rolando Baroni, to coordinate the project and the contracts.

Monsignor Baroni and two of his aides flew to Rome for an in-person update for the archbishop and the Board. They would fly back to Norway following the meeting.

Monsignor Baroni was a dichotomy. He was the epitome of both tact and hardness. He came highly recommended to Mario by the Cardinal of Madrid. Baroni lived up to his reputation as an accomplished linguist. A competent and organized negotiator and administrator, he relied on his training in both civil and Church law, and his history included serving most of his priesthood in the Vatican diplomatic offices.

The temperatures were warm for November, and they opened all the windows. They sat around an old inlaid oak table, one of the Vatican's ancient furnishings. Everyone leaned back on the modern, high-back chairs, which provided contrast to the table and afforded excellent back support. Monsignor Baroni opened the meeting with a prayer in

French, and then proceeded to address the Board in Italian.

"My initial observation is the Palestinian State will be more demanding of capital than we can initially assemble at our bargaining table. Our promises of financial development will only go so far. It is my understanding that they want to build a Palestinian empire in ten or twenty years."

Please keep in mind that this is only the preliminary report, and it is based as much on talk heard in the hallways as at the table. Senior Leckner's representative, Andres, also present for this Board meeting, seconded Monsignor Baroni's statement. Andres indicated his boss planned to sweeten the deal by gathering more chits. He added that many of the chits were the "wait and hope" type.

"In any case, we are inventorying all possible available sources of capital and investment, which might go into a settlement. We are sorting out the private sector, government, and philanthropic input and evaluating the probability of each. The methodology we employ calculates the manufacturing, and productivity areas of each country's economy. We use five-year increments for future projections. In all of our estimations, we develop accompanying worse case scenarios. It is an "iffy" formula, as you can all tell. Economists all differ on creating such projections. God alone knows all the answers!" concluded Baroni.

Archbishop Gutiérrez stood, as if restless. He stared out the window. He seemed almost ready to leave the room. He looked tired, distant, and drawn. His expression stood out amid all the eager faces at the table around him. He seemed to be gazing at some mystical vision, transfixed. He did not turn back to the table, but walked to the window, his back now to everyone, and he stood still, as if led by a gentle and strong light.

"Monsignor Baroni, Señor Andres, we thank you both for your frank observations. Let us go with the suggested plan, and use all the capital we can muster. Identify certain investors, the probable ones, as well as the possible ones, to include the distant possibilities and proceed. I want everything upfront and presented to all parties in this same manner. I believe the Lord will make up the difference. This is a moment of trust. God will bend the hearts of Palestinian States and Israelis, of their business people and government employees to realize living in peace is what their investments will mean to the process. I am certain God will bring peace." He spoke with the decisiveness of a general revealing a battle plan. He showed no hesitation, sureness, strength, and clarity.

Mario knew the net proceeds of the Vatican's limited contribution to this specific project provided only a start of the billions needed to establish this truce.

Psychological scarring held sway in the historical significance of ethnic and tribal differences. They may not be able to overcome memories of long-held hatreds. In its infancy, this prospect of peace proposed a magnificent dream, a divine gamble. In this peacemaking business, Mario compared the *Pope's Pipe Dream Team* to brash adolescents, who believe all is possible, given their wit and youth.

Señor Leckner scheduled meetings over three days with Pope Francisco and Archbishop Gutiérrez in the Vatican. He chose to stay again at the luxury hotel, the restored castle near the Vatican. Archbishop Gutiérrez invited him to lunch on the first day where they enjoyed a personal visit. They met at the hotel's restaurant.

"Señor Leckner, I think you are operating under some special inspiration, in this peace process. I believe God is using you to create this moment in history. Some men are destined to build universities, or governments or artistic empires. It appears that you are God's instrument for a new kind of peace-thinking in our world and you'll be remembered as such."

Leckner smiled, as the waiter bent to pour more wine. "I am flattered by your description of me in some mystical state. I assure you, my motives are much more mundane. I like your style too, Archbishop; I am sure you are a man of prayer and highest motivations. I marvel at how you keep everything going with such a small staff. In my corporate world, I employ thousands to make things happen. I must tell you that I am very satisfied with the progress of the team and the state of the negotiations. In any case, we are down to the final reckoning, putting our money where our mouth is, as the saying goes. How do things seem to you?"

"Close," Mario replied. "I have been given the impression that we can promise enough financial incentives to each side to proceed with the peace process. The economists on both sides envision future spin-offs, further developments, which serves to increase the appeal for both sides. They will make investments in infrastructure development, education, agriculture, medical care, social programs, manufacturing, and trade. These investments have the potential to lead to lasting peace. They will want all these things yesterday. Further investing by the Church, at this time, is out of our reach. However, I believe we can continue to attract enough investment to move this project forward, given your investment and that of your circle of friends."

"You are right, Archbishop. I agree with you. My hope is that this becomes a model for replication, not only for peacemaking, but also for developing nations, for instance in Africa and Central America. I am convinced private monies can serve to develop third world nations, without exploiting them, for the benefit of all. Quite a dream, as you know."

"Where this inspiration came from or how this came to me, is a mystery. Perhaps, through my sainted mother who raised me with genuine concern for those who are vulnerable? An inspiring woman, a wife and mother with a social conscience, she made a lasting impression on my life. She taught me well, and tried her best to bring me into the Catholic way. I have always been too stubborn, and independent for my own good, very much as I am now. I believe I helped to make her a saint, by the suffering I caused her. Despite the prayers she offered for my conversion, I remain a serious agnostic." Leckner sipped his wine, and smiled at Mario.

Mario found the conversation between them pleasant, relaxed, respectful and humorous. A genuine friendship formed, despite differences and preoccupations. Each would like to share more. However their relationship, like many enveloped in the realities of international business, prevented them from going deeper. This is a consequence of fast travel, and the information age. This pace of living left many influential people with many connections and acquaintances but little time to develop friendships and deepen relationships.

The following day, the Pontiff invited them to a working lunch. The lunch served lived up to expectations, healthful, flavorful and enjoyable. They reviewed the negotiations status with the Holy Father. A pleasant meeting, filled with hope about the direction of the peace project.

Pope Francisco asked Señor Leckner more about his religious upbringing. Mario glanced with some unease towards Leckner. He thought Leckner might believe a spiritual conspiracy underway.

"We priests love to explore people's spiritual origins and faith journeys. We want to discern where they are in their walk with God. They may be ready to invite into the fold. This interest is a professional pitfall, and yet, it is of God." Mario smiled.

Leckner did not appear troubled by the conversation with the Pope. His face held a gentle smile as he listened, as a boy listens to his granddad. Mario sat, somewhat transfixed, at the leading, and charisma of the Holy Father and the way he brought God's presence to the eyes of this powerful executive. The Holy Father led Señor Leckner to reflect on his upbringing and faith in a gracious and unforced, yet personal searching way. Mario, listening to the exchange between the two men, found their discourse touched his heart.

"Archbishop, I want you to take Señor Leckner on a personal tour of St. Peter's and perhaps the private museum collection as well as the Sistine Chapel while he is here. I think a tour is appropriate. Señor Leckner will enjoy seeing the inner workings of our household."

"Of course, you are right, Holy Father."

"Señor Leckner, will you please join me tomorrow?"

The meeting ended with this pleasant suggestion. Mario called Marie and Viktor to join them the following day on the tour. He thought their presence would add congeniality and more interest to the tour.

Mario took delight in the way Marie, Viktor and Señor Leckner shared their excitement about the tour. Viktor and Marie experienced some of the areas the outing covered for the first time. The excursion provided a backdrop for getting old friends together, and welcoming a new friend into their circle. The loss of personal touch in the never-ending daily grind, amid endless faxes, calls, letters and interviews happened often. Mario welcomed these more human moments of strolling and talking. He acknowledged moments like these as graced moments, given by God to cherish.

After Señor Leckner's tour, Viktor and Marie returned to the university. Viktor went back to his classes. Marie returned to her work where she brought the University to the forefront, this week, by heightening peace awareness in the Italian press.

Mario took Señor Leckner to his private jet the following day. Afterwards, he too returned to his respective busy, worldly activities. How sad, Mario reflected again, as he drove from the airport. There is so little time for real friendships. Did they sell themselves out for success and achievement, or did the busy means of communication and technology eat them all up. People did not have the time to walk, breathe, smile, chat, and sit and share about his or her life, share events or feelings. Something was missing."

The days wore on, and things settled into a comfortable routine for Mario. He continued to meet with Viktor every week for a walk, coffee or drinks. They made time for one another, carved out peaceful intervals for both to relax. Viktor kept in touch with what he termed the *new Russia* and shared his thoughts with Mario.

Mario kept his appointments with the Holy Father, met with staff, Board members, and conferred with the Swiss handlers on the art and museum sales.

They held the Consistory of the new Cardinals. Mario and Pope Francisco had agreed earlier not to announce his naming as a Cardinal. Mario would remain unknown and unannounced, a *cardinal in pectore*. It was a rare Papal move. The Pope planned to announce the proclamation at his death.

The Consistory made headlines around the world. The event also brought about a tremendous reunion of friends, new and old. Family came for the new, elevated Cardinals from places all around the world. They were accompanied by diplomats from their respective nations. Despite the secrecy of Mario's appointment, the days of the Consistory proved busy for Mario. The media asked for interviews with him about the University and operations of the Pax Internacionale Corporation.

Mario placed his responsibilities on autopilot. His duties with Pax Internacionale Corporation, the Pax Dei Pontifical University, the treasury and church holding sales settled easily into the capable hands of his subordinates. The Archbishop even found the time for tennis at his club, which he enjoyed. His energized life was filled with peace and manageability. He often thought of how far the Lord brought all this, in a few short years – this wonderful dream of peace was beyond his imagining.

Cardinal O'Rourke too found peace, and Mario wished him well when he saw him at the Consistory. Even his Japanese friend, Eiho Yoshino operated according to the rules. In fact, once the Board convinced Mr. Yoshino that fairness not only has a place in the world market, he discovered that making "fair and square deals" expanded his business.

All operations of Pax Internacionale Corporation stayed on schedule; the Israeli-Palestinian peace moved forward.

Señor Leckner rounded up unbelievable capital to pour into the project. Señor Leckner's participation in the Consistory receptions pleased Mario.

Peace contract opportunities arrived from all over the world.

They received applications daily from global perspective students to the Pax Dei Pontifical University.

Marie traveled the circuit of international University presidents, where she received much recognition.

He thanked God daily for the energy to get through those initial years, and for the excellent staff, which developed around him.

Life is good, Mario thought.

# Chapter 11

## Servants of Peace

---

God used Sister Helen Marie as the catalyst to bring the next genuine innovation to the ancient city and to one of the oldest religious institutions in the world, the Catholic Church.

Viktor and Sister Helen Marie visited one another routinely, most often at teatime. One day as they were seated at their favorite outdoor cafe, enjoying tea in the spring sun, "Viktor, in your peace endeavors have you ever worked with a community of religious dedicated to peacemaking? This is something that I recently researched, and I could not find such an order in our Latin western tradition. I thought with your background and history, you may be aware of such a group. This is most curious to me."

"No, Helen Marie, I have not. Professor Aleman, who teaches the history of peace, is a leading authority on this subject matter. He will be able to help you answer that question. Why do you ask?"

"Excellent, Viktor, I will visit the professor. The reason I ask is that I experienced a strange leading from the Lord, about a dedicated community of religious priests, brothers and sisters who would give their lives to peacemaking work, in both activity and prayer. These religious would be associated with a group of committed lay associates."

"What do you think Viktor?"

Viktor leaned forward over the small table. "What an inspiration! God must be keeping you awake at nights, Helen Marie, what did Archbishop Gutiérrez say?"

"Oh Viktor, it is much too premature to mention this wonderful dream of mine to the archbishop. You are the first person I have told about this. The Church has historically met unique needs in the world through religious communities. My Religious Order was founded in response to the need for missionary catechism work."

"Oh, this is a surprise to me. I thought the Pope appointed someone to do a project. I did not realize orders began at a grassroots level and worked their way up through the hierarchy."

"Viktor, things do not work the way you think. This dream will need someone to lead it; it will take a charismatic person, or movement to make it happen."

"Helen Marie, you believe this is a new idea for a Religious Order. It is my understanding that God worked with Saint Mother Teresa, to make something happen, didn't He? Sister, you must talk with Archbishop Gutiérrez, and listen closely to what he says."

"Okay, Viktor, enough of dreams. How is Magda? Is she enjoying Rome, settling into the new apartment?" With that, small talk took over.

Still, the notion would not leave Helen Marie. At the end of the day, she cornered the archbishop in his office. Mario stood before his desk as Sister broached her idea and asked for his thoughts. Mario said he would give this idea some thought and prayer. Tired at the end of a long day, he asked her to pray, and promised they would discuss her concept further.

The archbishop tossed and turned in his sleep that night. He prayed, "Lord, is this new direction in religious life of your design? Please enlighten me. Is this your answer to prayer for a group of intercessors to pray for peace?"

He woke early the next morning, and jotted down his ideas as quickly as they came to mind. First, speak to the Holy Father. Archbishop Gutiérrez believed His Holiness would endorse Sister's idea. Mario asked Mary, Queen of Peace, to intercede for them with this new dream and the challenge presented by it.

Professor Aleman was even more helpful than they expected. He gave Archbishop Gutiérrez and Sister Helen Marie ideas about how to design a group like the one they had in mind. Mario and Helen Marie quickly realized that they would need help. Mario thought a think tank group the best venue, with Sister Helen Marie included every step of the way.

Mario gathered a few key members from his staff and the University faculty to work with them. He picked eight people, men and women of strong religious community backgrounds. The Religious represented nations from around the world. Mario and Sister Helen Marie invited Sister Marta, Sister Mary Perpetua, Brother Elias, Father Benedict, Father Fidel, and Father Eymard. To his delight, this elite cadre agreed to meet for the initial brainstorming.

The small group decided to meet weekly. They gathered first in Mario's chapel to pray, and then moved to the discussion table in an open area outside his rooms. No one was able to relinquish any time from his or her daytime responsibilities, so the weekly meetings became evening challenge sessions. The religious group added appropriate Gospel reflections to each session.

The archbishop presided. Mario explained this historical moment in the Church. A Religious Order dedicated to peace was a first in the Church's history. The need for peace grasped clearly now using the interconnectivity of the world. Up to the minute information, available around the clock, wars and conflicts broadcast live 24/7 on the news. In countries where the media existed under government control, cell phones managed to transmit live video feed over the internet.

The archbishop acknowledged Sister Helen Marie's idea, and agreed that the formation should be both men and women. "My brothers and sisters, this is a new approach. A religious community formed from the true conviction of the need for peace in the world."

Initially, it was a lot of work keeping up with the reports and studies coming into the Archbishop's office from this brainstorming group. Mario found directing the categorization to Sister Helen Marie made the most sense. Sister's talents included a knack for organizing everything, and in this way, Sister was aware of all happenings.

Once a logistics plan, based on the strategic plan, was in place, the group was free to move forward. They began to deal with applicants, screening, formation, a center, a rule, spirituality styles, finances, officers and elections, administration, and noted all the details in the meeting minutes.

They developed an action plan, which the initial leadership carried out, guided by a strong, meaningful vision. The defining of the community's ministry and scope gave them a living document, which was subject to constant revisions. The overall plan was to serve the needs of peace building worldwide.

Pope Francisco encouraged the formation group to keep moving forward. "The Holy Spirit will walk with you in the months ahead, and He will lead you to a charismatic leader." The Pope spoke with absolute faith and confidence.

The archbishop contacted the leadership of the world's most recognized Catholic Religious Orders. He asked for names of people in their communities who had a history and sensitivity in the peace arena. Mario honestly explained he wanted to contact these individuals to ascertain their willingness to develop a new Religious Order in the Church.

This particularly unique charism of peace proved as exciting as it was challenging. Few outspoken, inner-driven religious community people existed in this arena. Many socially concerned religious persons worked in the Church for the unborn, or in charity relief, or for the sick, or on issues like immigration, or the homeless and poor. To be a peace-driven person in the Church equaled a luxury, which few religious communities can afford to underwrite. The cost in energy and supporters to be a prophetic voice in this rather invisible area of society provided the rationale for this lack. A peacebuilding Religious Order did not hold the promise of making a profit. The order would not be self-sustaining. Fortuitously, more people than ever before in Church history, were donating extraordinary financial gifts to peace projects.

The meetings involved endless planning. They tackled charisms, an overview, scope of work and possible outreach, the qualifications of candidates and leaders, a timetable, a budget and financial supporters; a headquarters location and satellite locations; organizational structure and a constitution; formation processes; the recruiting and screening; the spiritual routines, and many other lesser issues. They considered publicity and marketing, and ways to distribute the new Religious Order information worldwide. The days of forming a community as Saint Mother Teresa did, belonged to history.

Names and faces, graced and chosen by God, seemed like a tall order. To put these elements in motion was a daunting task.

The archbishop, neck-deep in the affairs of his current position, wondered if he possessed the time and energy to pull this Religious Order together? Was it Mario's desire to devote himself fully to the new order, or was it God's will? "I recognize that there is a difference, Lord.'

He prayed about the significant decisions facing him. "My God, please help me." Mario spent his early morning hours in the chapel, praying about how this might come about. He thanked God for giving Sister Helen Marie the inspiration. He asked God to support the new order, to lead Mario to those willing to be God's instruments, fools for Christ's sake. The turmoil in Mario's life led him to thinking about the anguish and the agony Christ endured in the Garden of Gethsemane. Mario's anguish significantly paled in comparison.

Mario discussed his involvement in the new Religious Order with few people. At this time, the archbishop still met with his regular spiritual director every other month. The wizened old Dominican, Fr. Vicenzio advised Mario not to rush his decision making; God would gradually put on his heart, the way to proceed. Used to the fast pace of the peace initiatives, the wait seemed agonizingly slow to Mario.

Mario spoke again to the Holy Father, counting on his support and endorsement. The Pope gently advised Mario to proceed as he thought best, after prayer and discernment. The Pontiff echoed the thoughts of his spiritual director. Pope Francisco asked Mario to talk with him often, and to keep him informed.

Archbishop Gutiérrez found his prayer life deepening daily. At times, Mario cried out to God, "Show me, Lord, what to do, what You want." This prayer quieted Mario. Mario spent increasingly more time simply seated and hearing nothing, only the cry for stillness and the longing for God, in his own heart and thoughts. He yearned for a clear answer. Finally, as he grew more patient, Mario saw a clear path on this project, and then he felt the Lord Jesus move his steps forward, which frightened him a little. He thought it would be easier to follow his own wisdom and insights, and label them as God's thoughts.

With three consecutive days open on his coming week's calendar, he flew to the Dolomite Mountains area for a retreat. Mario stayed at a little country villa where he had stayed on previous occasions. He found the air delicious and the sky endless, without a cloud in sight. He slept late, walked, ate and prayed. The vistas energized him, and he viewed the horizon in every direction. He concelebrated Mass at the small village church, late in the afternoon. In the evenings, Mario sat on the patio behind the inn, reviewed his outlines and assessed everything. The twilight turned the mountains and skies to a vivid purple, as he walked back to the inn on his last day. The archbishop took a moment to sit down on a wayside bench, praying and breathing quietly as he took in the sight of this beautiful valley.

The Lord chose that moment to begin echoing in his heart and head. "Begin, I am with you." That small, still voice: nothing too dramatic, nevertheless steady, clear and consistent. His sense of fear disappeared. Creativity took over. The ideas began to flow. God's Spirit filled his thinking, and he wrote notes furiously. Topics, questions and possibilities seemed to flow like a beautiful mountain stream. Mario began to design the steps needed to follow the dictum.

The archbishop retreated to his room as darkness fell.

He drafted needed steps for a group to develop the parameters for the new order. Mario listed people experienced in lay and religious communities, and those with charisms in peace building. There were overlapping names, which gave him a short list of candidates.

Mario worked up a budget, to include formation costs, needed space and equipment, and operational costs. Next, he took a similar approach to the way he developed the Pax Dei Pontifical University, he listed possible benefactors who might be willing to help sponsor such a group.

Mario laid out a plan for recruiting, screening, training systems, and identifying locations. Next, he outlined rules, structure, and spiritual expression of the order. He wrote down his inspirations, thanking God for each one.

Anna Malooff and Sister Helen Marie spoke each week. The activities status of the Palestinian-Israeli prospects for peace still interested Anna. She pumped Sister Helen Marie about rumors of a new Religious Order.

Anna surmised Archbishop Gutiérrez' network contained countless worldwide contacts. With Sister Helen Marie remaining silent about the rumors of the new order, Anna began her own research.

Once the new Religious Order was announced, she wanted to be ready to build a major feature story, if not a series of articles.

On his return from the brief, beautiful mountain interlude away, Gutiérrez found Sister Helen Marie in his Vatican office, breathing the city fumes through his opened windows. Sister handled all his correspondences, to include notes, dictation and transcriptions from tapes. His thoughts became so familiar to her that she completed his sentences. Together, they worked on an invitation list for perspective candidates.

Mario presented the list to the Pontiff during their visit two days later. Along with the invitation list, he offered an overview, and a personal letter, which he planned to send to each candidate.

"So Mario, you resolved your uncertainties with some prayer and clear mountain air?"

"Your Holiness, I believe the mountains helped, but I experienced so much more. I humbly ask for your insight. Is the new Religious Order too much of a dream? Does Christ approve the new order for His Church and the world? Your word will provide the seal for me. Are we overstepping the Holy Spirit? If so, not only will I be eating humble pie, but you will too, as our Supreme Pontiff." Mario could not believe he spoke his thoughts so abruptly to the Pope.

"Mario, like Saint Francis, we are to be fools for the sake of Christ, so being bigger fools than we can imagine, is not a bad risk. Let's leave something to God. Let's set aside our human cunning and calculating."

Mario and the Holy Father enjoyed an afternoon cordial, and afterwards they prayed together. Mario knelt for the Holy Father's blessing before he left.

The following day the Archbishop added a personal handwritten note before signing the letters to the influential Religious Order leadership. He enclosed the overview draft of the dream possibilities. They offered prospective candidates time off, living and traveling expenses, and asked for their prayers, notes and ideas. His question would not take most by surprise, since many on the list had helped to mobilize the University and the Contracting Corporation. Mario suspected most people of great faith possessed high energies, creativity, and loved a challenge from the Lord. They would likely accept his invitation. He set the rendezvous date for two months in the future, and invited their questions and draft ideas. Mario counted on his reputation, and the Holy Father's endorsement, to recruit hesitant participants. He was correct, and those who accepted made up an exceptional team.

They were from religious communities with years of experience and wisdom in worldwide peace issues. Much like his initial group, they formed a tight knit, enthusiastic insight group for spiritual brainstorming. The team included, Fr. Francois LaFrenz, S.J. of the Superior General's staff, Fr. Pedro Estivil, the Assistant Superior of the Capuchin Franciscans, and Sister Mathilde of the Sisters of Mercy of the Congo. Additional invitees included Bishop Vicente Mones, auxiliary of the Cardinal of Manila; Sister Rita of the American Maryknolls; Joseph Lenz, Australia's Director of Social Issues for the National Bishop's conference; other representatives from Korea, France, Britain, Germany, Croatia, Chile, and Morocco.

In the end, Mario's team unanimously agreed to a six-month commitment. The group planned to meet in the Vatican. All expenses were paid. They met in the World Peace Office main conference room.

First, they divided into small groups, which consisted of two and three members. One team drafted ideas in the areas of rules and a constitution, an organizational structure and lines of authority. Another team pulled together a formation process. Another team conscripted financing plans, candidate qualifications, and screening processes. Fr. Francois LaFrenz, S.J. of the Superior General's staff worked with his onsite staff to identify a headquarters and other site locations. Fr. LaFrenz also oversaw the committees on Canon Law and international legal questions. The other small groups devoted themselves to developing the spirituality of peace bringing, and its operational expressions in the lives of a community and their work in the world and for the Church. All team members prayed, studied, researched, and dreamed creatively together.

Mario found the scope of this project hard to believe. Given the expertise of the committee, Mario was not surprised that drafts started coming to him right away. To review the documents, they divided the larger group into sub groupings, for easier sharing and revising drafts in areas other than their own. Few inquiries came from the media, and the work proceeded under the radar. Mario kept the Holy Father informed.

"Helen Marie, please ask Father Rubio to read the drafts as they arrive, then pass them to me. Ask him to highlight what might be solid, versus questionable data, so I will be able to concentrate on what is important as I review the material. I value and trust Fr. Rubio's opinions, as I do yours. Sister, I grow weary of all this paper work, brilliant ideas and questions. Some days it is difficult to focus, and God only gives me so much energy for each day." Helen Marie simply nodded her agreement.

Mario telephoned Viktor to explain the new demands on his time. They made plans to meet for lunch as often as time allowed. At best, Mario's outside activities provided sporadic exercise. He played an occasional tennis game with some of the staff padres, and used his rowing machine several times a week.

Mario never missed his daily deepening prayer time with the Lord in his chapel. He needed his holy hour like the air he breathed and the food he ate to live.

Thank God, for his staff, especially Father Rubio. Father Rubio was a young priest who hailed from Mario's native Argentina. He was quick witted, as well as spiritual, and possessed a wonderful sense of humor. Rubio loved tennis and made a good partner, a bonus for both men. They enjoyed a close relationship.

The subcommittees met to highlight differences, common points, and questions from their respective areas. Next, they strengthened their work. For two days they listened to one another, and concluded with an open session of questions and input. A complete set of revised drafts circulated, and each member took home a set. After their review of the package, and redlines, they returned them to Sister Helen Marie and Fr. Rubio. A date was set for the near future for the final draft reviews.

Mario reviewed the drafts Fr. Rubio passed through to him. This became an evening routine. He marveled at the insights. They had managed to assemble a brilliant team. The next step was a three-day assembly set-up by Sister Helen Marie. Everyone was excited to share his or her research, thinking, and finished products.

In his inmost thinking, Mario remained in awe of God bringing such genius of the Spirit together. A final reminder to the group was to remind them God wrote through them, and they needed to retain this spirit of humility.

Mario kept the Pope informed of their regular meetings, and progress. He noted the key and recurring issues, and answered all of the pontiff's questions.

Looking at what attributes distinguished the peacemaking Religious Order from other entities, Mario determined that the mystical element provided the main difference between establishing a Religious Order versus a corporation. The order incorporated God's designs, an intangible sensitivity beyond human creativity.

The charism formulation would evolve from future challenges and with the help of a few past specific models. Mario wished formulating a mission statement came as easily. Many of the Church's historical charisms came from the statement of life from charismatic figures like St. Francis, St. Ignatius or St. Mother Teresa.

Mario, unaware of such a charismatic figure here, prayed for God to show him the way. To bring out a captivating dream for the Church, in this historical moment in time, required much prayer and discussion. This happened with movements, devotions, and historical trends, such as the missions to the new world, or monasticism. Not easy to define or pinpoint, he thought.

The spiritual brainstorming group used Mario's earlier notes to define the scope of work, ensuring each endeavor had parameters. They took care not to duplicate the peacekeeping work of the University or corporation. They referred often to the archbishop's file on "lessons learned."

The operation would begin with outreach to small conflicts in scale, and they would increase the size of their capabilities in a gradual manner. The work would begin by using the existing Catholic network throughout the world. This meant bishops and religious congregations and Catholic education institutions, publications and web sites. They planned to build a major network by identifying, cataloging and connecting the resources.

A Religious Order, they would consult in small ways, and for larger projects work with the University and its Corporation. They agreed upon their community's vision to achieve formation and development, through prayer and spirituality.

The new Religious Order included vowed men and women. The

Order would have separate accommodations, with common areas. They would come together in mission, prayer and liturgy.

They followed Jesus' instruction to the 72 in Luke 10. Sending them like lambs among wolves was never truer. Following the initial press release, the Vatican received threats of bodily harm as well as death threats, should the new Religious Order venture into unwelcome territories. Missionary work would be in teams of two or more whenever possible. Each member of the order was prepared to travel. They all had packed what they called a "ready bag."

The personal witness of being in the world's hot spots, unafraid of criticism or martyrdom held significant importance. The plan was not to intrude. They would draw attention to issues and places in need of attention, healing or peace negotiating.

The candidates of the new order would require much training, wisdom, and formation, as well as continual communal assessing that everything they did remained in a Gospel perspective, and in keeping with the inspiration of God's Spirit.

The design of daily prayer included the sacred liturgy of Mass and the daily Hours of Liturgy. The community was rooted in prayer, committed to a lifetime, much like the Buddhist monks gain from their collective centuries of reflection.

The initial cadre, mature and experienced, would come from existing religious communities of priests, sisters and brothers. The transfers would bring a wide variety of skill, experience to the order.

Archbishop Gutiérrez believed finances would not be a major issue. He counted on the Pope's endorsement and many generous groups and benefactors around the world supporting peace building. They were thankful for major donors committed to supporting the new Order.

The working group identified several international houses. There were places available in the Philippines, London, Chicago, South Africa, Argentina, Australia, and Germany. Rome, of course, would remain the headquarters.

They drew timelines for a five-year strategic plan.

A multilingual promotional brochure was designed to highlight the community's charism, inform and recruit possible candidates, and detail the services offered in the areas of building and maintaining peace. The pamphlet explained how the Religious Order would be available on a global scale, as well as locally. Humble beginnings dictated voluntary professionals, rather than hired professionals, produce the marketing materials and set up the website. Mario understood the importance of getting the word out, and ensuring the recruiting materials made it to the hands of people with an interest in the new order.

"Archbishop, this is our third key formation meeting, and many details are falling into place; with the exception of the two troubling factors that remain. One is the initial ministry leadership of the organization, and two, the mission charism statement of the Religious Order. These two issues remain difficult for us. Would His Holiness, provide any specific guidance for us in these questions?" Fr. Francois of the Jesuit community, leaning forward, in his comfortable conference table chair held a hint of anguish on his face as he spoke. "I believe I speak for the group when I voice these concerns."

Heads began to nod. Joseph Lenz of the World Lay Community spoke. "Our thoughts are too vague with the possibilities and suggestions we came up with so far on both. I agree with Fr. Francois, our thoughts are ambiguous, at best. Will you please bring these questions to the Pontiff, and ask for some inner, deeper wisdom? We are going around in circles on both of these issues." He took a sip of water to moisten his dry mouth, a reflection of his inner dryness.

"Yes, I will. You are both right and I will present these questions along with our suggestions, when I meet tomorrow with His Holiness. The Holy Spirit does sharpen his perceptions. This is an excellent idea!" "I am proud of our committee and how much work we have hammered out. God is doing something special for the Church, the world, and us. Let us conclude by praying together and giving our dry throats and minds a rest. We will reconvene tomorrow at lunch when I will bring a report from the Pontiff, for our 'planners' block.'"

He called following the meeting. "Your Holiness, we bring you a couple of special issues from our formation committee, and I need you prayers, and also to intrude on your schedule a bit, after your morning Mass and breakfast." "Mario, why don't you join me for a concelebrated Mass in my chapel, and with breakfast alone we can get a start on your questions. You can arrange breakfast for the others at your quarters."

Mario, relieved at the suggestion, praised God and asked this might be a hopeful step in resolving their stalemate. Christ did much over food and meals in finding answers to the confusion and dilemma of souls and life.

Breakfast began with a blessing of the table, followed by Mario's request for help. "Mario, I enjoy your humility and boldness, trusting prayer, me, and your team, in seeking direction. What seems to be the bottleneck? All your reports are excellent. How can I help?"

As they enjoyed coffee, fruit and bread, Mario began, "Your Holiness, we ran into an impasse trying to specify the charism of the new community and how to setup its initial leadership structure with positions and names. Your prayer, ideas and experience would help us. Gridlock is the long and short of our problem. We prayed to be enlightened about this."

"Well, Mario, Jesus said this best with His community of peace builders. Your team is active and in a positive phase. Nevertheless, these religious members are to live, breathe, speak, pray and construct peace at every opportunity. This will be their main vow, guiding their life thinking and energy. We want dreamers and theorists, researchers, prayer intercessors, and hands-on, on the scene workers, ready to die and be martyred for these causes. This is a charism of self-giving with the potential to change from issue to issue and from place to place. The charism demands a detachment and mobility. To paraphrase what Christ said, in the future you may find "nowhere to lay your heads," all for the sake of peace bringing without personal comfort. This is the call. All are united with the Prince of Peace and Mary, Queen of Peace as co-builders."

"Holy Father I wish I carried a recorder with me. Excuse my distraction, but I am going to make a few notes. "Mario drew out his little notepad and began to jot.

"Mario, as for the leadership, I want you to think and pray about the insight I offer you. Take some fresh coffee yours is getting cold. Eat something. You seem nervous. Do you want Sister to fix you an egg?"

"Well, Mario, you remember the night of your return from the United States and my announcement to you. You seemed upset by it, so we spoke only the one other time when we agreed that you would become a *cardinal in pectore*. At the following Consistory, I did go ahead, and name you as a new Cardinal, along with the others. You will remain unannounced until my death or until I might choose to do otherwise. I know that you understand this."

"Here is my suggestion, Mario. I want you to pray about it with me. In a prepared announcement, I will explain that you are stepping back from the University, the Corporation, and all your associated activities. I will announce your new title as the superior of the new Religious Order dedicated to peace. I will make clear the simplicity and poverty of this peace group vowed to a lifetime of praying and serving the cause of peacemaking. I will clarify that the order is still in the formation process. The Religious Order will be associated with the University and the Contracting Corporation, but not employed by either entity. The Church needs this Religious Order devoted to peace. Your replacement and transition to your new office as superior of the group will take several months, at least. We expect to release the constitution and bylaws of the order about the same time. Mario, we will keep all your needs in our ongoing prayers."

Mario stopped eating mouth ajar. He stared at the Pope. This offer took the wind out of him. Once again, the Pope hit him as if with a hammer. Mario's hope was to provide interim leadership for the order. He had prayed mightily that the Pope might allow him this temporary position.

"Mario, I see this comes as a shock to you, but I think you're the man the Lord wants, and I know that you are the one I want for this assignment. You will still be titular Archbishop, and an unknown Cardinal, and you are free to choose whatever structure and available people you need to set up an operational staff for the new order."

"Otherwise, Mario, this search will continue to go around in circles, waiting for an experienced, peace-aware, gifted leader to step forward. I think our Lord wants us to take the sacred bull by the horns and move forward. Our good and loving God worked to build you up over these years for an even greater work than your work with the University, corporation and peacekeeping. Other administrators can step into those offices. Mario, God is asking you to go deeper than you dreamed possible. You need the freedom and flexibility, not to be the initial leader for this charismatic community venture, but an ongoing shaper, shepherd and guide in the deep waters of peace-mobilization and spirituality for the world. This will be a monumental challenge. In other words, this role is a perfect fit for you, Mario."

"I'm flabbergasted, Your Holiness. This is beyond my imagining. Please understand I need time to think, pray and envision this call. My heart leaps with joy, as I think about this. This order lives at the center of all our dreams, with the hands-on way open to us. I do not want to be presumptuous. It was my hope to fill the role of the provisional superior of this group. Once again, Your Holiness, you have gone way beyond anything I expected."

Their breakfast finished, Mario went to his office and sat looking out his window over the Vatican garden, jotting down random thoughts and questions. He enjoyed enough ease and faith to bring these two insights of the Holy Father to the group. He would take the Holy Father's advice back to the ad hoc committee at lunch, and present it to their afternoon meeting, a challenging prospect.

They sat in a tight circle. Papers and reports scattered before each member in the small conference room. Mario spoke his heart. He relayed the Pope's suggestions.

The first papal suggestion to define their guiding charism was set out at each place around the table. They read the Holy Father's thoughts, and heads nodded in assent. This insight gave them a clear, succinct and beautiful guiding towards their mission statement. The best part of this guidance was the way the statement worked now as well as in the future for their order.

The second issue tore at Mario's heart as he explained what the pontiff told him. The Holy Father had asked him to give up his comfort zone of creativity at the University, the contracting corporation and their respective Boards. Mario explained Pope Francisco's request that he take on a new wandering style, much like Jesus, with nowhere to lay his head, as he traveled and ministered to people in structuring and shepherding this new Religious Order. Jesus, the Son of God, while on earth, never owned a pillow, much less a home, Mario thought.

His cardinal status remained unmentioned, in absolute confidentiality; known only to him and Pope Francisco.

The new position will be an honor and privilege, and a cross as well. Mario explained to the group how the Holy Father brought up the proposal. He shared with the group the way he found himself challenged by the role, which was open to serious consideration. He experienced joy, fear, and anxiety, not so much concern about leaving the Pax Dei Pontifical University and the Pax Internacionale Contracting Corporation, more a concern about the uncharted waters of the order. He considered the variables. He wondered about his own calm, mental peace and stamina to face these tough questions and to deal with people-issues, as he did with the University several years back.

The group sat back in silence, mulling over the options and consequences. They had all dealt with the complexities of religious communities and personalities.

At last, Fr. Francois, the Jesuit, spoke. "Mario, we are supposed to be burnt out incense for the Lord. The heat may be strong. Yet, this seems like God is calling you, through the Holy Father's invitation. This type of decision is tough. It is difficult for Religious like us to let go of favorite projects or assignments. Given our vow of obedience, when our Superior asks, we pack up and go. I am not so sure your bishops challenge you, diocesan men, as much as our orders challenge us, but this is standard stuff. Therefore, my insight is that our Jesus is behind this call, and I recommend you 'follow your heart.' Consider this another challenge and adventure for you."

They smiled at one other in knowing affirmation. No one else stated things like Father Francois, the Jesuit, did. Everything he said was true. This is the definition of serving Christ on His terms. They all understood the situation without question. Mario glanced around the room, and thanked everyone. It was a mentally and emotionally draining afternoon for everyone. With much settled, he would report to the Pontiff tomorrow.

They met the next morning in the Pope's office suite. Mario held in his hands the plan for withdrawing from his current positions. In his position as a Board Member, albeit in an emeritus position, he would remain accessible for major issues as well as to individuals who preferred to speak only to him. He outlined his succession plans, and they discussed his successor, continued projects, and reassignments.

The next challenge was the move to the new home and office combination of the order. Mario's new home came with a small inner patio that he already loved. The Holy Father had provided the operations headquarters for the new order. The new headquarters offered more than adequate accommodations for Mario and his staff, which consisted of Sister Helen Marie, Fr. Rubio, and a new hire, an administrative assistant named Sophia. The office came equipped with far fewer resources and certainly less staff than the Vatican or the University offices. Mario likened his new situation to returning to the trenches of his early priestly years.

Over the next four weeks, Mario ran between locations, in and out of the Vatican, through the traffic of Rome to the three-story eighteenth century headquarters for the Order. He met several times a week with the Holy Father, dreading that their time together would soon become less frequent. Mario delegated the responsibilities of the University as well as his World Peace Office responsibilities to the others as he and Pope Francisco agreed.

He found quantifying his closeness with the Pope impossible. The aging man, beyond titles, trappings, and formalities of his office, lived spiritually and simply as the Shepherd who struggled with the day-to-day problems of the Church and the world. Pope Francisco lived in a confinement with power, and aloneness. His isolation gave him a God-view of the smallest concerns of the world and people around him.

Mario would miss this touch of holiness. He trusted that they would stay connected by Jesus and through daily prayer.

"Mario, I send you off with these words and blessing. May the wisdom of Jesus slow your heart and thinking. Therefore, whatever threats or conflicts to peace arise, may you stand in an inner God-present stillness, and listen beyond the words and turmoil going on around you. Stillness with God will be your secret strength." The Holy Father gave Mario a fatherly hug, as they ended their final breakfast meeting. With the Papal household, they offered Mass together in the papal chapel, a touching farewell time. Mario left the papal apartments thinking to himself that this would be a long and strange walk in the days ahead.

Mario traded his bright robes of Archbishop for the gray turtleneck shirt and suit, the decided garb, for the order. Mario left his comfortable living quarters, his precious chapel, Vatican office, and chauffeured car without looking back. This turned into a humbling experience. "Jesus, I cannot believe this. What am I doing? Please, continue to walk with me."

Four of them moved into the three-story building, Mario, Sister Helen Marie, Fr. Rubio and Sophia. Sophia planned to become a lay auxiliary attached to the Religious Order. They shared a housekeeper who would be moving in the next week. There was a small chapel located just inside the entryway. They had a communal sitting room and study, which served as their library and meeting room. There was a parlor for receiving guests, and a recently updated kitchen. There were twelve individual bedrooms with a full bath and study space for each. Eventually visitors or staff members might share the five larger bedrooms, if needed.

Four additional religious, chosen by Archbishop Gutiérrez after conferring with the Holy Father, rounded out the nucleus of the new order. The housekeeper prepared the rooms in anticipation of the newcomers.

The new arrivals came with much enthusiasm, and little fear. "Thank God," Mario thought. They brought years of experience from their other communities to the new order. They would form the real core, the inner circle of disciples. The two priests, a sister and laywoman, made a two-year commitment, a temporary vow of sorts, to work with the community in its foundation years. Mario prayed much over the selection of these additional charter members, Sister Juana, Religious of Jesus and Mary, came from Columbia and held the office of Provincial Superior.

Sister Juana was fluent in Spanish, French, Portuguese and English with a background in teaching political and economic social areas, at the University level. She remained active globally in the areas of peace and social justice.

Fr. Charles Ngyuen born to Chinese-Vietnamese parents worked as a papal diplomat beginning with his ordination. He traveled the Asiatic world representing the Holy See. He spent much of his off-time authoring works on non-violence and the place of the United Nations in nation building.

Fr. Jacques Bissonette was a French Jesuit who represented the Jesuits of the International Generalate of the Order. He brought the skills and experience of administration and personnel management to the Religious Order. He spoke the major European languages. He possessed a wonderful sense of humor.

Georgina Smythe was a former executive of the International President of the PAX movement. She vowed her life to celibacy, and lived, in legendary, voluntary poverty. She possessed a deep sense of the sacredness of the world's ecology. Her forte lay with the Arabic world, its systems and languages, and she was fluent in Arabic dialects. Raised in Moroccan Africa, she worked indefatigably for the Church and United Nations in various positions dealing with the Muslim nations.

They were blessed with four secretaries, on loan from the University, and with the necessary computer and technical assistance needed. Moreover, the University lent the order a finance person. The additional staff was a luxury for what was best described as a bare bones beginning. Yet, in comparison, their beginnings were very different from the primitive conditions of Saint Mother Teresa's beginning.

The group began each day with community prayer and liturgy, and then moved into working sessions. The division of labor worked itself out; they met each morning and evening for a progress review. Mario directed the overall spirituality, and the developing decisions and policies. He also guided communications, to include publicity and contact with the Holy Father, the University and all other agencies. The division of responsibilities grew along the lines of individual expertise, experience and talent. They were a collegial team always in discernment.

In their search for a formation house, they located an empty convent, a few streets from their headquarters.

Mario turned once again to the dynamic team of Monsignor Rondeau and Sister Marta to screen and hire the faculty and support staff for the formation house of the Religious Order. The first two appointments came with ease.

Father Jacques was a new addition. He came onboard already having accepted the position of Rector for the Formation House. Fr. Jacques also took over the networking and research connections they needed to setup. An efficient computer-type, he worked with the volunteer web master, developed the web contacts, the library connections and a database of consulting experts.

Sister Juana accepted and moved into the position of Assistant

Rector for the Formation House. Sister took over screening applicants and developing formation plans. Intense and detailed, she zeroed in on formation candidates and preparations. The order decided they would accommodate forty to fifty candidates, per class, year round.

The original staff members found all of their roles expanded.

As the world slowly became aware of the new order and many in need of peacemaking applied, Fr. Charles set up processes for screening applicants. Father Charles coordinated proposals and requests for mediation. His computer knowledge helped everyone.

Ms. Georgina Smythe relished her work with the house and formation center operations. She took the responsibility for overall budget planning in stride. She used her numerous global connections with funding sources, and contacted anyone and everyone she thought might be helpful.

"Holy Father, how good to be with you." Mario gave Pope Francisco a respectful brotherly embrace and greeting. It was enjoyable to be back in such familiar surroundings in the Vatican.

"I miss you Mario. You must be awash in decision-making. I hope in prayer too. I pray for your community. I want you to bring them with you next time; we will celebrate Mass in the chapel and enjoy breakfast together. They are special to me."

"I apologize. Your Holiness time seems to be speeding away, with so many 'hands on' concerns each day, and fewer opportunities to delegate. The new order is exciting and creative. The Holy Spirit has charged our small community with energy. We are sorting out our prayer time together. Holy Father, we even held discussions about using incense as a sign of peace, and an electronic chant and bells also, as part of our prayer. These are not earth-shaking issues. Yet, it seems we are constantly excited and always making plans."

"Mario, you are relaxed, I suppose these are different kinds of pressures for you than before. The change has been good for you."

"Holy Father, we stay on our knees and humble."

"Mario, I wonder how you are handling requests for help. What is your process for screening?" Mario told the Holy Father about Father Charles' processes for handling requests from groups and governments around the world.

"Are your finances adequate? I understand you now live with the vow of poverty. Nonetheless, I want your community to be established, and not distracted by concerns of financing. Peace building should cost us all something of material goods and sacrifices. The new Religious Order is an excellent investment, pleasing to God."

Mario assured him about their financing in more detail, and explained how they handled the screening and formation for the candidates. "I was so pleased that the decision to take the vow of poverty was unanimous."

"Holy Father, there are a couple of other things I want to mention. Our initial requests have been situations like prison hostages; a hospital strike; an ongoing University demonstration, and a food-aid protest focused on an African dictator. In response to these appeals, our Religious Order while still in the formation process stepped forward in an effort to bring reconciliation to warring parties. We formulated a process, which eliminates the waiting time for one or the other parties to move towards the other in peace. In other words, we choose the party who is comfortable making the first move toward reconciliation and then we support them. We are so few in number, we experienced a couple occasions when we brought in negotiating support. We worked with a negotiator from the contracting corporation on two occasions, and once we pulled in an appropriate professor from the University to bring about peaceful settlements. Even though, we're not officially founded, our order seems to be on the right track."

"Your Holiness, we've determined that our initial community council will serve for three years, followed with rotational elections. With your approval, we selected the title 'Servants of Peace' for the order, 'Servant' for members of our community, and 'Servant in Charge' for our leader. We did not want President, Superior, Chairperson or similar titles. The religious men and women will commit for two years in temporary vows to the Order. It will be the same for the candidates in the formation process.

We realize we will be the first coed community in Church history. We will write guidelines and monitor this development with care to safeguard our religious and ensure no scandal arises from our vows of celibacy. In addition, we are forming an association of married couples, and single lay people as auxiliaries, to assist us by prayer and advocacy. They are to be an important voice with God and governments worldwide. Our hope is to rotate traveling service teams of two or more, on assignment locations, for short terms in the beginning."

The Pope allowed Mario to finish, and then leaned forward with excitement in his voice. "I approve of that title, Mario, Servants of Peace! The first Religious Order dedicated only to peace building, which includes both men and women members. I prayed much over this. The order will be dedicated to the Lord of Peace or Father of Peace."

"Mario, your order is ecumenical. With a focus on unity, I want you to form your community using peace texts from the world's religious writing. Keep the Quran, Confucius, the Bhagavad-Gita, in mind. In addition, I would like you to include peace music and prayer forms from around the world. The Religious Order will need to understand the peace documents of governments, history and literature too. Though I am certain computers make research easier today, you will need to establish your own community libraries. We must build peace through the common civic and political human experiences of justice everywhere. The library will be your repertoire and treasury."

"Mario, I want to commission a painting of the 'Dove of Peace,' with the Baptism of Jesus, for your community. Tell me when to come, to visit and bless your quarters and dine with you. I want you to continue to report directly to me. I understand your second location will be in London, and the third, possibly in central Africa. Do be conscious of the Arabic world."

"Your Holiness, we are getting many requests for publicity and interviews. We try to minimize these, in a sense of humble service as well as confidentiality. The Lord will bless our efforts with time, and without lots of hype."

"By the way, our meals are frugal, and we fast on Fridays for the intentions of world peace. We live as vegetarians for the most part, with some exceptions, in solidarity with the poor of our world."

Mario returned to the residence center in the afternoon, and he relayed all the information and sharing he enjoyed with the Pontiff to the group. Excited to learn about the meeting, and relieved the Pope approved the title of Servants of Peace. Mario shared with the group that the Pope said their Religious Order was a true inspiration of the Holy Spirit.

Mario cautioned the group about receiving too much publicity for their work. They planned to visit with local bishops and always pray with the local church about their mission. He announced the Pope's plans to offer Holy Mass with them. At the same time, the Holy Father planned to bless their residence and share a meal with them. Things were clear as to their directions and work.

Mario marveled at the way the plans came together. He prayed daily about the self-surrender God wanted. "Let this be Your dreams, hands, and work, Lord, and not ours." His awareness of God on his shoulder, in all kinds of little daily decisions, inspired him. There was no hesitation on his part, to pause and ask the Holy Spirit, alone or with others around him, about what to do. It was a charming companionship like a child with a make-believe friend. He lived full of joy as he faced thrilling and exciting challenges each day. The Holy Spirit made everything inspired, happy, and easy. Nothing seemed like a burden. Mario acquired a bounce in his steps as he enjoyed this new chapter in his life.

The gray shirts and neckpiece proved comfortable for everyone, and the sisters had a choice of suits with a skirt or slacks. They wore a medallion, which consisted of a cross, molded by crossed hands. The cross spoke to the vision of peace and the hands to building of peace among all peoples. For a human flesh sign, they decided to take the Eastern Indian sign of joined hands and a head bow, recognizing Christ in every person. They chose a smile to be their greeting symbol. In addition, they adopted a blessing in the form of a cross as their hand gesture. These flesh peace signs marked the new order.

They adopted the "Prayer of St. Francis. Make me a channel of your peace ..." To walk together in peace was another gesture they discovered and used to symbolize their order. They discovered a fifteen or twenty minute walk in peace, shared or alone, with no words brought them closer to God, and to one another. The silence gave significant value to their work. Such walking to or from sessions, or work occasions, became their trademark. No driving up in cars and jumping out, instead they parked at a distance and walked to and from places of ministering, for fifteen or so minutes, in a group or alone. They came together in daily reflection at the end of each day. They sat around the table, family style and spoke of their day, their plans, and any problems they incurred.

They accomplished a lot using this format. They established informal rules for one another. For example, they planned to match interactive peace work with an equal amount of time devoted to quiet activities like prayer, research, reflection and writing. This plan gave them a good balance in their work and allowed the order to turn to the voice of the Holy Spirit. The family-style sharing around the table produced a lot of their best work.

The dedication of their residence, took place without much publicity or fanfare. The Pope presided in beautiful simplicity at a Mass in their garden patio area. Their chapel was too small to hold the attendees. The Servants of Peace dressed in their simple gray shirts and blouses as they always did. The media admitted by invitation only. The Pope and Servant in Charge Mario, along with all Servants of Peace made themselves available for photo ops and brief interviews with the invited *Vaticanisti*. Sister Helen Marie and Anna Maloof had visited with one another the day before as they helped set things up for the simple reception. Anna, never without her camera, seemed comfortable moving around and gathering little notes as she visited with those in attendance for the dedication. This would make a wonderful feature item. She had gained a deeper understanding, after months of research about the spiritual mystery of a Religious Order.

Day by day, decisions for the Servants of Peace, as well as their working and living relationships and shared spiritual life grew stronger.

As they prepared for their official outreach assignments, their daily meditation was Luke 1:79, "And, to shine from the heaven on all those who live in the dark shadow of death, to guide our steps to the path of peace."

Mario found a deep peace, content with God's designs.

# Chapter 12

## Apostle of Peace

---

The Pope's diagnosis of pancreatic cancer came as a shock. In the six months following the cancer diagnosis, the Holy Father went through opinions, chemotherapy and radiation treatments, and now palliative therapy. This type of the disease limited his treatments and time.

The media kept a respectful distance. Nonetheless, they expected information daily. The Vatican chose instead to issue weekly updates.

Mario, Servant in Charge of the Servants of Peace, enjoyed flexibility in his position that allowed for the accommodation of the Pontiff's request for his daily presence. Mario helped the Holy Father to celebrate Mass each morning in the Papal chapel. The Mass was the highlight of the Pope's day, his daily pleasure. These days, the Holy Father spent more time in bed, and the nursing sisters provided a continual presence, helping with his daily needs.

Mario kept up with his Servants of Peace work via delegation, his computer and phone. Mario considered backing away from his work to spend time with the Holy Father, a wonderful blessing.

Mario, with his servant's heart, listened to the Lord Jesus about what he might do with each concern of his day. Prepared for what might come, he lived each day in a quiet peace. Much of the anxiety of his former lifestyle vanished. Mario seemed to be at the center of life, so close to a dying friend and holy man. The Pontiff's fragile frame was to the point of a skeleton.

Time passed quickly for both men from the first time the Holy Father told Mario of his cancer until now. Pope Francisco asked Mario to stay with him through the end of his illness.

"Mario, I left my funeral notes in the second drawer of my big desk. We reviewed them before, remember?" "Yes, Your Holiness, I remember."

"Mario, will you please ask Secretariat of State Cardinal Casavantes, followed by the Cardinal Prefects to come by and visit with me for a few minutes in the next two or three days. It is most important that I visit with Cardinal Casavantes. The visits will take about all the energy I can summon." Pope Francisco's exhalation breathing was short and labored.

"Of course, Your Holiness. The prefects have requested a visit with you. Following Cardinal Casavantes, I will schedule Cardinal Rostani, and then, Cardinal Eugenio. We will continue for the next couple of days until you have met with each one of the prefects. Each will want your blessing, and to offer you theirs."

Mario asked the sister-nurse to step in as he exited the room.

Servant in Charge Mario became more and more removed from his own life. His focus remained with his dying friend, the Pope. Mario relied on his religious community, the Servants of Peace, his underpinning. Servant in Charge Mario shared most with his confrères in the Peace community. Mario hoped his dear friends Viktor and Marie understood how his life had changed given the care of the pontiff. He knew the Religious understood the way of hierarchal living in the Vatican.

Jesus became Mario's only true confidant. He gave his love and concerns to the Lord daily. Mario's life grew silent, deep and peaceful, which he did not mind at all. His life had been intense for so long, he wondered where God would lead him, next. Mario's daily routine left him very little time to think about the future.

Anna Malooff called Sister Helen Marie frequently following the Vatican's announcement about the status of the Pope's ill health. Anna's mother died of the same illness four years earlier. Sister Helen Marie spoke with Servant in Charge Mario several times a week, and she prayed for him and Pope Francisco.

Anna had worked out of Cairo for the last several months. She continued to monitor the Palestinian developments and published numerous articles, to include the brutal fighting that occurred just prior to the opening day of the Norway peace talks. While the activists, churches, and governments cried out for peace, it seemed as if evil capitalized on the lack of it.

Anna visited her aunt and several cousins safely, for a few days, in

Beirut, thanks to her press credentials. The entire region remained dangerous. The main office of World Wide News appreciated her consistent reports, interviews and insights. The weekly press briefings by the Vatican press officer, Father Giovanni, generated few questions, the press corps stayed quiet and respectful in these last days of a holy man's life. The people filled the Basilica and parish churches, day and night with prayers and candlelight vigils.

Sister Helen Marie and Anna got together for lunch at their favorite Trattoria near the Vatican. Sister shared with Anna that His Holiness' Dominican confessor, Father Juan Diego, gave the Pope the last rites of the Church earlier in the day. While at lunch, Sister received an alert about the Pontiff's family visiting.

Servant in Charge Mario led the Holy Father's final visitors, a few remaining family members, in prayer. During that prayer, the Pontiff passed away peacefully in a beautiful and quiet manner with loved ones gathered around him. Mario wept with the family.

Sister Helen Marie informed Anna a short time after the Pontiff's death and she came at once to the press briefing held in the Vatican Assembly Hall.

The Pontiff left the instructions for his funeral with Mario, who hand carried them personally to Secretariat of State Cardinal Casavantes. The Pope reviewed the instructions several times with Servant Father Mario. In addition, they reviewed the Pope's instructions for the election conclave, and Mario passed these too to the Cardinal.

The Secretariat of State, Cardinal Casavantes announced the funeral arrangements, and informed the press of the availability of media places at the funeral. Cardinal Casavantes concluded the press conference with the announcement that Pope Francisco had named an *in pectore cardinal* at the last Consistory. Cardinal Casavantes went on to explain the title was derived from Latin meaning "in the heart." Servant in Charge Mario was officially a cardinal, albeit an unnamed cardinal, as of the last consistory. The Cardinal explained that Pope Francisco had given him a sealed envelope when he visited him on his deathbed with instructions that the Pope's wishes were for the new cardinal to remain unannounced until his death. With that, Cardinal Casavantes announced Servant in Charge Mario Gutiérrez, Archbishop Gutiérrez, was the *in pectore cardinal*.

Sister Helen Marie and Anna called one another on the phone as the press conference ended. They asked one another, what this meant.

The simplicity of death impressed Mario. He tried to prepare for his spiritual father's going forth in a reverent manner. As the visitors came and prayed over the pontiff, Mario thought this would be the perfect time for music, so he arranged for some of the Pope's favorite liturgical music in the background.

Now, he found the large bedchamber resoundingly empty upon the passing of the Holy Father. Stillness, gray and quiet, and the somberness of a monk's cell, existed in those last days, in the room, despite the loving people surrounding the Pope.

The loving grieving process resides in each person, whether rich or poor, in his or her human poverty, as death comes. Mario's thoughts echoed Job's: "I came into the world naked and I leave naked, from my mother's womb." We all go alone. The pomp of the papacy meant nothing!

The Pontiff told Mario not calling an Ecumenical Council on Peace and Poverty for the twenty first century remained his biggest personal regret. Mario and Pope Francisco shared the council dream. Servant in Charge Mario wished he could have promised the council to the Holy Father.

The world media covered the funeral. With deepest solemnity, the Cardinal Angelo Casavantes, Secretariat of State presided. Government representatives from around the world assembled. Officials from Muslim and Communist nations attended. Kings and queens, presidents and prime ministers and more than two dozen leaders of other religions attended. Protestant, Eastern Orthodox Christians, Jewish, Islamic, and Buddhism leaders offered prayers and memorials. The Pax Dei Pontifical University and the Pax Internacionale Corporation had become well-known entities, and presented a strong presence in peacemaking efforts around the world. Both organizations added their dignitaries to the funeral. The press recognized the Pope's funeral as the largest single gathering of Christianity in history. The mourners were estimated at between four and five million. Memorial Masses celebrated made headlines throughout the world.

The day of the funeral dawned still and dreary with a gentle drizzle. It rained as the Holy Father joined many of his predecessors when he was laid to rest in the crypt below St. Peter's Basilica.

Saint Peter's throne sat empty.

With the papal election Conclave fast approaching, Anna accepted Sister Helen Marie's invitation to stay with her at the Servants of Peace residence. Sister invited Anna to join her community each evening in prayer for the election of the new Pontiff, which Anna did most nights. She realized how distant and inactive her faith life had become, given her busy life. Anna grew up in a devout Lebanese Catholic family. Her days with the Servants of Peace gave her the opportunity to return to the roots of her faith.

Anna did not join in the speculation, or track much of the "papabile guesses" made popular by the press. She chose instead to interview Sister Helen Marie and President Marie Mobatumbo about their memories of Pope Francisco.

The press, especially the *Vaticanisti* heralded Pope Francisco as a unique voice for world peace among all nations. A voice, listened to as never before. Some members of the press reported Pope Francisco's voice; even in death would not be stilled. Peace would be forever his hallmark. This recognition pleased Mario.

Pope Francisco was proclaimed a *Man of God* who lived the luxury of raising awareness of "peace through justice and mercy," throughout the international community. Mario realized the Holy Father supported this consciousness with action, commitment, finances, and the dramatic investing in this cause. Mario was humbled, blessed to have been a part of this papacy.

The second day after the funeral Mario called Viktor. "Viktor, I have missed you. Forgive my long absence. The papal funeral days, caring for Pope Francisco and our new religious community responsibilities have kept me too busy. I received your note of condolence. Thank you. How is Magda? Can you come by and lunch with me tomorrow. I am going to stop by Marie's office in the morning to catch up on recent developments." Mario hardly stopped talking long enough to wait for an answer. Conversation seemed like a release from the prison of death and solemn burial, he thought, as he hung up the phone.

The next day before lunch, Mario went by Marie's office where they sat for nearly an hour as she briefed him on what was going on in her work and with her family. He shared some of his experiences of the Servants of Peace with her. Their friendship remained intact, and he appreciated her respect and professionalism. Their roles now clearly defined as experienced professionals in the area of world peace. Their names and credentials had grown together in the world of peacebuilding. Servant in Charge Mario and Dr. Marie Mobatumbo shared a mutual respect, and enjoyed a comfortable relationship.

Mario and Viktor enjoyed their lunch. They lingered over coffee as they caught up with the happenings of their lives over the past months. Their meeting seemed like a debriefing. Mario spoke with admiration and animation as he shared his experiences of time with Pope Francisco.

Viktor told Mario of the unprecedented expansion in the areas of world peace, thanks in large part to the agreements developed between the Israelis and Palestinians. An achievement of monumental proportions, slow but still moving forward, and, Viktor said with certainty, a miracle.

As they talked, the realization dawned of how their lives had diverged from their previous professional association. Their friendship remained, but they used different vocabularies now, and spoke of experiences less understood. They finished their lunch and conversation as a strange, unspoken realization came over them. Something had passed and others appeared to be passing for them. As Viktor and Mario released their past association, they held fast to their friendship.

Servant in Charge Mario spent the afternoon in his community's chapel. He examined in prayer the grief and sadness from the loss of the Holy Father. The darkness in the chapel comforted him. It seemed to enclose his mind in peace.

Mario grieved. He missed his mentor, friend, and leader. He prayed for the future, for the Servants of Peace. Mario dared hope the new Holy Father would want him to continue to lead the Servants of Peace. "Not my will, Lord, Thy will be done."

At sixty-six, Mario neared retirement age. His energy was no longer that of a young man. The Lord consoled his heart and reassured him. "Be not afraid, Mario, I give you my peace."

Mario planned to visit his family, and to make a personal retreat. He wanted to travel and enjoy the outdoors. He missed his hobbies of hiking and nature photography. He had put them aside for far too long. His time had been severely limited since the earliest days of the peace project.

He still read outdoor, mountain, photography, and travel books, when time allowed. His photography with all its detail and study had gone by the wayside. The last time he experimented, he worked with black and white natural shadings, and all the delicate light and settings to be recorded in this.

Mario planned to spend five days in Argentina. Following that, Mario scheduled a retreat for his Servants' community. They would meet at the Grand Chartreuse in Switzerland for the retreat with the Carthusian monks.

The Secretariat of State would oversee the coming Conclave for the new pope. Mario would be present, as would every able-bodied Cardinal. His having been named a *cardinal in pectore* by Pope Francisco created little stir when released to the public at the death of the Pontiff.

Mario needed the space to get away from everything "churchy."

These past months brought a deluge of hierarchy, cardinals, bishops, meetings, ceremony, documents and all kinds of administrative bureaucracy, as well as his personal contact with the Holy Father. He had surrendered all space of his own. He was grateful that the Servants of Peace provided a tremendous support for him in prayer and friendship. Yet, he knew Jesus wanted his servants to live in a personal integrity and peace, rather than poured out in exhaustion.

Mario left his contact information with the Vatican reception office, but he did not expect notification to come so soon after the funeral. He hoped for ten days or even two weeks.

The conclave announcement came early. So, Mario knew the trip to Argentina would be briefer than he planned. Mario visited with his family and managed a short visit with Moises Leckner while in Buenos Aires. The two men discussed the Holy Father's passing, and the status of the Palestinian and Israeli peace talks. In the end, they acknowledged that Moises, the skeptical agnostic and Mario, the archbishop had become genuine friends.

Mario sat on the international flight returning to Italy, he thanked God for his wonderful family and prayed about his guilt for paying so little attention to them. Mario was refreshed by his family. María Elena, Fidel, and the children all loved him so much. Mario returned their affection. He would always be close to his sister and her family.

He liked flying to and from Argentina. Like a mini-retreat, the flight gave him time to reflect on the Vatican, his work, the Servants of Peace, his family, his life and his soul. He enjoyed the vast expanse of seas and clouds beneath him, and seeing the Alps as they approached Rome. He fell into a prayer of repeated praise in his soul, as he thought of all God allowed him to enjoy and accomplish with his energy and years, family ties, friends and work.

Our lives change, he reflected. God speaks to us and leads us through these calls of life. God would provide direction for the Servants of Peace. Mario was glad they were able to continue with the planned retreat.

Mario thanked the Lord, as he thought of responding to God and His corresponding peace. Mario did not live with regrets; he lived clear, strong and peaceful in changing times. He experienced the satisfaction of a life well lived, with God in the center. God blessed his life.

Stacks of mail waited for him at the Servants community residence. He made quick work of the distribution.

He telephoned Monsignor La Vertu of Cardinal Casavantes staff, next. He asked the Monsignor to explain the way in which conclave protocol pertained to him, as a previously unnamed cardinal. Monsignor La Vertu explained that Mario had the full privileges of cardinal with regard to the upcoming conclave. In fact, his right of precedence dated back to the day of reservation *in pectore.*

Mario recalled recent historical moments, such as when he established the University, with the Holy Father, and again when they founded the Servants of Peace. No longer in a hidden way, he would be included in the naming of a papal successor. He thought his name surfacing as a voting cardinal, would surprise, and perhaps affront some of the other cardinals. Mario noted his name was missing from the lists noted as "papabile."

Mario believed the Secretariat of State was the leading candidate. The secretary served the last three popes. He served in diplomatic areas since his days as a young priest. He understood the papal role. Mario would vote for him.

After his personal prayer the morning of the Conclave opening, Mario went to the hall where the Cardinals met. They gathered in small groups as the wait staff served coffee and tea to the cardinals. A pleasant gathering on this historical morning, everyone a little subdued, yet relaxed, as Mario moved among his brother cardinals with "good morning" greetings.

Most cardinals of Mario's acquaintance worked in Vatican offices. Retired cardinals under the age of 80 were eligible to vote. Cardinals over 80 were entitled to attend, and participate in all activities except the vote. He met the newer Cardinals, like himself, at the elevation ceremony held two months ago. The cardinals from distant countries were the least familiar to him.

The most vocal and yet gracious of the cardinals was the loud American who had been his nemesis for a while, Cardinal O'Rourke. He made much to do, as they shook hands and exchanged small talk. Mario enjoyed the warm greeting, showing none of the former tension. Something must be going well with all the financial concerns of the United States church, Mario smiled with the thought.

Their first call would be to prayer, followed by an explanation of the process by Cardinal Casavantes, who would serve as Camerlingo-Coordinator of the Conclave.

The cardinals collected all cell phones, i-pads and similar electronics. They allowed no outside calls. They conducted all business in complete confidentiality. They made no public announcement of voting results after each balloting. Nothing went public except the black chimney smoke after each ballot until the time that the white chimney smoke would broadcast, "We have a Pope."

After the morning prayer of the divine office, they received an outline of the process they would follow in the balloting. Written in several languages, the material contained a list of the names and addresses of all the cardinals. The list indicated those absent by health, which reminded the cardinals to facilitate calls or visits in the off hours. Reminded of secrecy, the cardinals were aware of the danger of any leaks to the press who hovered outside.

Mario arrived at the conclave filled with a deep sense of peace. He had the Lord's assurance. God will arrange for an empathetic man, one of sensitivity to continue with the work of peace, which remained his greatest concern.

Mario chanced to read the newspapers. He read of the front-runners predicted by the world press. The article named the Secretariat of State along with other old-time Vatican administrative names. They were Italians for the most part, which meant nothing new for the election. His own name came into the press, in two publications, both described him as a dark horse. He saw no other South Americans mentioned. Most considered Mario as part of the Italian establishment.

They held the first ballot in the afternoon, which went as expected. The Secretariat of State's name was followed by other traditional officer's names who served in various Vatican positions. The vote showed a mark of respect and appreciation to those names submitted and voted for in the early balloting. It was recognition of faithful service.

Everyone expected this recognition. Mario's name received nine votes as a thank you.

To Mario, this seemed pro-forma. The second ballot got a little more serious with some of the traditional older names dropping from the count. About half-dozen names surfaced. Mario, surprised by his name appearing again, became a little upset and disturbed. This time he received sixteen of one hundred and eleven possible votes. He served less than two years in the Servants of Peace and never in a cardinal's gathering. Mario pictured himself as unready and unfamiliar for any serious consideration.

The cardinals retired after Vespers. Not sequestered, they went out to various lodgings around the city. Some met for dinner at private locations. Mario dined alone, and spent an hour of prayer in the adoration chapel of his community. He cherished the time spent alone with the Lord. The other Servants of Peace were still at the retreat.

Mario turned on the late evening news just as someone knocked on his apartment door. It was unusual for someone to come by without a phone call at this late hour. It must be a messenger or a housekeeper, he thought. He opened the door, and found two brother cardinals, which surprised him. Cardinal Meier of Buenos Aires, a distinguished man, a cardinal for some twenty-three years stood in the hallway. Next to him, Cardinal Liáng, Prefect of the Oriental Church Office, a man in his late fifties and part of the Vatican bureaucracy for all his priestly years.

"Your Eminence, please forgive the lateness of the hour and our calling. We enjoyed our dinner, lingered too long over it. We would like to speak with you."

This must be the behind-the-scenes politicking rumored about over the years. He ushered in the distinguished visitors and showed them to chairs around the fireplace.

"Your Eminences: may I offer you an after-dinner cordial?"

"No thank you, Mario," Cardinal Meier replied. We would rather get right to the point, since the hour is late."

"We represent cardinals on the Vatican staff and others from South America and Africa. With your permission, we would like to begin circulating your name in the balloting. We believe you understand the Vatican and its workings, and that you are in touch with much of the world, through your University and now Servants of Peace work efforts. You also enjoyed the complete trust of our recent and much loved Pontiff."

"I am not sure if you are aware of the depth of confidence Pope Francisco placed in you. Prior to his death, he called most of us in and he wrote to others around the world. Pope Francisco stated if he could vote for his successor, he would cast his vote for you. The Holy Father assured everyone, Mario; you best understood all the issues and needs of the Church, as well as being a holy man of many gifts. He championed you. He referred to you, Mario, as the apostle of peace. We loved him, trusted his judgment. We have witnessed your work in the Church over the years as well. Many are confident of your gifts. We want to entrust the Church to you. Your Eminence, did the Holy Father speak about any of this to you?"

Mario recalled his discussion with the Pope about his appointment as a Cardinal in secret, and the twinkle in the Pope's eye. His Holiness had indicated his appointment would gain significance in the future. Mario questioned this information. Is this the way of the Holy Spirit of God, or did human politics operate this way. It may be that this was some strange combination of both.

"Your Eminences, I am surprised by your statements. The Holy

Father suggesting my name surprises me. I had no idea of his thinking about this. This would almost disqualify me from consideration, in the sense of someone trying to use influence on a papal election, albeit a deceased pontiff. Your consideration of me as a possibility honors me. However elected to the pontificate on the coattails of another Pope, does not. I hope I have more to qualify me than a Pope's wishes. I think you understand what I am saying. This is disturbing to me. Please let me think and pray about your suggestion and invitation tonight. I promise that I'll get back with you first thing in the morning."

After some other small talk, and their leaving, Mario sat in silence, staring into the flames from the fireplace. He loved the quiet and reflective mood, the fire brought. For these times of introspection, the fireplace became his second favorite place, right after the chapel.

The Pontiff's suggestion that Mario become his successor seemed in bad form, disturbed him and made him uneasy. He lacked understanding. In times past, did the Church, the cardinals, handle a pope's election in this manner? He came into this process at the last minute. This was a spiritual surprise, quite like the Lord choosing Paul for the Gentiles. Some will resent this intrusion and may react badly to this gerrymandering. Mario thought about his freedom, and his self-assessment. At least the cardinals came to talk things over. Perhaps he would be a backlash victim of some presumptive faction. Numerous questions surfaced as Mario tried to grasp the implications of this overture.

He left the fireplace, and retreated to the chapel.

He spent the next four hours in prayer, and discussion with the Lord about this possibility and pleaded for divine guidance. He analyzed each point as they came to him, prayed with pencil and paper, as he often did, and wrote down his thoughts, and reflections with the Lord. He expressed his sadness, anxiety and anger, over the whole thing, as well as his confusion. He sat in total silence, as he listened for God, Mario experienced a calming as each new image, or memory came to him, or a new question arose. The strong and quieting presence of the Lord, always present, comforted him. Sometimes he knelt, sometimes sat, and finally he prostrated himself at the altar steps.

The Lord led Mario to recognize his weariness. At the same time, he realized his growth and experience in international awareness and his involvement in church issues made him as well versed as any of the cardinals.

Mario's personal spiritual growth, which is hard for any person to calculate, eluded him. The Lord assured him of his spiritual growth, through daily prayer, humbling mistakes, theological study, reading, his daily faithfulness, and his loving and caring interactions with all the people he encountered.

Mario lived in Gospel simplicity, with justice and peace always on his mind and Jesus in his heart. He loved kindness and walked with humility. He realized, however, in the last year he missed confiding in a personal spiritual director. He needed someone with whom to share his soul. He was faithful to the examination of his conscience and confession of his sins.

Mario wearied, and the Lord assured Mario he would receive new energy from God's Holy Spirit for the task. He asked for a confirming direction of the voting as with the election of Matthias from the "Acts of the Apostles." He still did not understand the meaning of suggesting his name in advance by the former Pontiff, or the significance of the Cardinals talking to him. This still seemed like crass politics, but even the Lord might use such means if He chose. In the end, God would speak through the voting, and Mario believed in this. God's will be done!

The holy hours of prayer renewed his strengths and identified his weaknesses, his spiritual and career history, the state of the Church, the friends and connections of the years.

Finally, God spoke to him. Jesus assured Mario that He wanted the peace efforts to continue. He left the chapel, clear in his resolve, strong about his candidacy, and humbled.

The morning ballots will be in God's hands.

Mario slept for almost five hours. He woke up, and enjoyed a cup of coffee, and a brief prayer visit to the chapel. Mario called Cardinal Meier because he was closer to him than to Cardinal Liáng. He kept his misgivings about the political mechanisms to himself. After all, he was still new in this realm of Cardinal politics. Mario simply told the cardinal "yes."

He hung up the phone. He chuckled, thinking of God's divine humor. He, Mario, might end up as pope. This is far-fetched. He came from Argentina, not part of the cardinal-level office holders ranking. He was a dark horse, and a brand new cardinal, a relative outsider.

The first ballot of the morning narrowed the candidates down to five names. Mario's name was in the middle of the ballots counted. By the end of the day, three names remained on the ballot with his name still in the middle. The cardinals prayed, reflected, and held discussions. Mario was nervous and restless. He prayed to himself throughout the day, asking God's will be done, and leaving all in the hands of the Lord. He did not rest any easier as the day ended with his name in serious contention.

A number of the cardinals smiled at him and nodded, as they left the chamber for the day.

He walked out with Cardinal Meier.

"I suppose you prayed through much of this day, Mario. I prayed too. This is a strange business, the election, one of the only democratic processes in the Church, dating back to the times of the Acts of the Apostles. They believed in this process, and we do the same. I often wonder how we do not bring voting into more things of the Church. Of course, as we bring personalities, diplomacy and politics together, we complicate everything. How are you doing, Mario?"

"Pretty drained, Your Eminence." Mario spoke the title of respect for his senior. He remembered Cardinal Meier with affection from his days as a young priest. Mario mentioned needing a little siesta and some quiet time.

Cardinal Meier nodded. He also needed to rest. "Mario, you might gather some thoughts for yourself, on an acceptance address to the cardinals. This will sound presumptuous, but I think that tomorrow the voting will shift more and more toward you. Remember, as human as this sounds, God works through us. In any case, everyone will be waiting to learn about your style, goals and hopes for the future. Pray, Mario."

Mario and Cardinal Meier went their separate ways at the top of the stairs. Mario wished he could run home to his apartment, not far away, to weep in private. This day, the magnitude of the conclave, numbed him. He hoped a small group of cardinals, with ulterior motives, was not planning to use him. He did not want to be a pathetic straw man.

Mario wearied as he walked slowly home. He sought and found the solitude he needed when he reached his chapel. He had tried to pray throughout the day, but so many conflicting thoughts crept into his mind. He assessed one cardinal against another – for him or against. He hoped they prayed for God's guidance as he did.

Mario, so naive about politics, wondered if the cardinals were labeled liberal or conservative. What did they want in a Pontiff?

Many such questions had raced through his mind all the day. He remained interiorly distracted, as they voted on each ballot and assessed the count.

He clung to the teachings that his beloved mentor, Pope Francisco, instilled in him for the direction of the Church for the future. This thinking distracted him, yet he believed the same held true for every cardinal present. They all had ideas and thought about the way they would like the Church to go in the next ten or twenty years.

"Lord," he prayed, yet again, "Thy will be done." This is such an easy prayer to mouth, and even seemed trite sometimes. To pray this with true conviction went so much deeper. You understand, Lord. I am weary of this process, thoughts, my own analyses, and myself. Father, into your hands I commend my spirit, the final words Jesus spoke before he died on the cross. This seemed much more real and appropriate. Mario questioned what he was doing. Doubts aplenty arose. He again sat and knelt in silence, for what seemed like hours. He listened as the Lord spoke in a most gentle way.

Pope Francisco and he had worked to simplify the Vatican's accumulated wealth. The process started with material things and styles. Now, the Church was experiencing an emptying, dismantling process, a disenfranchising from holdings of power, position, and bureaucracy. Mario wondered what this meant for the future of the Church.

He kept picturing the naked Christ, the humbled and lonely Christ. The Church was to imitate Christ, to be unspectacular, a quiet voice and an example, to be present among the poor and suffering and the oppressed of the world. Any show of resources or pomp, needed to be let go, in favor of humble simplicity, and sharing of resources. This deepened and echoed the way of his predecessor.

Should Mario be elected, he would announce the Church as the unprofitable servant in the Gospel, never to glory in its accomplishments. The Church will be the servant of the world in its struggles for order and peace, and its mission as a healing power. Peace must be brought into homes, families, and the workplace, as well as to governments and ethnic divisions.

His personal dream was for Servants of Peace to rise up around the world, and help peace to succeed, in neighborhoods, families, individuals' lives, and in institutions and communities.

Cardinal Meier called him the next morning to remind him in a gentle manner today might be the day. He asked if Mario was prepared. Mario hung up the phone thinking he had no response to the cardinal's question.

They gathered in the Conclave Hall, as more smiles and nods came in Mario's direction than had on previous days. He felt like the object of some conspiracy. They sat to pray, and he surveyed the hall and interiorly blessed all the heads and faces in the room. He smiled to himself, as he thought, "Lord I don't understand, this is like a dream, but I surrender the dream to you. Somehow, I believe you are in all this.

Lord. If you want this for your Church, your people and for me, Thy will be done."

The balloting came down to Mario and the Italian Cardinal Cifferelli of Milan early in the afternoon. On the second vote of the afternoon, the announcement came. The white smoke emerged from the Sistine Chapel.

The cardinals elected Mario the new Pontiff.

He stepped into a dream, of past and future. He wept as he stood, with the final calling of his name.

Mario spoke his words of acceptance. "Beloved Brothers, I hope we all realize well, what has happened. Paul wrote about how God chose the foolish of this world to confound the wise. I feel like the most foolish of all men. How confounding of the wise, I might be, will be in the hands of God and history."

"I owe so much to my beloved predecessor, Pope Francisco, who perhaps did the original choosing of the foolish, when he asked me to work on the peace development plan on behalf of the Vatican. I cannot begin to fathom how God chose me, in so many small ways, leading to this day."

"Your confidence humbles me. I am a servant of God, and of the Servants of Peace."

"You are aware my style will be simplicity, the poor, and moving toward peace, in every way. I will take steps so that we will be the humble servant Church of the world, with a focus of bringing peace."

"Jesus' words best sum up my thinking and hopes for the Church, in the world in the coming generations. From the Gospel, we are the unprofitable servants, doing all we are supposed to do and looking for no reward, or recognition. Our profit and gain will be in eternal life. Our treasure stored in heaven. This world will be toil and sacrifice, and simplicity and sharing with the suffering."

"Pray for me, dear brothers, and come to me with any of your questions or suggestions. We are to be collaborators everywhere in the world, for simplicity and peace, in Jesus' way." I chose my name for this serving time of papacy and shepherding, to honor my predecessor. I choose the name of Pope Pacis."

Mario came to the center of the room and knelt. He asked for a few minutes of prayer from them, and asked that each man might come forward, and give him a simple blessing.

# Epilogue

Pope Pacis stared into the crowd in St. Peter's Square with an expression Anna Maloof later described as a combined sense of holy fear and humility. The new Pope was ready to move forward on the balcony to take his place in history.

Deep in his heart, he felt love – the love of God. He thought of the papal lineage tracing back to Saint Peter "the rock" on which Jesus built His Church.

Church history flooded his thoughts. He recalled the violent crusades, power struggles, oppression, excommunications, executions, and manipulation of people and ideas. Pope Pacis shook his head to clear his mind, and thought instead of the way the Church carries Christ at its center. He thanked God for healing the brokenness of the Church. He thanked God that despite promises broken repeatedly, God's promises remain unshaken even in our world today.

Mario Gutiérrez was no longer the archbishop who began the tsunami for peace in the world or the man who started the first Religious Order dedicated to peace or, the newly recognized Cardinal. Mario was the newly elected Pope.

Anna admired the way that the new Pope stepped up to one of the loneliest and most difficult positions of authority in the world. Given the progress for peacemaking accomplished by this man, she wondered what wonderful things to expect from his papacy.

Pope Pacis smiled and waved at the throng in St. Peter's Square. The Square was a wall of people, a beautiful mosaic. The jubilation and joy expressed by the crowd, gave him more time to pray. He wanted peacebuilding to outlast his papacy, to last for generations to come. "Lord, my prayer is for you to walk beside me every step of the way. Thank you, for your presence daily as well as the journey used to bring me to this place in my life. I am confident that You will not abandon me now."

He gathered his thoughts, prior to addressing the crowd. He thanked God for his predecessor who paved the way for the world to consider genuine peace. Mario made a solemn vow that he would carry on the work begun in the world towards peacebuilding.

To those who say peace is impossible, Pope Pacis planned to remind them that it is only with Jesus that we know real peace in this life. Only when Jesus comes again, will there be real peace on earth. In the meantime, we have His words in John 16:33, "I have told you this so that you might have peace in Me. In the world you will have trouble, but take courage, I have conquered the world."

Pope Pacis planned to call a World Congress right away, an Ecumenical Council addressing peace and eliminating poverty. The World Congress was the next step in peacemaking and one of his first tasks as the new Pope. It would include delegates from ecclesial movements, religious communities, bishops, cardinals, and representatives of all faiths who wished to participate.

The Pax Dei Pontifical University, Pax Internacionale Corporation, the Peace Encyclical, and founding the Order of the Servants of Peace were partial expressions of the search for peace, which bound him forever to his predecessor as brothers in the Lord.

Mario experienced a personal aching because so much remained to speak to the world about seeking peace using the Gospel perspective. Jesus led Mario to this juncture of his life, to this time in history. The new Pope wondered where his papacy would take him.

Jesus never traveled more than 200 miles outside the little village where He was born. Yet, no one ever made such a positive impact on the world, as had the man from Nazareth. Pope Pacis was committed to Jesus. He would always follow his gentle Savior.

Marie Mobatumbo was in St. Peter's Square, standing with a group of trusted friends, Sister Helen Marie, Anna Malooff, Magda and Viktor Fiderev, and Señor Leckner. It was a short walk from Marie's office in the Vatican. While she walked to the Square, Marie reflected on all that happened since the day she witnessed on television Archbishop Gutiérrez as he stepped up to the microphones and onto the world' stage.

Marie now occupied the archbishop's former position and offices in the World Peace Office. When Mario took over the leadership of the Shepherds of Peace, Pope Francisco appointed Marie to take his place as Director of Operations of the World Peace Office.

Pope Francisco appointed Marie's former assistant, Father Jules Mattosha, to be the second President of the Pontifical University dedicated to peace. When Dr. James Whitney retired, Viktor Fiderev moved easily into the position of Vice-President of the Pax Dei Pontifical University.

Servant Helen Marie was the new Pope's first phone call. Pope Pacis wanted her to know that she was the new Servant in Charge of the

Servants of Peace, and that her selection would be one of his first papal announcements.

Moises Leckner was in the Square, and he was thrilled for his friend Mario. He thought, "This man may make a believer of me, yet."

Fr. Rubio stood just behind Pope Pacis on the balcony. Pope Pacis had summoned Fr. Rubio moments ago and asked the young priest to be his personal assistant, to accompany him on this new journey. Fr. Rubio's joy knew no bounds.

Pope Pacis shook his head to clear his mind, and then stepped forward to address the waiting crowd here in the square, and around the world. Deep in his heart, he felt again – the love and the peace of God. Though he could not see them in the crowd, he knew his closest friends were there, and always would be. His smile grew even wider thinking about his sister María Elena and her family watching.

## Glossary

**Angelicum** – the University is composed of Faculties and Institutes of specialization erected by Apostolic Authority.

**Apostolic Nunciature** is a top-level diplomatic mission of the Holy See, equivalent to an embassy.

**Apostolic Nuncio** is the Pope's representative in a country. As a diplomat, he carries out functions within his competence with the Government of that country. At the same time, serves a pastor in special relationship with the national episcopate.

**Apostolic Delegate** is a representative of the Pope in a country that has no regular diplomatic relations with the Vatican.

**Archdiocese** is the head of a group that forms an ecclesiastical province. While the diocese is governed by a Bishop, Archdiocese is governed by an Archbishop.

**Bishopric** is a district under a bishop's control. It can also refer to the position of bishop.

**Breviary** is a book containing all of the daily psalms, hymns, prayers, lessons necessary for reciting the office in the Roman Catholic Church. Please refer to Liturgy of the Hours for further explanation.

**Canon Law** is a group of ecclesiastical laws (canons). Since the early days of the Church, there prevailed the custom, by private initiative, to gather all the laws mainly dictated by the councils and the Popes.

**Camerlingo** is the Cardinal who presides over the Apostolic Chamber. During the vacant seat, he is responsible for temporal administration of the Vatican. He formally establishes the Pope's death and arranges the conclave.

**Cathedraticum** is a certain sum of money contributed in an annual sum paid by a Roman Catholic parish for the support of the bishop.

**Catholicism** is one, holy, catholic and apostolic Church, which transcends boundaries of race, people, language and traditions and is universal in Christ.

**Catholic Social Teaching** has developed since the end of the nineteenth century with the awakening of a sense of justice for inhuman conditions. Later, it expanded to social aspects such as peace, relations between people, family, education, consumption, democracy, human rights, and work. Key principles include social doctrine, solidarity, subsidiarity and the common good.

**Celibacy** in the Catholic church means priests and religious take vows of absolute chastity.

**Christus Pantokrator** is a conception of Jesus as the Almighty, Ruler of All Things, and is a common depiction of Jesus in the Byzantine or Eastern Orthodox churches.

**Codes of Canon Law** are the systematic collection of all general laws of the Church.

**Conclave** is from the Latin, *cum clavis*, with key, room that can be locked. The name comes from the fact that for centuries the place where the cardinals were gathered and lived until the election was concluded was locked from the outside. Since the last reform established by Saint John Paul II in 1996, seclusion is in effect over because the cardinals reside in Santa Marta house, and go to the Sistine chapel twice a day to vote.

**Consistory** refers to assembly of Cardinals convened and presided over by the Pope. All the cardinals present in Rome participate in the ordinary consistory. For the extraordinary consistory, cardinals of the world are summoned in secret session for serious matters.

**Curia** is the administrative and judicial body needed for pastoral operations. The diocesan curia assists the bishops in running the diocese.

**Diocese** is the portion of the people of God entrusted to the pastoral care of a Bishop.

**Divine Office** is also called the *Opus Dei* (Work of God), please refer to Liturgy of the Hours

**Ecumenism** unites the various Christian churches and all faiths.

**Encyclical** is a document of the Pope under the form of a letter addressed to the bishops and all of the faithful, all humankind, on a particular theme, usually of a doctrinal character.

**Hierarchy** is from Greek, "sacred government." It consists of the Pope, the bishops that are in communion with him and the priests and deacons, who embody the authority in the Church.

*In pectore* is a Latin expression that means "in the chest," inside. It is used in cases where the Pope makes someone a Cardinal whose name remains secret for reasons that are appropriate until the moment in which making it public will not cause any inconvenience.

**Liturgy of the Hours/Divine Office/Breviary** – all three names refer to the official prayer of the Church offered at various times of the day in order to sanctify it. Clergy and Religious have a canonical obligation to pray the Liturgy of the Hours as official representatives of the Church.

**Liturgy of the Hours** – From *liturgia horarium* (L) and the Greek *litourgia*.

**Breviary** – From *breviarium* (L), a compendium of the Canonical hours.

**Magisterium** is the authoritative teaching exercised by the Pope and the bishops. The Ordinary Magisterium is exercised in the normal and ordinary life of the Church. It is different from the Extraordinary Magisterium, which is exercised in circumstances of particular relevance, as a council or a dogmatic definition.

**Monsignor** is the title the Holy See grants to bishops and other clerics to recognize the importance of their function. Pope Francis has abolished the conferral of the Pontifical Honor of 'Monsignor' on secular or diocesan priests under the age of 65.

**Nuncio** is an ordinary and permanent representative of the Pope, vested with political and ecclesiastical powers, accredited to the court of a sovereign or assigned to a definite territory with the duty of safeguarding the interests of the Holy See.

**Papabile (Papabili)** a term used to describe those thought likely to be elected Pope.

**Patriarch** is the honorific title of some bishops or in relation to their episcopal office, or by personal concession in today's world. Patriarch refers also to the biblical fathers of the human race, especially Abraham, Isaac, and Jacob.

**Pontifical Status** refers to higher education institutions established under a papal charter. The Catholic University of American received its papal charter in 1887 from Pope Leo XIII. Only universities that have pontifical status are allowed to confer ecclesiastical degrees, which are accredited and certified by the Holy See.

**Quinquennial** refers to status reports to the Vatican given by all bishops in the world.

**Vatican Bank** is the only branch of the *Istituto per le Opere di Religione* (IOR), otherwise known as the Vatican Bank. Most recently, Pope Francis executed reforms to the Vatican Bank that are comprehensive and implemented by lay experts who are creating a system of controls that do not depend on just a few people being honest and competent.

**Vatican City,** officially Vatican City State is a walled enclave within the city of Rome. It is an area of approximately 100 acres and a population of 842. It is the smallest internationally recognized independent state in the world by both area and population.

## Religious Glossary

**Religious** in the Catholic Church refers members of religious orders who make a final profession of solemn vows and members of religious institutes or religious congregations who make a final profession of perpetual simple vows, after a period of temporary simple vows. They serve the Church in a special way; work for the salvation of the world; strive for the perfection of charity in their own lives. They are a witness to Jesus Christ.

**Priests** are also known as "presbyters" or "elders." In fact, the English term "priest" is simply a contraction of the Greek word presbuteros. They have the responsibility of teaching, governing, and providing the sacraments in a given congregation.

**Brothers** take the simple vows of poverty, chastity, and obedience, live in community, and share in a particular apostolate, like education, health care, or other charitable work.

**Monks** live in religious community and make a final profession of the solemn vows of poverty, chastity, and obedience. A monk may be a priest or a deacon, who has received the Sacrament of Holy Orders, or a religious brother, who is not ordained. Monks live in a monastery. They may have a very strict contemplative, cloistered lifestyle.

**Nun** is member of religious order who takes the vows of poverty, chastity, and obedience. A Religious Sister denotes a woman religious under simple vows who is a member of a particular religious congregation.

**Supervisor General** or **General Superior** is the leader or head of a religious institute or religious order in the Roman Catholic church.

**Roman Curia** consists of Secretary of State (including the General Affairs Section and the Section for Relations with States), congregations (may be compared to the Ministries of a country), Ecclesiastical tribunals, Pontifical councils, Offices, and then Institution connected with the Holy See, such as The Vatican Secret Archives and the Vatican Library.

**Stipend** is a fixed pay, retribution for work in ecclesiastical living. In canon law stipend is a general designation of means of support provided for the clergy.

**Suffragan** refers to a bishop appointed to help a diocesan bishop; a bishop in relation to his archbishop or metropolitan.

**Synod of Bishops** is an assembly of bishops, chosen from different regions of the world, who come together to promote a closer union between the Roman Pontiff and the bishops themselves. They are elected by the episcopal conferences of different nations, in proportion to the number of their members; some are appointed directly by the Pope. The ordinary synod meets every three years.